P9-CJJ-318

MURDER AT THE FITZWILLIAM

By Jim Eldridge

Murder at the Fitzwilliam
Murder at the British Museum

MURDER AT THE FITZWILLIAM

JIM ELDRIDGE

Allison & Busby Limited
12 Fitzroy Mews
London W1T 6DW
allisonandbusby.com

First published in Great Britain by Allison & Busby in 2018.

A CIP catalogue record for this book is available from
the British Library.

First Edition

ISBN 978-0-7490-2366-9

Typeset in 11/16 pt Adobe Garamond Pro by
Allison & Busby Ltd.

The paper used for this Allison & Busby publication
has been produced from trees that have been legally sourced
from well-managed and credibly certified forests.

Printed and bound by
CPI Group (UK) Ltd, Croydon, CR0 4YY

To my wife, Lynne

CHAPTER ONE

Cambridge, 1894

Daniel Wilson stood before the Fitzwilliam Museum in Cambridge, taking in the wide stone steps that led up to the eight tall white pillars that supported the ornately sculpted frieze at the front of the building. *Impressive. Imposing. But not to me*, he thought as he carried his small suitcase up the steps. During his time as a member of Abberline's team of detectives he'd been in many impressive and imposing buildings, including the Houses of Parliament at Westminster, and even Buckingham Palace – although, he had to admit, that had been via a side door rather than the front entrance. After those, even the magnificent building that housed the Fitzwilliam tended to appear slightly less imposing.

He reached the top of the steps and the large green door of the main entrance. It was shut. He checked his watch. A quarter before eight.

He tugged at the bell pull beside the door, and waited. He allowed a minute to pass, then, when there was no sign of the door being opened, he tugged at the bell pull again, longer this time.

The door opened just enough for a woman, wearing an apron and a headscarf and holding a broom, to peer out at him.

'We're closed,' she said. 'It opens to the public at ten o'clock.'

She began to push the door shut, but Daniel shoved his booted foot into the gap, halting the door's progress.

'My name is Daniel Wilson,' he said. 'I'm a private enquiry agent and I'm here at the request of Sir William Mackenzie.' He paused, then added, 'About the body.'

He saw the woman give a shudder at the word. Recovering, she shook her head.

'Sir William ain't in yet.'

'I'm aware of that,' said Daniel. 'But he asked me to call as soon as I arrived to make my inspection.'

The woman hesitated, then reluctantly said, 'I suppose you'd better come in.'

She pulled the door open wider, and Daniel stepped in.

'You got anything to prove who you are?' she demanded, her face showing her suspicion. 'Only we've been warned to watch out for people who just want to take a look at where it happened.'

Daniel reached into his pocket and took out a buff envelope containing the telegram he'd received the previous evening from Sir William, along with his card.

'Here,' he said, holding them out to the woman. 'These will prove I am who I say I am.'

The woman looked at both items suspiciously, but didn't take them. Instead, she muttered, 'You wait here. I'll go and get Alice. She's in charge.'

With that, she locked the outer door, then headed down

the marble stairs, still toting her broom, with a last warning to Daniel: 'Don't touch anything!'

As he stood, surveying the opulent adornments of the interior, Daniel wondered if he would have received a different reception if he'd announced that he was a detective from Scotland Yard. He doubted it. Even when he was with Abberline's squad, their arrival at any establishment, whether as grand as this or a filthy illegal drinking den, was usually met with obstruction. People didn't like the police poking their noses into their business. And they liked private enquiry agents even less.

He stood there, surveying the tall, wide columns of mottled green and black marble trimmed with gold that reached up to the high, decorated vaulted ceiling. Opulence. Money. Prestige. Grandeur. But it still needed the little people, the cleaners and the attendants, to keep it going.

The cleaner reappeared, accompanied by a stern-looking woman, also wearing an apron and a headscarf.

'Mr Wilson?' she demanded brusquely.

'Indeed, ma'am.' Daniel nodded, and again he held out the envelope with the telegram and his card. This time, they were taken. The woman took out the telegram and read it, then studied the card, before returning both to Daniel.

'Very well,' she said. Turning to the cleaner, she ordered, 'Take Mr Wilson to the Egyptian Room, Mavis.'

Mavis shook her head.

'I ain't goin' in there,' she said. 'Not after what happened. Anyway, the p'lice said no one was to go in there.'

'Don't be ridiculous,' rebuked Alice. 'The police have finished their examination.'

'Yeah, but *he* may still be there,' said the woman with a shudder. 'His ghost.'

'There are no such things as ghosts, Mavis,' snapped Alice.

'I ain't goin' in there,' said Mavis doggedly. 'My Bill says I shouldn't have to. It's not right.'

'If you'd just take me to the entrance to the Egyptian Room, I'm sure I can find my way around,' offered Daniel, keen to make peace between the two women.

But Mavis shook her head again, firmly.

'I can't stay 'ere after what 'appened,' she said. 'That's what my Bill says, and 'e's right. I'll finish 'ere today, Alice, but that's it.'

Alice stood looking at Mavis, a grim expression on her face.

'Very well,' she said. 'But I am *very* disappointed.' She turned to Daniel and gestured. 'If you'll follow me, Mr Wilson.'

As Daniel followed Alice down the marble stairs, he said apologetically, 'I'm sorry if my arrival has caused this upheaval.'

Alice shook her head dismissively. 'Mavis is a halfwit. She's always finding things that seem to prevent her doing her work properly. And now this talk about ghosts. It's just brought things to a head that have been simmering for a while.' They arrived at the bottom of the stairs, where a pair of massive stone lions – or some creatures partly resembling lions – flanked a wide entrance.

'This is where he was found,' said Alice.

Daniel followed her into the room, past rows of artefacts stacked, possibly awaiting display, to a large heavy grey stone box: a sarcophagus. The lid had been removed and was now leaning against it.

'He was inside here,' said Alice.

'I see,' said Daniel. 'And who exactly discovered the body?'

'I'll let Sir William answer your questions, if you don't mind,' said Alice primly. 'I've got to get my work done.'

'Fine.' Daniel nodded. 'Perhaps you'll be good enough to leave a message with Sir William's secretary to let him know that

I'm here. And also, I'd appreciate it if you could advise everyone that my orders are for no one to come in here until I've finished.'

She hesitated, as if about to argue with him, then nodded and left, heading out of the room and back up the stairs.

Alone, Daniel Wilson took the time to take in the vast array of Egyptian artefacts that filled this room. And the next, because Daniel could see that the Egyptian Room went on from this room into another, and from there into yet another.

The items in this room were a veritable treasure trove. Some attempt had been made to bring order to the assembly: ornamental statues had been lined up along one wall, and an unusual group at that, all life-sized with humanised bodies, but some with heads of falcons, some with those of cats, others with wings on their backs, all carved in stone, with the faded colours of their original paint still adhering to some of them. Mostly, his eye kept being drawn back to the mummified bodies, the cloths that covered them yellowed and worn. Some of the mummies were very small, infants, their tiny cloth-wrapped bodies in crumbling wicker baskets. Others were larger, adults, their bodies laid in wicker or stone coffins. Daniel noticed that the cloth covering on one of these larger mummies had eroded to the extent that a bony foot poked through. *How old?* he wondered. *Three thousand years old? Four? Five? More?*

His reverie was interrupted by a woman's voice snapping angrily at him, 'You dare to bar me! This is intolerable!'

CHAPTER TWO

Daniel turned and saw a tall, well-dressed – and, he had to admit – attractive woman in her mid-thirties stood glaring at him.

'I beg your pardon, madam?' he said. 'But, for the moment, the Egyptian collection is closed to visitors.'

'I am not a visitor. I am making an inventory of the collection for the museum,' she said curtly.

'That may be,' he began, 'but a body was found here and I have been asked to look into it. My name is Daniel Wilson—'

'I know who you are,' snapped the woman. 'You were formerly Inspector Wilson of the Metropolitan police, Chief Inspector Abberline's assistant on the notorious Jack the Ripper case, now operating as a private detective. Sir William advised me yesterday that he would be telegraphing you.'

'Private enquiry agent,' Daniel corrected her politely. 'In that case, you have the advantage of me, madam.'

'I am Abigail Fenton, archaeologist, with an honours degree from Girton College in the Classics. I am not just some nosy local busybody. As I informed you, I have been asked by the Fitzwilliam to make an inventory of the Egyptian collection, and it was I who found the body.'

'I see,' said Daniel. 'In that case I would be most interested to hear what you have to say, Mrs Fenton . . .'

'Miss,' Abigail stressed firmly.

'Miss Fenton,' Daniel corrected himself. He gestured at the sarcophagus. 'Would you show me how you discovered the body, and what position it was in?'

Abigail joined him.

'It was yesterday morning, Wednesday, at about ten o'clock. I had been examining the object the day before, both externally and internally.'

'Did you have assistance in removing the lid?' asked Daniel. 'It's very heavy.'

She shook her head.

'The lid had been slid partly to one side, enough to enable me to see inside. On Tuesday the sarcophagus was empty. I know that because I was particularly keen to see if there were any decorations on the interior; the ancient Egyptians were very keen on colour and adornment.'

'Yes, so I see.' Daniel nodded, indicating the other objects in the large room, many of them colourfully painted.

'In fact, as you will have observed, the interior of this particular sarcophagus has not been decorated; the ornamentation has been kept to the outside. However, when I left the museum on Tuesday evening, I left the lid pushed to one side so I could carry out a more detailed examination of the interior the next day, in case there were holes in the stone that might show where a different form of decoration had been used.'

'And when you returned on Wednesday morning . . .'

'The lid had been pushed back in place. I assumed it was one of the museum staff who'd done it, possibly for reasons of safety, although I can assure you I had not left the lid in an unsafe or precarious position . . .'

'No, I'm sure you didn't,' murmured Daniel.

'I started to push the lid to one side – it moves surprisingly easily because the Egyptians had used highly polished stone on the top of the actual box – and saw at once that there was something inside. At first I thought someone had dumped a pile of old clothes inside it, but then I saw the man's head . . .'

'If it distresses you . . .' began Daniel gently.

'Of course it doesn't distress me,' Abigail snapped at him. 'Life and death are facts of nature. I've not long returned from an archaeological dig at Gaza in Egypt, and out there human life is far more precarious than it is here in Britain. Death is an everyday fact of life there.'

'I apologise for being overprotective of your feelings,' said Daniel.

She sniffed, but appeared to be slightly mollified.

'I apologise for the sharpness of my tone,' she returned. 'But I am fed up with being treated as some kind of fragile flower just because I am a woman. We do not all swoon at the sight of death or injury. If we did, there would have been no Florence Nightingale or her nurses to bring comfort and aid to soldiers during the Crimean War.'

'No, indeed,' agreed Daniel, making a mental note that this woman would be a formidable adversary, but at the same time could be a very useful ally in the right circumstances.

'At first I thought he might be drunk, but I smelt no alcohol. And then I noticed the unnatural angle of his head and realised that his neck looked as if it was broken.'

'You have medical training?' asked Daniel.

She shook her head. 'While I was in Egypt I saw the body of a man who'd been hanged. His head was at the same angle to his body.'

This is a formidable woman indeed, Daniel thought. *Unafraid, not easily put off.*

'I immediately went to see Sir William Mackenzie and reported my discovery to him. Sir William came down, confirmed what I had found, and called the police.' Her expression hardened. 'Some idiot called Inspector Drabble arrived, who promptly ordered me to leave. He said the dead body meant it was no place for a woman.

'I pointed out to him that we are surrounded here by dead bodies with all these mummified remains, but he was adamant, and he actually called for a constable to escort me from the premises. I complained to Sir William, but he told me that the site was under the jurisdiction of the police. Inspector Drabble didn't even ask me about the body, despite the fact that I was the one who discovered it.'

'There was a reason for that,' snapped a voice, curtly.

They turned to see the short, round, moustached figure of a man descending the steps, bowler hat firmly wedged atop his head, the buttons of his suit jacket straining over his ample stomach.

'Inspector Drabble, I presume,' said Daniel. 'My name is Daniel Wilson—'

'I know who you are,' said Drabble brusquely.

15

'I assume you have finally come to talk to me about finding the body,' said Abigail, her disapproval clear in her tone.

'You assume wrong,' said Drabble. 'I gained all the information I needed from Sir William Mackenzie and the other staff.'

'But I found the body!' exploded Abigail angrily.

'I am aware of that, and it was noted,' said Drabble coldly. He turned to Daniel. 'I've been advised by Sir William that he has brought you in to investigate this case.'

Daniel nodded. 'That is correct.'

'I have advised him that your presence is unnecessary, and also could be a distraction.'

'Really?' said Daniel.

He'd been expecting this. So often, when he was called in, he encountered hostility from the local police force, who resented him.

'The reason I say your presence is unnecessary is because our study of the situation, and of the premises, indicate that the man broke in during the night of the Tuesday. With all the external doors and windows being secure, this suggests he gained entry by climbing a drainpipe up to the roof, then traversing the roof to the courtyard area, down another drainpipe into the courtyard, where he was able to access the interior of the building, the doors and windows from the courtyard being less secure.'

'That seems a very circuitous route,' mused Daniel.

'We have examined the building and it is the only answer,' said Drabble tersely.

'Unless someone let him in?' suggested Daniel.

'We've spoken to the nightwatchmen who were on duty during the night and they both insist that no one entered the building while they were here,' said Drabble. 'As I say, all the evidence so far points to the fact that this man had come to steal some artefacts, and he was in the act of climbing into the sarcophagus when the heavy lid fell down on him, killing him.'

'And that's your conclusion?'

'It is. However, we shall continue with our investigations in case new evidence arises, and if it does, we shall reappraise the situation.' He stepped close to Daniel and thrust his face forward. 'If anyone's going to solve this case, Wilson, it's me and my men. Local bobbies using proper police procedures, not a so-called private enquiry agent. If you ask me, you and Abberline have done a disservice to the police by setting yourselves up the way you have, just because you had a bit of luck on some high-profile cases.' He sneered. 'The fact is, you never brought Jack to justice, did you. It was all hot air. You and Abberline were chancers, the pair of you.'

Daniel was used to attacks like this and they didn't bother him, but the jibe at his much-loved former boss stung him.

'Chief Inspector Abberline received eighty-four commendations and awards for his excellent work during his years on the force before he retired,' he growled. 'How many have you received?'

'You don't fool me, Wilson,' snapped Drabble. 'You call it private investigation, I call it taking money under false pretences. You're not wanted or needed here.'

'Sir William obviously disagrees with you, or he wouldn't have contacted me,' replied Daniel coolly, having regained his temper. 'But you may rest assured that anything that Miss Fenton and I discover, we will impart to you.'

Drabble's mouth dropped open in bewilderment. He looked from Daniel to Abigail, then back again.

'Her?' he burst out, stunned.

'Miss Fenton is not only the person who found the body, she

17

is also an expert on the ancient Egyptians and as such will be able to offer valuable insights into the reasons why the victim was here, and why he may have been killed.'

'I've told you, it was an accident!' raged Drabble. He pointed a stubby accusing finger at Daniel. 'You're just spinning this out to make more money!'

'On the contrary, I'm intending to get to the bottom of this, as a proper policeman – current or former – should.'

Drabble glared at him. He was obviously boiling with rage and doing his best to not let it spill out.

'A chancer and a woman!' he spat. 'Well, I'm warning you now. You interfere with this investigation and I'll have you both arrested!'

With that, the inspector turned on his heel and stomped up the stairs.

Abigail waited until he'd gone, then turned to Daniel, her face showing her bewilderment.

'Me?' she said.

'If you're agreeable to work with me,' said Daniel.

She smiled. 'It will upset Inspector Drabble?'

Daniel nodded. 'Most certainly.'

'Then count me firmly in.'

CHAPTER THREE

'If I am to be a detective with you, what is our next move?' she asked.

'I'd like to talk to the nightwatchman who was on duty on Tuesday night.'

'We have two who alternate,' she said. 'Harry Elder and Joseph Ransome. Miss Sattery, Sir William's secretary, will be able to let you have their details. One of them will be on duty at half past six this evening, but I'm not sure which.'

'Thank you,' said Daniel. 'The other thing is to view the body. Although, if Inspector Drabble has taken charge of it, that may prove problematic.'

She smiled. 'Fortunately, that is not the case. With no known friends or relatives to lay claim to the poor man, his body was taken to Gonville and Caius.'

Daniel gave her a look of enquiry.

'Is that a hospital?' he asked.

She laughed.

'I'm sorry,' she said. 'One gets so used to talking to people who know Cambridge. Gonville and Caius – it's pronounced "Keys" but spelt C-A-I-U-S, after its founder, John Caius – is a college with a very strong medical tradition. And when I suggested to Dr Keen—'

'Dr Keen?' asked Daniel.

'Dr Thomas Keen,' explained Abigail. 'As Inspector Drabble was refusing to accept the dead man was a case of murder, I thought it would be acceptable for Dr Keen to conduct an autopsy to try to ascertain the cause of death.'

'And Dr Keen was willing?'

'Very much so. Dr Keen has a wonderful enquiring mind. We are lucky to have a man like him in Cambridge: someone who's not held back by hide-bound convention. A free thinker.'

'You sound as if you have great respect for this Dr Keen,' said Daniel. 'An acquaintance?'

She shook her head.

'Not really, I've only met him a couple of times, both times through my sister, Bella. She's a librarian at the public library and he attended an event she organised to find ways to encourage the poor to become literate. My sister is very keen on reshaping society along more socially equitable ways, something she shares with Dr Keen. Although his passions are more in the areas of improving the health of the poor.'

'Very creditable,' said Daniel. He was about to ask for more on Dr Keen, and Abigail's sister, when the head cleaner, Alice, appeared.

'Sir William is in early,' she announced. 'He asks if you will join him, Mr Wilson.'

'Certainly,' said Daniel. To Abigail, he said, 'After I've met with Sir William, perhaps we could go to see Dr Keen at Gonville and Caius and see if he's had a chance to examine the body.'

'Excellent.' She nodded. 'I'll see you here.'

Sir William Mackenzie's office was on the top floor of the museum, tucked away down a maze of corridors. Daniel was grateful that the formidable Alice had accompanied him, otherwise he might have wandered, lost, among the corridors, particularly as there was no sign to indicate where the office was located.

Alice arrived at a dark oak door, rapped at it with her knuckles, then opened it and called, 'Mr Wilson for Sir William, Miss Sattery.'

'Do come in, Mr Wilson,' said a middle-aged lady, rising from behind her desk. 'Sir William is ready for you.'

Daniel thanked Alice, who withdrew, then turned his attention to the office as Miss Sattery strode to an inner door. It was a small room, but very neat, everything orderly. As was Miss Sattery herself. About fifty, Daniel guessed, and very much the efficient organiser. It struck Daniel that Sir William had surrounded himself with a team of strong-willed, formidable women, if Abigail Fenton, Alice and Miss Sattery were anything to go by.

'Mr Wilson,' announced Miss Sattery.

She gestured for Daniel to go in, but before he did he asked, 'If I may, I'd be grateful if you could furnish me with the details of your two nightwatchmen, Mr Elder and Mr Ransome.'

'Of course,' she said. 'I'll have their details for you after you've seen Sir William.'

Sir William Mackenzie's office was very different from his secretary's: books and papers of all sorts were piled high on his desk and every other available surface, including the wide window ledge.

Sir William was in his sixties, tall and thin, white-haired, and Daniel observed that the front of his dark waistcoat was freely speckled with cigar ash. Ash also featured on the desk, and Daniel guessed that this must have been very painful for the neat and tidy Miss Sattery.

'Sir William,' said Daniel.

They shook hands, and Sir William gestured Daniel to a chair on the other side of his desk.

'Thank you for attending so quickly, Mr Wilson.'

'I find it helps an investigation to examine the scene of the occurrence as soon as possible, before any trail goes cold. I caught the early train from London.'

'I understand you have met Inspector Drabble?'

'I have, sir.'

'He insists it was an accident of some kind.'

'Yes, he was very strong on that point.'

'Have you reached any conclusions yet as to whether it was an accident, or something more sinister?'

'I have only just begun to examine the scene where the body was discovered. But it occurs to me that whether it was an accident or not, the discovery of a dead man in a sarcophagus is a mystery that needs investigating. I hope to have more information after I've spoken to the person carrying out the autopsy on the dead man.'

'Ah yes, Dr Keen at Gonville and Caius,' said Sir William. 'An excellent man.'

'So I understand from Miss Fenton,' said Daniel.

'Yes, she is a most . . . determined person,' said Sir William. 'It was partly her dissatisfaction with the way she believed that Inspector Drabble responded to the matter that decided me to ask you to undertake enquiries on our behalf.' He paused, then added, 'You were recommended to me by Sir Jasper Stone at the British Museum. He told me about the incident of the missing Saxon jewels, and how you'd unmasked the culprits responsible. He said that if we ever found ourselves in a similar predicament then he suggested we get in touch with you. And, as it turns out, we do indeed find ourselves in such a situation.'

'I am very grateful to Sir Jasper,' said Daniel.

'It is important that we get to the bottom of this,' said Sir William. 'The Fitzwilliam has built up a very high reputation, and something as . . . unorthodox . . . as this can have an adverse impact on that reputation. Instead of it being lauded as a place of education and knowledge, it becomes known as a place where bodies are found. Such things can put serious people off.'

Including wealthy patrons, reflected Daniel.

'You may rest assured, Sir William, I will do my best to bring this to a satisfactory conclusion as swiftly as possible, and with the greatest discretion.'

'Yes, Sir Jasper did say your discretion was particularly invaluable to the BM,' said Sir William. He opened a drawer in his desk and took out an envelope, which he passed to Daniel. 'We've made arrangements for you to stay at a small and very respectable boarding house during your time in Cambridge. It's run by a Mrs Loxley, a widow, a very efficient lady. Whenever we have visiting speakers, they stay there, and all have reported very favourably on the accommodation, and her manner. At this moment I understand she only has two other gentlemen staying there.'

'Thank you, Sir William,' said Daniel, taking the envelope. 'I very much appreciate your hospitality.'

CHAPTER FOUR

As Daniel and Abigail walked to Gonville and Caius along Trumpington Street, continuing along King's Parade, Daniel couldn't help but reflect how different the air was here, compared to London. Two cities, but vastly different. The London of his birth and residence was smoke-filled, the buildings darkened with soot and grime from the thousands of coal fires, domestic and industrial. And his own particular area, a terraced house not far from Mornington Crescent, was close enough to the three main railway termini of Euston, St Pancras and King's Cross to receive coating after coating of coal dust from the succession of trains that steamed in and out of the stations, their smoke carried on the winds to form a black layer. And all too often this smoke mixed with fog to create a thick pea-souper of smog, choking the life out of everyone who ventured out in it.

Cambridge, however, was clean by comparison. Yes, there was some smattering of smoke from chimneys on some of the buildings, but slight by comparison. Possibly it was because Cambridge was set on a vast flat plain of agricultural countryside, whereas the centre of London was constructed of tall buildings rammed close together, allowing no space for the smoke and stench of the inner city to disperse. Certainly, as they walked along King's Parade, beyond the university buildings all Daniel could see were swathes of open countryside.

Daniel had half expected a history of the various magnificent ancient buildings they passed from Abigail, especially the huge and glorious architecture of what he discovered – from a large noticeboard they passed – to be the chapel of King's College, a magnificent structure that in Daniel's eyes easily rivalled Westminster Abbey. But Abigail seemed oblivious to these wonders, possibly because for her they were just part of everyday Cambridge life; she just strode onwards, obviously eager to get to grips with the next stage of their investigation: the results of the autopsy.

As Trumpington Street had become King's Parade, so the same thoroughfare now became Trinity Street.

'Here we are,' said Abigail, stopping before an ancient building of light brown sandstone, the stone around its doors and windows carved in the medieval style. 'Gonville and Caius.'

'Very old,' observed Daniel.

'Founded the first time by Edmund Gonville in 1348,' said Abigail.

'The first time?' queried Daniel.

'Alas, it ran into financial difficulties over the next two hundred years and was on the point of closure before a rich doctor called John Keys came to its aid and refounded it in 1557. In fact, his name was actually Keys, just as it sounds, but he decided to Latinise it to be spelt Caius because he felt it sounded far grander, as befitted his new status as the creator of a Cambridge college.'

'"Vanity of vanities,"' quoted Daniel.

Abigail regarded him. 'Ecclesiastes,' she commented. 'Do I take it you are a religious man, Mr Wilson?'

'Not necessarily,' replied Daniel cagily. 'I just think some quotations are apt, and the story of Dr John Keys seems to suit.'

She headed in through the main door, Daniel following, and after making their way along and down a maze of corridors and stairs, they found themselves in a basement room which had been turned into a small operating theatre. The body of a man lay on a large table, a sheet covering him to the shoulders. Examining the cadaver was a man in his early thirties, who looked up as they approached.

'Miss Fenton!' He beamed. 'I got your note to say you would be calling, so I've got everything ready for you.'

So Abigail had sent a note ahead while he was meeting with Sir William, Daniel realised. Very efficient.

'This is Daniel Wilson, Dr Keen,' said Abigail, introducing them.

'My pleasure, Doctor,' said Daniel as the two men shook hands.

He turned his attention to the body. A man in his forties, Daniel guessed, with something in his features that suggested he wasn't English. The shape of his nose and his high cheekbones, along with the pallor of his skin, reminded Daniel of some of the Arabs he'd come across during his time at Scotland Yard, especially in the areas around the London docks.

The body had been packed with ice to delay composition, but already after just three days there was the unmistakeable odour of decaying flesh. Daniel glanced at Abigail, and was impressed by the way she seemed unmoved by the sight of death. When he'd been in the Met, there had been many a constable or sergeant who'd been unable to cope with the sight and stench of violent death. Although that was at first; if they got past that and continued in the force, their constitution hardened. Not to death, emotionally – that was something that had never eased for Daniel – but physically: to the smell and the sight, the ripped flesh, the gore, eyes torn from their sockets.

He assumed that Abigail's lack of shock came from her time in Egypt, where – according to her – death and sights such as this were a daily occurrence. Much as they had been for Daniel when he was working in Whitechapel and the East End of London.

'Thank you for letting us view him, Doctor,' said Daniel. 'I suspected that Inspector Drabble might have given instructions that we weren't allowed.'

'He did,' said Dr Keen, 'but this is one area where he does not have any authority. And when I received the original note from Sir William requesting I give my assistance, and who it was for, I was only too happy to oblige.'

'Sir William mentioned me?' said Daniel, feeling flattered that his name had registered this far from London.

'Yes, but it was his mention of Miss Fenton that persuaded me this was not a frivolous request. We sometimes get what I describe as thrill-seekers wishing to view a cadaver, often ladies. But when Sir William mentioned that Miss Fenton was involved in the investigation, any doubts I may have had were erased.' He turned to Abigail and said, 'As a patron of the Fitzwilliam I am very impressed by your scholarship with the Greek and Roman antiquities, and now with the ancient Egyptian.'

'Thank you, Doctor,' acknowledged Abigail, and Daniel noticed that she coloured slightly. *Embarrassment at being praised in this way, or is it the fact that Dr Keen is a young and handsome man in his late thirties? Is he married, or single?* Daniel wondered. And then mentally kicked himself. It was of no matter – he was here on business.

Dr Keen lowered the sheet covering the body to waist level, so they could get a better view.

'I'm guessing his age at somewhere in his early fifties,' said Dr Keen. 'From his skin colouring, and certain facial features, I'd say he was from the Middle East.'

'I would agree,' said Abigail. 'There is a strong resemblance to many of the people I met while I was in Egypt.'

Daniel pointed to the hands.

'The hands are soft, no hard callouses, unusual for a man of his age.' He bent down and peered at the hands closer. 'And on the right hand index finger and thumb you can see traces of ink. Faded, but there.'

'A person who writes,' murmured Abigail.

'It is a broken neck, I assume, Doctor?' asked Daniel.

Keen nodded. 'There was a contusion at the base of the skull, caused by a hard object.'

'Could it have been the lid of the sarcophagus falling on him?' asked Daniel.

Keen gave a tight smile. 'Inspector Drabble's theory?' He shook his head. 'The object that killed him was heavy, but narrow. Possibly an iron bar, or something similar.'

'Have you informed the inspector of your conclusion?' asked Abigail.

'I have,' said Keen. 'He has informed me that I am wrong.'

'Do you have his possessions?' asked Daniel.

'Only his clothing. There was nothing else. No wallet, no money.'

He led the way to a cupboard, opened it and took out a tray which contained a grey suit, a white shirt, socks, male undergarments and a pair of polished black leather shoes. A white celluloid collar and a tie, decorated with a series of small red crescents on black, rested on the other items.

Daniel took every item out of the tray and examined them in detail. He pointed out the tailor's label inside the jacket.

'Cairo,' he observed. 'Egyptian. But the words are in English.'

'So, a tailor patronised by the English.' Keen nodded.

'And Egyptians of a higher class,' added Abigail.

'Which adds to the hands not being those of a labourer. The material is of good quality, as are the shoes. But the traces of ink on his hands show that he is not a man of leisure, one of the idle rich.'

'A professional man,' observed Keen.

Daniel nodded. 'Would it be possible to get a photograph of the man?' he asked. 'Just his face.'

'You think you might be able to identify him?'

'It's possible,' replied Daniel.

'Certainly,' said Keen. 'I'm only too happy to help if it helps to discover what happened to this unfortunate man.'

As Daniel and Abigail left the hospital and entered the warm Cambridge sunshine, Daniel commented, 'We were lucky to be dealing with a man like Dr Keen. Others might have been more obstructive.'

'He's an intelligent man,' said Abigail.

But, again, he noticed that she coloured slightly as she said it. *So,* he thought, *she has a soft spot for the doctor.* He wondered if it was reciprocated, then told himself off for being too inquisitive. *You are here on business*, he reminded himself sharply.

'So?' he asked. 'What are your conclusions?'

'Not a common burglar,' she said. 'A professional man of some sort, I believe we all felt that.' She frowned. 'But no identifying documents of any sort.'

'Whoever killed him removed them to stop him being identified,' said Daniel.

'Then why didn't they simply remove the body?' asked Abigail.

'Perhaps it was too difficult to get it out of the museum, for some reason,' mused Daniel. 'So, to recap: a professional man, most likely Egyptian, one who writes a great deal, with an interest in Egyptian artefacts serious enough to make him break into the Fitzwilliam at night.'

'An academic,' said Abigail.

'Yes, that's what occurred to me,' said Daniel.

'And you intend to take the photograph from Dr Keen around the colleges to see if you can identify him?'

'That was one thought,' said Daniel, 'but the problem with that is, if he didn't have anything to do with the colleges here, if he'd recently arrived, for example, we'd be drawing a blank. But it's likely he would have stayed somewhere. A lodging house or hotel, or with someone he knew.

'So my intention is to take an advert in the local paper, his photograph with the caption: "Do you know this man? If so, please contact . . ." with my name and the address of where I'm staying, and the address of the Fitzwilliam.'

'Why an advert instead of letting the newspaper cover it as a story?'

'Because that way, I control the wording,' said Daniel. 'Sometimes I've discovered when newspapers tell a story, the facts can be wrong. Sometimes they leap to conclusions, which can also be wrong. If we try and give them this as a story, they'll be keen to put in all we know, or guess, and if we don't give them anything, they'll very likely make it up.'

'Yes, that makes sense,' she said. Then she turned to him. 'Can I suggest you add my name to the advertisement, Mr Wilson. After all, you could be all over the place conducting your enquiries, and I will be mostly at the Fitzwilliam. So, if anyone does have any information . . .' She smiled. 'And you did tell Inspector Drabble that we would be working together on this case.'

'Yes, I did, and thank you. That would be excellent,' said Daniel. On a sudden impulse, he asked, 'Actually, Miss Fenton, and forgive me if it seems forward, that's not my intention, but I wondered whether you might be free to show me some of the sights of Cambridge. I am a stranger here, and . . .'

He saw immediately the look of worry and doubt that briefly crossed her face; then she smiled – but a polite smile this time, not one of genuine warmth as when she had thanked him a few seconds ago.

'Of course, Mr Wilson. But could we make it some other time? I really need to get back to the Fitzwilliam to continue with the inventory. That, after all, is my prime occupation at this moment.'

'Certainly.' Daniel nodded. 'But perhaps you would be good enough to point me in the right direction for the lodgings that Sir William has arranged for me.'

He produced the envelope that Sir William had given him and passed it to her.

'Ah yes, Mrs Loxley.' She returned the envelope to him, and pointed at a side street opposite the college. 'That's Green Street. Go down there and take a left when you reach the end and that's Sidney Street. Walk along, past Sidney Sussex College on your right, and cross over Jesus Lane. Sidney Street becomes Bridge Street, and you'll find Mrs Loxley's house just along there on your right.'

'Thank you.' Daniel smiled, with a slight bow. 'If I discover anything, I'll make contact at the Fitzwilliam.'

As Abigail hurried away, she felt herself reddening, and cursed herself for a fool. He had made it clear that he had no untoward intentions on her, so why had she reacted the way she did? Certainly, he seemed genuine. And honest.

But Edgar had seemed genuine and honest, and she had responded to him. Given herself to him. And then he'd abandoned her, heartlessly, cruelly. A plaything, that was all she'd been to him. Despite his promises and the look in his beautiful blue eyes that had appeared to reveal his honesty and warmth at that time.

I was a fool. A gullible fool. But I won't let it happen again.

Daniel was still feeling puzzled as he thought about Abigail Fenton's sudden and antipathetic reaction to him, as if he'd made an improper suggestion to her. He'd genuinely just meant it as a request to show him around the city so that he could get his bearings; the knowledge of a local was always superior to that of a map. But the expression on her face suggested he'd alarmed her.

Why? It had to be something he'd said, or done; his manner. She'd misinterpreted it in the worst way. Obviously he'd have to watch his step with her, be more reserved. From now on he'd make sure he stayed at arm's length from her, kept it purely professional. No personal questions. No intrusion of any sort.

CHAPTER FIVE

Mrs Loxley's house was a very neat semi-detached with a small garden at the front and a colourful hanging basket of white and yellow flowers by the front door. It looked warmly inviting. Mrs Loxley herself was indeed the picture of friendly welcome, a far cry from some of the landladies Daniel had encountered when he'd been forced to travel away from home. He remembered one in particular who vented her anger loudly on her temporary lodgers for the smallest infraction of behaviour, the worst of which was apparently adding another lump of coal to the open fire in the sitting room.

From the glow of this friendly fire in the hearth, the light decor of the flowered wallpaper and the cheerful smile of Mrs Loxley herself – a plump lady of about fifty – Daniel knew he would feel at home here, and he made a mental note to express his thanks to Sir William for arranging these lodgings for him.

'I only keep a small house, Mr Wilson,' Mrs Loxley told him, 'just the three rooms. So there's yourself, a Mr Barron, who's a businessman – trades in precious metals, I believe – and a professor, Wynstan Hughes. He's here in Cambridge researching a book on the Civil War.' She smiled. 'I'm sure he'll tell you all about it. It's a topic he's very passionate about. Sir William said you're here to help him with this dreadful business at the Fitzwilliam.'

'Indeed.' Daniel nodded, inwardly remarking that there would be no secrets kept while he was lodging at Mrs Loxley's. But often on an investigation, that was no bad thing. People with information would need to know where to find him, and once Mrs Loxley had spread the word of her latest lodger ('He's a detective investigating that dead body they found at the Fitzwilliam'), those with what might be vital information wouldn't have to search for him.

After he'd been shown his bedroom – again, friendly, cosy and welcoming, warm colours and not too many decorative ornaments – Daniel made suitably flattering compliments to Mrs Loxley about the accommodation, then set out once more into the streets of Cambridge, promising that he would return in time for supper.

He made his way back to the source of his investigation, the Fitzwilliam.

As he entered the building, he thought about letting Abigail Fenton know he was there, but decided against it. After her somewhat surprising reaction to his suggestion about showing him the city, he didn't want her to think he would be imposing his company unnecessarily on her. Instead he explored the rest of the museum: the upper floors, which mostly consisted of displays of Italian and Spanish painting, with some British, and then the courtyard, an open space in the centre of the main building. This was the way the man had come in, Drabble had said. Up a drainpipe on the outside of the building and over the roof, then down one of the drainpipes into the courtyard.

It seemed to Daniel a very involved action, especially because – according to the attendants – nothing had been taken from any of the display cases or exhibits.

And had the murderer followed his victim along that route? If so, he'd obviously done it without being spotted by his victim. Or had both arrived at the Fitzwilliam and broken in together, then some sort of altercation broke out between them and one was killed?

Daniel thought of the dead man he'd seen at Gonville and Caius, the professional academic from Egypt, and tried to picture him scaling a drainpipe up two very tall floors of the Fitzwilliam, then crossing the roof, before making a perilous climb down another long drainpipe into the courtyard.

No, it didn't add up. The dead man had been slightly podgy, not a physique that went with such a dangerous sequence of climbs.

But if that wasn't how he'd got in, with all the doors and windows reported as being untampered with, how had he made his entrance?

CHAPTER SIX

As Abigail let herself into the neat terraced house she shared with her younger sister, Bella, she could hear Bella practising scales on the piano in the drawing room. Abigail gritted her teeth as she heard the same error, the same missed note, that Bella made every time.

She does it to annoy me, thought Abigail. *She heard the door open and immediately played the wrong notes on purpose.*

'I'm home!' she called.

The piano stopped and Bella appeared in the hallway. She was shorter than Abigail, but decidedly – at least, in Abigail's eyes – more *feminine*. It was a cultivated image, of course, intended to make men look at her admiringly, and women purse their lips in jealousy. Bella had always been the same, even as a teenager. The blonde curls were the key to it. And the deliberately narrow waist, courtesy of what must surely be a painfully tight corset.

But then, that was Bella: superficiality over substance. Abigail loved her sister – after all, one had to love one's sister – but there was so much about Bella that annoyed her.

'How are you, Abi?' asked Bella, her voice showing concern.

'Annoyed,' replied Abigail. 'I had to deal with that idiot, Inspector Drabble, again.'

Bella shuddered. 'Honestly, Abi, I don't know how you can be so blasé about this. You found a dead body!'

'I'm not saying it was a pleasant experience, I'm just angry that Inspector Drabble seems to be so dismissive of me just because I'm a woman! Fortunately, an intelligent man has appeared on the scene to take part in the investigation.'

'Oh? Who?'

'A man called Daniel Wilson. He's a private investigator, a former detective inspector at Scotland Yard in London. Sir William says he comes highly recommended, and so far he seems to be an improvement.' She snorted derisively. 'Though, compared to Inspector Drabble, that isn't too difficult.' She took off her coat. 'How was your day?'

'Not as exciting as yours,' said Bella. 'We had a slight panic when it seemed that a book might have been taken illicitly, but fortunately it had just been misfiled. It was Ibsen's *Hedda Gabler*. It had been filed under "G" instead of under "I".' Bella worked at the public lending library in the Guildhall. 'We also had a visit from Lady Restwood.'

The tone of excited satisfaction in Bella's voice made Abigail ask, 'Who?'

'Lady Restwood. The wife of Lord Restwood. Of Restwood Manor.'

Abigail shook her head. 'I don't know them.'

'Oh, Abigail, you surely do! Especially Lady Restwood.'

'Is she anything to do with the Fitzwilliam, or one of the colleges?'

'No, she's a very vocal advocate of votes for women. I thought you'd have been aware of her. You're very vocal yourself on the position of women in our society. Listen to you just now, talking about this policeman and the way he was dismissive of you just because you're a woman.'

'Inspector Drabble is a moron. Fortunately I do not receive the same Neolithic reaction from people like Sir William Mackenzie, or many of the people I work with.'

'But that's because they are frightened of you, Abi.'

'Nonsense! They treat me as an equal because they respect me as a person.'

Bella shook her head. 'I have seen their faces. You frighten them. You are very domineering. You frighten *me*.'

'Obviously not very much, otherwise you wouldn't be lecturing me on what you consider the negative aspects of my personality.'

'Because this is important, Abi. Lady Restwood wants help to form a women's group to canvass for proper suffrage. The right to vote for women. Surely you agree with that.'

'Of course I do, but on a list of priorities, whether social or personal, I do not rate it as of the greatest importance. Women do – and have – exerted influence. For heaven's sake, our monarch is a woman, and I think you'll agree that her predecessor, Elizabeth, was the most influential person of her time.'

'But they are privileged people, Abi. Protected by their position. Lady Restwood feels we can work to make changes for *all* women.'

'How? By marching on Parliament? If that's the case . . .'

'By all manner of ways. Lady Restwood asked if she could put some leaflets in the library for members of the public to read. She's already arranged a public meeting.' She sighed. 'Unfortunately, I was reluctantly forced to inform her that I would have to ask permission of the library committee, and as the committee is exclusively male . . .'

'Bella, do I get the impression that you are considering becoming involved in radical politics?' asked Abigail, with a concerned frown.

'And why shouldn't I?' challenged Bella.

'Well, for one thing, you would be putting your employment at the library at risk,' said Abigail. 'It's all very well for people like Lady Restwood, who have no need to earn their own living, but for people like us, involvement in radical politics could be precarious.'

'I'd hardly call votes for women "radical",' responded Bella curtly.

'It is to those in power, whether at national or local level,' said Abigail.

'Well, Dr Keen is supportive of the cause,' said Bella. 'He said as much to me when he was in the library yesterday, seeing if the campaign to increase literacy amongst the poor had had any discernible effect.' She smiled. 'I reassured him that it was a long-term project, and results may take some time.'

'Thus encouraging him to return to the library with greater frequency,' commented Abigail drily.

Bella glared coldly at her sister. 'Might I ask what you are suggesting?' she demanded.

'Oh really, Bella, it is obvious that you are smitten with Dr Keen . . .'

'I am not!' snapped Bella, colouring.

'Well, you give all the signs of harbouring such feelings,' said Abigail. 'However, if you want my opinion—'

'No, I do not!'

'—when I saw Dr Keen today it struck me again that he is a single-minded person with his sights devoted to things other than romance; namely: social equality and science.'

Bella stared at her sister, shock on her face. 'You saw Dr Keen!'

'Yes,' said Abigail.

'Where? Did he come to the Fitzwilliam?'

'No, we visited him at Gonville and Caius.'

'We?'

'Mr Wilson and I. Mr Wilson wished to view the body of the dead man I found, and Dr Keen is conducting the autopsy.'

Bella still stared at Abigail, dumbfounded.

'You went to Gonville and Caius?'

'Yes, I've already said so.'

'And did you . . . look at the body?'

'Both Mr Wilson and I did. We examined it, along with Dr Keen.'

Bella gave a little gasp.

'Tell me the body was clothed.'

'Of course it wasn't clothed, Bella. For heaven's sake! How can anyone carry out an autopsy on a body wearing clothes?'

'So you and Dr Keen were looking at the naked body of a man . . .'

'Dr Keen had covered his private parts with a sheet,' said Abigail. 'To be honest, it wouldn't have bothered me if he hadn't, but I assume he felt some form of decorum was needed.'

Bella glared at her, furious. 'How can you!' she demanded, shaking with anger. 'You tell me you are aware that I have feelings for Dr Keen, and yet you deliberately place yourself in a private situation with him and a naked man!'

'Hardly private,' said Abigail. 'Mr Wilson was with us.'

'The fact remains—' burst out Bella.

'The fact remains,' cut in Abigail firmly, silencing her sister, 'that I am investigating this murder along with Mr Wilson. To that effect I will do whatever is necessary, and if that includes examining the naked body of the victim then so be it. And I can assure you, Sister, that that the smell of a decomposing body in a mortuary is not exactly conducive to romance, even if I did have designs on Dr Keen. Which I do not.' She looked at the clock on the mantlepiece. 'Now, has Mrs Standish given an indication of when she'll be serving dinner? It has been creeping ever later these last few evenings.'

CHAPTER SEVEN

Daniel waited until a quarter before seven before pulling the bell pull at the Fitzwilliam. As he had done first thing that morning, he stood by the large green door and waited. On this occasion, the door was opened with greater alacrity, and an elderly man dressed in the uniform of a nightwatchman looked coldly out at him.

'Do I have the honour of addressing either Mr Elder or Mr Ransome?' asked Daniel. 'My name is Daniel Wilson. I've been asked to investigate the recent tragedy here. The discovery of the body in the Egyptian sarcophagus.'

The man nodded. 'Yes, sir. Sir William mentioned that he'd contacted you. I'm Harry Elder.' He gestured for Daniel to enter, then closed and locked the door behind them. He pointed towards two chairs in the main reception area. 'If you don't mind, sir, we'll sit there and talk. That way I'm not far away in the event of someone arriving.'

As the two men walked to the chairs, Daniel asked, 'Does that happen often? People calling after the museum has closed?'

'Only after the first hour or so,' said Elder. 'People who've realised they've left an umbrella or something behind. I usually sit here for the first hour of my watch, in case, before I do my rounds.'

'Were you on duty on the Tuesday night?'

Elder nodded. 'I was on first shift. Joseph Ransome took over from me during the night.'

'And what are your shift times?' asked Daniel.

'Six and a half hours,' said Elder. 'First shift is half past six in the evening until one in the morning. Second shift is one in the morning until half past seven. That's when the day staff come on.'

'Do you always do the same shifts? You the first, Mr Ransome the second?'

Elder shook his head. 'One week I'm on first shift, him second. The next week we work it the other way round. So next week, he'll be on first shift.'

'Did you notice anything unusual during your shift on Tuesday evening?'

Elder shook his head firmly. 'No, sir. I did my rounds as usual, and I can swear that there was no sign of any intrusion.'

'Inspector Drabble has said that he thought the man gained access through the courtyard, coming over the roof, then down into the courtyard and breaking in through a door or a window.'

'If he did, it wasn't on my watch,' growled Elder. 'No one came in during my shift.'

'And you didn't let anyone in?'

Elder glared at Daniel, affronted by the question. 'Certainly not.'

A very proud and firm man, thought Daniel.

'Did you go into the Egyptian Room during your rounds?'

'I always go into every room, every corridor, every nook and cranny,' stated Elder. 'I am very meticulous about my duties.'

'What about during Mr Ransome's watch?' asked Daniel. 'Do you think this intruder came in then?'

'He must have,' said Elder. 'He didn't come in during mine.' He hesitated, then added, 'Ransome'll be here from one o'clock tomorrow morning. I'm sure he'll be able to answer your questions about his activities better than I can.'

As Daniel walked away from the Fitzwilliam, heading for Mrs Loxley's, he decided not to bother with calling on Ransome in the early hours of the morning, once he'd started his shift. His questions could wait until a more reasonable hour. He'd call on Mr Ransome at home, during the day.

He'd be interested to meet Joseph Ransome. There had been something disapproving in Elder's tone when he'd talked about Ransome. Why? Was it just a clash of personalities, or was there something more? Hopefully, tomorrow, he'd find out.

CHAPTER EIGHT

Abigail entered the Fitzwilliam early the next morning, determined to get a good start on her work. The murder – tragic though it was – had severely disrupted her schedule, and she was determined to get back on track.

Alice, the head cleaner, was wielding her mop at the top of the stairs as she entered, and greeted her with a clipped, 'Good morning, Miss Fenton.'

'Good morning, Alice.'

Alice stopped mopping and Abigail could tell by the look of serious intent on her face that she was about to make an announcement.

'Just letting you know, Miss Fenton, we've got a new girl started today. Ellie, taking Mavis's place. But I've told her not to go into your rooms or touch any of your things.'

'Thank you, Alice. That's much appreciated.'

Alice nodded, satisfied, and Abigail headed for the area that housed the Egyptian collection. *Good for Alice*, she thought. The last thing she wanted was some new cleaner blundering into her domain and messing things up. Possibly picking up a small but rare artefact and throwing it into a rubbish bin because it looked dirty. Or, worse, attempting to clean and polish the newly arrived sepulchres, and removing the precious gilding. She shuddered with the memory of it happening before. Fortunately, on that occasion, she'd come in and spotted what was happening, and ordered the cleaner out before too much damage was done. Perhaps she'd been a bit too sharp with her, she had to admit, because the cleaner – what was her name? Millie? Margaret? – had quit, saying she 'wouldn't be spoken to in that way'.

Abigail made her way through the items awaiting cataloguing towards her own small office at the back, where her desk – although organised, after her own fashion – was deep in paperwork, the latest items to be examined and listed. As she neared it, she was irritated to see that the door was ajar. She knew she'd left it closed the day before. She assumed the nightwatchman must have been poking around in there, and the thought made her anger rise. Her own private inner sanctum invaded.

If this was the case, it would be the creepy one, Ransome. The older one, Mr Elder, was a respectable and respectful man. She couldn't imagine him violating her private space.

She pushed open the door, and stopped. A booted foot was sticking out from behind her desk. She saw the cloth of the nightwatchman's uniform on the section of leg attached to the boot.

What had happened? Had the man fallen and hit his head, knocking himself unconscious?

She moved further into the office and stopped, her hand going involuntarily to her mouth. It was Ransome, the nightwatchman, sure enough; but he lay on his back, his eyes and mouth wide open, his tongue poking out from between his lips. And wrapped around his neck was a bandage, a very ancient bandage, and Abigail knew immediately it was from one of the mummies.

'You seem to have a habit of finding dead bodies at the Fitzwilliam, miss,' said Inspector Drabble, looking down at the body of the dead nightwatchman. A uniformed police constable stood beside him, pencil poised, notebook open.

'I can assure you it is not intentional,' said Abigail. 'And it has only been two.'

'Two more than for most people, I think you would agree,' said Drabble stiffly.

'Is there a point to this observation, Inspector? I assume you are not accusing me of being responsible for their deaths. If I were, I would hardly have brought the deaths to the attention of the police.'

Drabble glowered at her, then asked, 'That bandage around his neck. It looks old.'

'It is,' confirmed Abigail. 'I believe you will find it has come from the wrappings of one of the mummified bodies.'

Drabble looked puzzled. 'You're saying he was strangled with the bandage from a mummy?'

Abigail shook her head. 'No, that's not what I'm saying at all. Just that I believe the cloth is from one of the mummies.'

The clatter of booted footsteps from outside made them turn, and they saw Daniel appear in the office doorway.

'My apologies for being late, Miss Fenton,' he said. 'I've only just got your note.' He stopped as he saw the dead body lying on the floor. 'Strangled?' he said.

Drabble gave a sarcastic snort.

'There you have it, Staines,' he said to the constable, with heavy sarcasm. 'The mark of a true Metropolitan Police former inspector. He sees a dead body with a bandage wrapped round its neck and straight away his lightning brain says "Strangled!" Whereas it would take we poor mere mortal coppers a long time to reach that same conclusion.'

'He was not strangled with that bandage, Inspector,' said Abigail.

They both turned to her, Drabble scornful, Daniel curious.

'How can you tell?' asked Daniel. 'Have you examined the body?'

'Certainly not,' said Abigail firmly. 'I would not dream of disturbing the scene of the crime and incurring the inspector's wrath. It is merely that if the bandage round the unfortunate man's neck is from one of the mummies, then it would not have been possible to strangle him with it. It is three thousand years old and would not be able to stand the pressure of being used for such a purpose. If you do not believe me, perhaps you'd care to test it.'

Drabble frowned, then went to the dead body and took a free end of the bandage in one hand, then held it tightly a few inches further down. He gave a tug, and immediately the bandage frayed and parted.

'See, Inspector?' said Abigail.

'But if he wasn't strangled with it, why leave it wrapped round his neck?'

'That, I leave to you,' said Abigail. 'You are the detective.'

CHAPTER NINE

With the body taken to Dr Keen and the police departed, Abigail had her office back. Daniel sat in the visitor's chair and studied her.

'Are you sure you're alright?' he asked. 'That must have been a terrible shock for you.' He held up his hand to stop her as she was about to say something. 'And, please, don't tell me about the bodies you've seen in Egypt. Finding a dead body, especially a murdered one, is always a shock, and I've seen many in my career.'

She hesitated, then nodded.

'Yes,' she admitted. 'Somehow it's worse when it's someone you know. Even if I didn't know Mr Ransome well, we used to see one another occasionally, if I was working late and he was on the early shift, for example.'

'Have you any idea why someone would want to kill him?'

She shook her head. 'Two bodies in such a short space of time. And both murdered.' She looked enquiringly at Daniel. 'Is it the same murderer, do you think?'

'I must admit it would be too much of a coincidence if it wasn't,' replied Daniel, adding thoughtfully, 'but then, as I've discovered over my years as a detective, anything is possible. The telling thing is that there seems to be no sign of a break-in. The same as with the previous victim.'

'Perhaps Mr Ransome let his killer in?' suggested Abigail.

'That does seem likely.' Daniel nodded. 'Which raises the question, did he do the same before?'

'But why would he do that?' asked Abigail. 'The police talked to him after that event, and he said nothing untoward had happened during his watch.'

'He was hardly likely to say if it had,' Daniel pointed out.

'What's our next move?' asked Abigail.

'To see Dr Keen,' said Daniel. 'His opinion on how Mr Ransome was killed will be vital. And I'm also hoping he might have the photograph of the mystery dead man for us.' Carefully, so as not to startle her into rebuffing him again, he asked, 'I hope you will accompany me? After all, Dr Keen obviously greatly values your observations.'

'I think that may be an exaggeration,' said Abigail, but Daniel saw by the slight flush that came to her cheeks that she was flattered by his comment.

Once again they were in the mortuary in the basement of Gonville and Caius, standing beside Dr Keen as they looked down at the dead body of Joseph Ransome. Abigail was relieved to note that so far only the dead man's upper garments, his tunic, shirt and undervest, had been removed. She did not fancy another altercation with Bella if she revealed that, yet again, she had inspected the naked body of a dead man in the presence of Bella's hoped-for paramour.

'Cause of death: strangulation,' said Dr Keen. 'But not by the bandage around the neck. That seems to be stage dressing for the crime. He was strangled by the use of a pair of hands.'

'Strong hands?' asked Daniel.

'That's a good question,' mused Keen. 'Because I also found traces of chloroform in his nose and mouth, which suggests he was anaesthetised first.'

'So the murderer wanted to make sure the nightwatchman was unconscious before he—'

'Or she,' interrupted Abigail. 'The use of chloroform to disable Mr Ransome suggests the murderer needn't have been a strong man, it could have been a woman.'

'I'd be careful about saying that,' said Keen drily. 'Inspector Drabble has already mentioned that you discovering both victims is . . . well, a very large coincidence.'

'Inspector Drabble is an idiot,' said Abigail.

'That may be, but there are certain facts about this case that raise questions for him; in particular that both men were found in the Egyptian Room, and there were no signs of a break-in on either occasion.'

'He suspects an inside job,' said Daniel. 'That someone inside the Fitzwilliam may well be responsible.'

'That's the impression I get.'

'If that's the case, as the bodies died at night, that would suggest the nightwatchmen,' said Abigail.

'Or someone who knows the nightwatchmen's rounds,' said

Daniel. He turned to Keen and asked, 'By the way, did you get a chance to take the photograph of the other victim?'

'I did, but I haven't had a chance to develop it yet,' said Keen. He gestured at the dead body of Ransome. 'I intended to do that this morning, but . . .'

'Understood,' said Daniel.

'I'll see if I can get it done today,' said Keen. 'Perhaps if you'd call back at – say – five this afternoon?'

'Thank you,' said Daniel.

As Keen pulled the sheet over the body of Ransome, he said to Abigail, 'By the way, Miss Fenton, please pass on my thanks to your sister for the handbill informing me about the public meeting on Sunday. Unfortunately I have another engagement, otherwise I would be delighted to attend.'

'This Sunday?' said Abigail in surprise.

'Yes. Voting rights for women,' said Keen. He smiled. 'Do I assume your sister has omitted to tell you about it?'

'She did mention it, but not the details,' said Abigail. 'We have both been very busy. I shall make sure to pass on your thanks to her.'

'And my best wishes for the occasion. It is a cause I support, and not just for women. Despite the recent Representation of the People Act, nearly half of men in this country don't have the vote, either, unless they pay rent of at least £10 per year. There are large numbers of the population whose tenancy is part of their employment. It's a restriction to stop the poor from voting and should be challenged. Alas, with most of our politicians only concerned about their own vested interests, the likelihood of social justice can only come from people like your sister in their demands for equal suffrage.'

* * *

Afterwards, as Daniel and Abigail walked back to the Fitzwilliam, Daniel commented, 'So you weren't aware of this meeting on Sunday?'

'There was talk of a public meeting, but not that it would be this Sunday,' replied Abigail. 'My sister doesn't always share her activities with me.'

'Because you disapprove?'

'Of votes for women?' asked Abigail. 'Not at all. It's just that sometimes I question my sister's motives.'

Daniel, intrigued, was about to ask her to explain, but before he could she asked him, 'And you, Mr Wilson, where do you stand on the issue?'

'I echo Dr Keen's sentiments,' said Daniel. 'Votes for all. Votes for women, by all means, but also votes for all men. At this moment only men of a certain financial class have the vote. To exclude all women and half the men from the voting process is a recipe for social unrest.'

'Perhaps even revolution?' enquired Abigail.

Daniel shook his head.

'I doubt it,' he said. 'Unrest and upheaval in some areas, possibly. But as we saw with the Tolpuddle Martyrs, at the first hint of serious revolution, the ruling British establishment moves in and crushes the leaders.'

'You sound as if you disapprove, yet you are a part of that same ruling establishment.'

'I *was*,' Daniel corrected her.

'Is that why you left the police?'

Daniel hesitated before answering. 'I believe that the work the police do as protectors of the population is vital. I don't endorse it when the police are used as political tools.'

'To suppress the population? To protect the corrupt elite?'

Daniel laughed. 'With respect, Miss Fenton, you sound like a political tract.'

To his surprise, Abigail joined in his laughter. 'To be frank, I was making mock.'

'Of who?'

'My sister, I suppose. She is becoming more radical in her beliefs.'

'And you disapprove?'

'I would approve if I felt she was doing so for the right reasons.' Then she shrugged. 'But let's return to the matter on which we came.'

'Indeed,' said Daniel. 'At least we know that the killing of Mr Ransome was premeditated, and not a reaction to being caught by the nightwatchman.'

'How?' asked Abigail. And then she nodded. 'Of course, the chloroform.'

'Exactly. Our murderer intended to kill someone at the Fitzwilliam, but was his target Mr Ransome, or was Ransome just unlucky and in the wrong place at the wrong time?'

'You think his murder may have been done just to confuse the situation and throw us off the scent?'

'I don't know,' admitted Daniel. 'If Inspector Drabble is right and an inside person was involved in the first murder then, in my opinion, suspicion falls on Ransome.'

'Why him? Why not Harry Elder?'

'You said yourself that Harry Elder seems respectable and responsible. That's the impression I got when I met him, too, yesterday evening at the Fitzwilliam during his night shift. If he'd committed the first murder I think I'd have picked up something from him.'

'Guilt?'

'Guilt manifests in different ways with different people. Successful criminals are able to conceal it completely, if they even have any. Respectable citizens, on the other hand, struggle to conceal it.

'Of course, there could be many other reasons why Ransome was murdered, and he may have been quite innocent, just in the wrong place at the wrong time. I'll go and see his family, see if they can throw any light on the mystery of his death. What can you tell me about him, so I'm prepared when I see them? Was he married? Did he have children?'

'I'm afraid I was unfamiliar with him outside of work,' admitted Abigail. 'Possibly the best person to talk to about him is Harry Elder.'

Daniel nodded. 'Agreed.'

CHAPTER TEN

Abigail tried to concentrate on the article in the magazine on her lap, but was finding it difficult. The subject matter was so dear to her heart – an article by William Flinders Petrie disproving Piazzi Smyth's theory of the Great Pyramid – that it should have absorbed her completely, but as she shot a look at her sister on the other side of the hearth, engrossed in a book of her own, the fact that Bella hadn't told her about the public meeting that coming Sunday irritated and disturbed her. Why the secrecy?

Bella laid down her book with a sigh.

'Truly remarkable!' she said.

'What is?' asked Abigail.

'This. A novel, *Germinal*, by Émile Zola. I'd heard such wonderful things about it, and I've been desperate for it to come out in English.' She gave a happy sigh. 'It does not disappoint! I recommend it to you, Abigail.'

'What is the story?'

'It's set in a mining community in northern France, where the miners go on strike for justice.'

'Of course,' said Abigail drily.

'But there is much more to it than that!' burst out Bella. 'It is a love story, a love triangle!'

'Is it long?'

'It is,' said Bella. 'Satisfyingly so.'

'Then I shall leave it until I have more time to spend on relaxation,' said Abigail. 'By the way, you did not tell me this public meeting of yours is happening on Sunday. Votes for women.'

'Did I not?' said Bella. 'Actually, it's not *my* meeting. It's being organised by a committee of which Lady Restwood is chair. I just promised to pass on word about it to people I thought might be interested.'

'Like Dr Keen.'

Immediately, Bella stiffened. 'Why do you say that?' she demanded.

'Because it was Dr Keen who told me about it, saying you had sent him a handbill.'

'You saw Dr Keen *again*?' said Bella, agitated and rising to her feet.

'For heaven's sake, Bella, calm down!' snapped Abigail. 'I saw him again, with Mr Wilson, because we had yet another dead body at the Fitzwilliam.'

Bella fell, rather than sat, back on her chair.

'Another . . . ?' she whispered, aghast.

'One of the nightwatchmen. He'd been strangled. It was I who found the body when I arrived at the Fitzwilliam this morning. The body was taken to Gonville and Caius for examination, and naturally, Mr Wilson and I, as investigators of the case, accompanied it.'

'Yet you didn't tell me!' said Bella accusingly.

'I am telling you now,' said Abigail. 'Anyway, you do not always tell me everything, Sister. I repeat, this public meeting on Sunday, for example.'

'One can hardly compare a public meeting about voting with the discovery of a dead body!' exploded Bella indignantly.

'Really, Bella, there is no need to be hysterical about this,' Abigail reprimanded. 'Anyway, I was about to tell you in order to pass on Dr Keen's message.'

'His message?'

'He thanks you for the handbill and offers his personal support for the cause. However, he offered his apologies, he would have attended but he has another engagement on Sunday.'

'What engagement? Who with?' demanded Bella.

'I have no idea,' said Abigail. 'He did not offer the information, and I did not ask. It did not seem relevant.'

'It may have been relevant to me!'

'Then I suggest you ask him.'

'No!' said Bella, horrified at the suggestion. Then, nervously, she began, 'This man who died . . .'

'The nightwatchman.' Abigail nodded. 'A man called Joseph Ransome. I'm sure it will be in the newspaper tomorrow. I've asked for the early edition to be delivered here.'

'You say he was strangled?'

'Indeed,' said Abigail.

Bella looked at her sister, horrified. 'Aren't you at all frightened?' she asked.

'Of what?' asked Abigail. 'Dead bodies? They cannot harm me.'

'Of it happening to you.'

Abigail frowned at her, puzzled. 'Why would anyone want to murder me?' she asked.

'Why would anyone want to murder the nightwatchman?' countered her sister.

'That is what Mr Wilson and I are trying to determine,' replied Abigail.

But as she said it, she thought: *Why, indeed?* Could it be that there was no logical reason for the latest murder? Or even the first? That someone was killing people inside the Fitzwilliam indiscriminately?

I shall discuss this with Mr Wilson, she determined.

At the thought of Daniel Wilson, another decision came to a head for her. *I will escort him around Cambridge and show him the city*, she decided. *After my traumatic experience with Edgar, I allowed my perception of men as primarily sexual predators to dominate my reaction to his suggestion. Daniel Wilson is not like Edgar.*

At least, she thought, *I hope so.*

CHAPTER ELEVEN

This time, Daniel's tug at the bell pull of the main door at the Fitzwilliam was opened by a man he didn't recognise, but a man who wore the same nightwatchman's uniform as Harry Elder. In fact, Daniel was sure it was *exactly* the same uniform.

'I'm looking for Harry Elder,' he said.

The man regarded him suspiciously. 'Why?'

'My name's Daniel Wilson and I've been hired by the Fitzwilliam to look into the recent deaths here. I saw Mr Elder here yesterday evening, and I need to continue our conversation.'

The man shook his head.

'He's not here. Him and his missus have gone to a wedding of his wife's cousin in Thetford. He asked me to do his shifts for him.' He sighed. 'But with the other bloke getting done in, it looks like I'll be doing both shifts tonight and tomorrow.'

'When will he be back?'

'Sunday morning, he said.'

'Do you happen to know what time he left for the wedding today?'

'They were catching the early train.'

Daniel frowned, thoughtfully. If Elder had caught the early train out of Cambridge, he wouldn't have known before he left that Ransome had been murdered. Unless Daniel had completely misread the man's character and Harry Elder was the killer, and had now made his escape.

He needed to check if there actually was a wedding, or if it was simply a ruse to buy Elder time to get away.

'Do you know the name of his wife's cousin?' he asked.

The man looked at him suspiciously. 'Why would you want to know?' he demanded.

'Because I am tasked with looking into the recent deaths here, and it's important I talk to Mr Elder very soon. If necessary I shall travel to Thetford to see him, but to do that I need to know where they will be. The name of the church. Who is getting married. Where Mr and Mrs Elder might be staying.'

The man shook his head.

'Sorry, I can't help you. I only know Harry casual-like. We go to the same chapel. But who his wife's cousin is, I've no idea. All I know is the wedding's in Thetford, and he's coming back early on Sunday morning.'

'Thank you,' said Daniel. He was about to leave when he stopped and asked, 'Is your substitution official? Do the Fitzwilliam know that he won't be here tonight and tomorrow?'

The man looked uncomfortable.

'Not exactly,' he said. 'I don't think he wanted to upset things for himself by telling them. He's got a good job here.'

'So when did he make this arrangement with you? Recently?'

'Yesterday,' said the man. 'Thursday.'

'Short notice,' observed Daniel.

'Yes, well, I don't think Harry was sure if he should go to the wedding. He's very duty-conscious.'

'But he decided to go, and at short notice.'

The man nodded. 'I got the impression he was under pressure from Ettie, his wife, to go. It can be difficult for a bloke, torn between wanting to keep his wife happy, and doing his duty.'

As Daniel walked away he mulled over this new and unexpected development. Harry Elder hadn't mentioned anything to him about the wedding, but then, there was no reason why he should.

Was it suspicious? Or was it, as the man had said, that Harry had been torn between duty and his wife, and had chosen to accompany his wife, but kept it a secret from the Fitzwilliam rather than put his job at risk.

The first thing was to call at Elder's house and make enquiries of the neighbours about this wedding in Thetford, to see if they knew anything about it.

Daniel found the terraced house in Petworth Street that Miss Sattery had given him as the address for Harry Elder. There was no answer to his knock – exactly as he'd expected – so he began knocking at houses on either side. His first calls drew blanks – again, expected because it was a Friday night, and Friday night was traditionally a time for spending the week's wages in the pub. It was the fourth house he tried where he found a chatty and cheerful woman who was happy to let him have the details he was after.

'Ettie's cousin, Victoria,' she informed Daniel. Then she leant close to him and told him in a confidential whisper, full of scandal in her voice, 'She's marrying an Irish bloke and he's a Catholic!'

'A Catholic?'

'Exactly!' She nodded. 'Harry swore blind he wouldn't attend, him being so firmly chapel. But Ettie's always been so fond of her cousin, Vicky. Like sisters they were, before she lost touch.'

'So Harry wasn't going to go to the wedding, but at the last minute he changed his mind?'

'That's right,' said the woman. 'He did it for Ettie. He knew it would break her heart if he didn't go. He's a hard man, but not so hard that he'd upset Ettie. I think he's going to stand outside the church while Ettie goes in.'

'And they'll be back on Sunday.'

'Sunday morning,' said the woman.

As Daniel headed back to Mrs Loxley's, he reflected that – on the evidence – there was no need to consider Harry Elder a suspect. Everything added up.

Unless, of course, when Daniel returned to Petworth Street on Sunday morning, there was still no sign of Harry Elder.

CHAPTER TWELVE

Abigail went into the kitchen to put the kettle on to make a pot of tea. As it was a Saturday, Mrs Standish would not be arriving to make breakfast until half past eight, rather than her usual weekday starting time of seven o'clock.

The kettle on, she went into the hallway. Yes, there it was on the doormat: the *Cambridge Gazette*, as Horden's the newsagent had promised. Perhaps she would place a regular order for their newspaper to be delivered as Horden's had proved efficient.

She unfolded it, and as her eye fell on the headline blazoned across the front page, her eyes widened and her mouth dropped open in shock, before closing tightly in outrage.

'This is appalling!' she fumed.

'Did you say something, Abigail?' Bella asked as she came down the stairs.

But her sister had already snatched her coat from the rack, put it on, then stormed out of the house, slamming the door shut behind her.

Daniel sat at the breakfast table he was sharing with Professor Hughes as they tucked into their kippers. Daniel still hadn't set eyes on the third lodger at Mrs Loxley's, Mr Barron, the businessman who traded in precious metals. So far he hadn't appeared at breakfast or for supper, nor been seen in the comfortable lounge.

'He's very busy,' Mrs Loxley had told them, explaining his absence. 'Lots of important meetings.'

Professor Hughes, however, was a constant presence at mealtimes. Elderly, genial, but with an air of abstraction about him, as if his thoughts were elsewhere. Daniel guessed him to be in his late fifties. A pale complexion and slightly round-shouldered, which seemed to go with spending most of his time poring over old books in darkened archives.

'Are you a Cambridge man, Mr Wilson?' enquired Hughes, pausing between mouthfuls and happy to make conversation.

'Er, no,' said Daniel.

'I was at Peterhouse,' said Hughes. 'Many years ago, although sometimes it seems like only yesterday.' His face took on a look of pride as he added, 'It's the oldest college in Cambridge, you know.'

'Really?' said Daniel politely.

'Founded in 1284,' affirmed Hughes, and then proceeded to give Daniel a potted history of his old college.

Everyone here in Cambridge seemed to be constantly referring back to the city's historical past: Professor Hughes with Peterhouse, Abigail Fenton with Gonville and Caius,

Sir William at the Fitzwilliam surrounded by the past. It was as if this history was vital to their very existences. No, to their status.

Cambridge was important, and by their association with it, they too were important. Or, felt important.

Professor Hughes' mini-historical lecture was interrupted by the appearance of Mrs Loxley, who seemed to be slightly flustered.

'Excuse me, Mr Wilson, but there is a lady to see you,' she announced.

'A lady?'

'A Miss Abigail Fenton.'

'Ah yes, from the Fitzwilliam Museum.'

'Which is next door to Peterhouse,' put in Hughes. 'One of Cambridge's oldest buildings next door to one of the most recent.'

'She says she needs to talk to you, sir,' said Mrs Loxley.

Daniel nodded and put down his napkin, pleased that he'd finished his breakfast kipper before this interruption.

'Would it be possible for us to have our conversation in the parlour?' he asked. As he saw Mrs Loxley hesitate, he said, 'I know the rules on entertaining ladies, but Miss Fenton has been asked to act on the investigation with me by Sir William Mackenzie, so you can rest assured that this is with his authority and there is no question of any impropriety.'

'No, no, of course not,' said Mrs Loxley hastily, still obviously slightly flustered but keen not to upset Sir William Mackenzie in any way. 'By all means, I'll show her into the parlour.'

'If you'll pardon me, Professor,' said Daniel, 'but business calls.'

'Absolutely,' said Hughes cheerfully.

Daniel left the breakfast room and entered the parlour, where Mrs Loxley had installed an obviously very angry Abigail.

'Miss Fenton.' Daniel smiled in greeting.

'Have you seen this?' she demanded, barely containing her anger as she thrust the newspaper at him.

Daniel took it from her and saw the headline blazoned across the front page: KILLER MUMMY ON THE LOOSE IN CAMBRIDGE.

'No,' he admitted.

'It's ludicrous!' exploded Abigail. 'Absolute rubbish! She snatched the paper back from him and began to read aloud, her voice trembling with indignation. '"Is an ancient murderous Egyptian mummy on the loose in Cambridge?"'

'Perhaps if I read it myself?' suggested Daniel, but Abigail was so enraged she continued reading aloud, her voice full of scorn.

'"The horrific murder at the Fitzwilliam of nightwatchman Joseph Ransome was particularly gruesome because of the fact that he was strangled with the bandages of one of the mummies recently brought over from Egypt. According to an eminent Egyptologist who has spoken exclusively to this newspaper, recent acquisitions by the Fitzwilliam include the mummified bodies of an Egyptian princess and her private bodyguard. The bodyguard was buried in the same tomb as the princess to protect her in the afterlife. Could it be that the bodyguard is doing just that, wreaking revenge on those who desecrated the princess's tomb and brought her to England?"'

'It's an interesting thought,' mused Daniel.

'It is not interesting at all, it is absolute tosh!'

'The paper quotes "an eminent Egyptologist",' said Daniel. 'This story of his must be based on something.'

'Yes, and it's the plot of a story by Arthur Conan Doyle called "Lot No. 249", published two years ago in *Harper's*, an American magazine. The story's about a reanimated murderous Egyptian mummy commanded by a vengeful university student.'

'At Cambridge?' asked Daniel.

'No. He was from . . .' She hesitated, then said, 'The *other* place.'

Daniel gave her a puzzled frown. 'Hell?' he asked. 'The netherworld?'

She looked at him coldly. 'Oxford,' she said curtly. 'The point is that whoever came up with this story obviously read it in the magazine.'

'An American magazine?' he said.

'Yes, that's what I've already said.'

'Well, that cuts the list of possible suspects down,' said Daniel. 'That suggests we're looking for an American, or someone who's been in America recently.'

'Not necessarily,' she said. 'I came across the story while I was in Egypt on a dig. Someone had left a copy of *Harper's* there. The story's not to my taste, but there was very little else to read.'

She handed the paper to Daniel. 'Ludicrous!' she said.

'I don't know,' said Daniel.

She stared at him. 'You're surely not giving this nonsense credibility?'

'"There are more things in heaven and earth, Horatio, than are dreamt of in your philosophy,"' quoted Daniel.

'There is no need to quote Shakespeare at me,' said Abigail. 'Anything coming from a man who wrote about fairies does not convince me of the existence of the supernatural. And I am surprised that you, as a detective, would consider it.'

'When I was working as a detective in London, we encountered many strange things that were not easily explained,' said Daniel. 'Especially amongst the immigrant communities: the Arabs and the Chinese, for example. Reports of strange apparitions, the dead coming back to life.'

'The results of an excess of opium,' said Abigail curtly.

'Not everything can be so easily explained,' insisted Daniel. 'I have seen things that have made me doubt my senses. Or, certainly, doubt concrete reality. And I have never taken opium or hashish.'

'Then I would suggest beer or strong drink were the root of it.' Abigail sniffed. 'Or possibly too much cheese. The mould in cheese is a fungus, and fungus can play tricks with the brain's mental abilities.'

'You sound very definite,' observed Daniel.

'I am very definite,' said Abigail. 'There is no basis in proper science for the supernatural.'

'But Arthur Conan Doyle is a scientist, a doctor, and, from interviews with him I've read, he seems to believe in many aspects of the supernatural. He's a member of the Society for Psychical Research and attends seances, that sort of thing. And this story of his . . .'

'"Lot No. 249",' said Abigail.

'He must have based it on something.'

'He's a writer with an overactive imagination,' said Abigail.

'One question,' said Daniel. 'Did the mummy of an Egyptian princess arrive from Egypt recently?'

'Yes, but that means nothing. The mummy is said to be that of a princess, but the term "princess" could mean anything.'

'And was that mummy accompanied by that of a bodyguard?'

'The mummified body of a bodyguard, if she had one,

would not have been identified as such. Only the elite were identified as individuals, not servants.' She stood up. 'Come with me to the Fitzwilliam and I'll prove to you that this talk about a reanimated murderous mummy is nonsense.'

CHAPTER THIRTEEN

The first room of the Egyptian collection seemed to have been further organised since the first time that Daniel had seen it; the artefacts had been separated and arranged in a kind of chronological order, from the identifying cards that had been placed with each item. The statuary had been erected so that dog-headed lions towered protectively over smaller objects: earthenware bowls and other items of pottery.

'Where do they come from?' asked Daniel.

'Egypt,' said Abigail.

'I know that,' said Daniel, annoyed. 'I mean, how does the Fitzwilliam get hold of them? Are they donated by the archaeologists who've discovered them?'

She gave a rueful laugh.

'If only that were possible,' she said. 'No, the unearthing

of these artefacts costs money, as does transporting them to England. But the principal cost is in purchasing them from the site owners in Egypt. Different people own different sites. Money changes hands for the right to dig, with more money being paid if anything is found.'

'It all sounds a bit dubious,' commented Daniel.

'I can assure you everything is done legally and above board,' said Abigail. 'Bills of sale, receipts, everything correct. Although things are complicated by the fact that the Egyptian government have authorised the French to be in charge of the Antiquities Service, which officially has responsibility for all antiquities found in Egypt.

'The reality is that, until 1886, the individual items in the Egyptian collection at the Fitzwilliam, although impressive, were small in number. It was Sir Wallis Budge of the British Museum who felt the museum should have as large a collection of the culture of ancient Egypt as possible, and private funds were raised in order to achieve this objective. Have you heard of the Reverend Greville J. Chester?'

'No,' said Daniel. 'Should I have?'

'Possibly not, unless you are interested in Egyptology. In 1890 and 1891, it was the Reverend Chester who presented a number of important items to the museum, and by last year, with others being added, the Fitzwilliam's Egyptian collection now totals some 600 items.'

'Very impressive,' said Daniel.

'With more items coming all the time, which is why curating the collection is so time-consuming. Recently there has been a surge of such artefacts arriving as the result of new digs. Edward Hardwicke, in particular, has been responsible for a great many of the recent imports.'

'Another name unfamiliar to me,' commented Daniel.

'One of the new generations of archaeologists,' said Abigail. 'And a scholar, as well as a digger. In fact, the last consignment that arrived was from him. And, coincidentally, it was that consignment that included the mummy of an Egyptian princess.'

'Interesting,' mused Daniel. 'How many people were aware that this recent consignment included a mummified princess?'

'Well, me, of course. But no one else that I can think of.'

'Except this Edward Hardwicke, obviously.'

'Mr Hardwicke is still away. He sent the artefacts on ahead, with a note explaining that he would be taking a different route back to England.' Then a thought struck her, because she exclaimed, 'The carters!'

'The people who delivered the artefacts?'

'Yes. I think the delivery note listed details of some of the more precious artefacts.'

'Do you have a copy of that delivery note?'

Daniel followed her to her office, where she rummaged through a pile of papers, and produced a crumpled sheet of paper.

'Yes!' she cried triumphantly. 'There!' And she handed it to Daniel.

Daniel looked down the list, which mostly consisted of Roman numerals against items to identify them, such as 'mummy from Khufu – XXII', but some had more details against them: 'scarab beetle', 'head of Ra'. Halfway down the list was 'mummy of Princess Ka'.

'So the cartage company would have known about this.'

'Yes, but I cannot see them being the source of the story. The carters are quite rough and ready men. To be honest, I'm not sure if they can actually read.'

'But the people in the office can.'

She looked doubtful. 'It all seems a bit far-fetched.'

'More far-fetched than the story of a murderous reanimated mummy?' He made a note of the name and address of the cartage company, Peebles and Co., then followed Abigail out of her office and into the second display room.

Here the mummified bodies had been put on display, most of them inside glass cases, although there were two still unprotected.

Abigail went to one of the unprotected mummies.

'This is the mummy said to be that of Princess Ka.' She took hold of the end of a piece of bandage from the packing around the foot of the mummy and gently unfurled a short length, which she held out to Daniel. 'Take this in both hands and pull at it.'

'You've already illustrated your point with the inspector, earlier,' said Daniel.

'And now I'm doing it again, with you, so there can be no mistake.'

Daniel tugged at the bandage, and – as before with Drabble – the bandage separated, fraying easily. Abigail took the frayed end of bandage and very gently tucked it into a fold.

'The cloth is far too fragile to have been used to strangle the nightwatchman.'

'At least we can make a good guess as to why the bandage from the mummy was left around his neck, to lend credence to the story that the murder was done by this supposed bodyguard of hers,' said Daniel.

'So you believe me that this was no supernatural event, a reanimated mummy?' said Abigail challengingly.

'I always like to keep an open mind,' replied Daniel. 'But, in this case, the fragility of the bandage makes your point.' A thought struck him, because he asked, 'Where is the mummy of this supposed bodyguard?'

'I've already said, the mummified bodies of servants were not identified as individuals,' said Abigail.

'How many of these unidentified mummies were with her in her tomb?' asked Daniel.

'According to the list that was brought with them, four,' said Abigail. 'I've kept them in a storage room for the moment until I've examined them properly.'

'May I see them?'

'You mean you're still not convinced, Mr Wilson?' said Abigail archly.

'Please, humour me,' said Daniel.

She led Daniel into another, smaller, room. There were wooden crates with the lids off, filled with small objects, and laid on the floor against one wall were three mummified bodies.

'I only see three,' said Daniel.

'One's been moved,' said Abigail.

'Or it's walked,' said Daniel.

She shot him a sharp, cold glance.

'That was a joke,' he said.

'Excuse me,' she said, and left the room, returning a moment later looking puzzled. 'The attendant says no one's moved the other mummy.'

'Then, obviously, whoever killed Ransome also removed one of the mummies to add credence to the story about a murderous mummy being on the loose.'

'That seems very risky.' Abigail frowned. 'Someone may well have seen the mummy being removed from the museum.'

'It might be a case of knocking on doors to ask if anyone saw anything suspicious, and at what time,' said Daniel.

'Surely that's a job for the police,' said Abigail.

'It is,' agreed Daniel. 'Would you like to make that suggestion to Inspector Drabble, or shall I?'

When Abigail hesitated, he smiled and said, 'Allow me. But first, I suggest we go in search of the person who wrote the newspaper article.'

'Why?' demanded Abigail. 'The man is an obvious fantasist.'

'Because he mentions an eminent Egyptologist "who has spoken exclusively to this newspaper". Which suggests to me that this mysterious Egyptologist may have had a reason in planting this story in the newspaper.'

'To divert attention away from the real motive for the murder!' exclaimed Abigail, with sudden realisation.

'Exactly,' said Daniel. 'Do you know where the offices of the *Gazette* are?'

'I do,' she said.

'And the name of the writer of this report?'

Abigail took the rolled-up newspaper from her pocket and read the byline aloud. '"By our special correspondent, Hector Blades."'

'Excellent. Then let us go and find Mr Blades and see what he can tell us.'

CHAPTER FOURTEEN

The man on duty at the outer office of the *Gazette* shook his head at their request.

'Sorry, Hector Blades doesn't come into the office on Saturdays.'

'He doesn't work on Saturdays?' asked Abigail. 'I find that odd for a journalist.'

'Well, he does, but on Saturdays he's the racing correspondent. With a big meeting at Newmarket, that's where he'll be today.'

'Will he be in tomorrow?' asked Daniel.

The man shook his head. 'Never on a Sunday. If he's had a big win, he'll be nursing a hangover. If he's had a bad day, he'll still be nursing a hangover. He'll be back in on Monday.'

'Could you let us have his address?'

The man shook his head again. 'Sorry, not allowed. See, I'm

only really here to pick up letters and things for the paper, which I pass on.'

'Most unsatisfactory.' Abigail scowled as they left the offices.

'It will keep till Monday,' said Daniel. 'Until then, we have other courses of enquiry: my reporting the missing mummy to Inspector Drabble, and tomorrow I shall talk to Mr Elder again.'

Now is the right time, decided Abigail. *I shall suggest I show him more of Cambridge, as he first asked. Purely as working acquaintances, of course, but it would be interesting to find out more about him.*

'Actually, Mr Wilson,' she said.

'Yes?'

'I was wondering—'

'Miss Fenton! Mr Wilson!'

They turned and saw Sir William Mackenzie hurrying towards them. In his hand they saw that he was brandishing a copy of the *Gazette*.

'I'm glad to have spotted you both! Have you seen this?'

Abigail nodded. 'We have, Sir William.'

'It's outrageous, and it will do the reputation of the Fitzwilliam no good at all! I've come here to see the person who wrote it and demand a retraction at the very least.'

'I'm afraid the person responsible is not here today, Sir William,' said Daniel. 'We've just been advised of that, and our request for Mr Blades' home address has been met with a refusal.'

'Yes, I can understand that,' said Sir William. He sighed. 'Very well, I shall write a letter to the editor expressing my disquiet. In the meantime, it is fortunate that we have met. This would be a good time to receive an update from you, Mr Wilson, on your enquiries.'

'Of course, Sir William,' said Daniel. 'I was intending to report to you on Monday morning.'

'I'm afraid I have a meeting of the board on Monday morning, where they will be expecting some answers,' said Sir William. 'Are you free now?'

'Of course. Let us go to the Fitzwilliam now and I'll give you my verbal report.'

'And at the same time, Miss Fenton, perhaps you could accompany us and update me on how the cataloguing is going. It's very important for the museum that we have a proper display in the Egyptian Room as soon as possible, especially in view of the recent dreadful events. It's vital that we revert to a position of normality, and the board will be looking for answers to that position as well.'

'Absolutely, Sir William,' said Abigail.

Sir William elected to receive Daniel's verbal report in the Egyptian Room. As concisely as he could, Daniel summarised what they'd discovered so far, which he had to admit wasn't a lot. 'We have established one of the mummies seems to be missing,' he ended.

Sir William looked confused. 'You mean someone's taken it?' he asked. 'Why?'

Daniel shrugged. 'I'm afraid that's yet another mystery.'

Sir William looked at Abigail and asked, 'Are you sure it hasn't just been mislaid?'

'Absolutely not,' replied Abigail firmly.

'What on earth would anyone want with an Egyptian mummy?' asked Sir William, still bewildered by this turn of events.

'Hopefully we'll find that out when we get to the truth of what happened with the deaths,' said Daniel. 'Now, if you'll excuse me, I'd better go and see Inspector Drabble.'

'Of course.' Sir William nodded. 'So, Miss Fenton, shall we look at the cataloguing?' And he walked off to begin examining the latest deliveries of artefacts.

'Just before we met Sir William, you were about to say something,' said Daniel quietly to Abigail.

'Was I?' She smiled. 'I can't remember, so it can't have been that important.' She gestured towards where Sir William was waiting impatiently at the other end of the room. 'I'd better go. Do let me know how you get on with Inspector Drabble.'

'I will,' Daniel assured her.

Inspector Drabble's expression when Daniel told him about the missing mummy was as bewildered as Sir William's had been.

'A missing mummy?'

'It appears so,' said Daniel.

'Why?' asked Drabble. 'Who'd want to take it?'

'I have no idea,' said Daniel. 'I just thought I'd bring it to your attention.'

Drabble looked thoughtful. 'You think that someone was stealing the mummy when Ransome interrupted him, and that's why Ransome was killed?'

'No,' said Daniel. 'I spoke to Dr Keen earlier, and he told me about the traces of chloroform found in Ransome's nose and mouth. That suggests that the murder was premeditated.'

'You spoke to Dr Keen without my permission!' snapped Drabble, outraged.

'I didn't see him to ask about the murder of the nightwatchman, but another matter, concerning the first body,' said Daniel. 'It just so happens that the issue of the second death came up in our conversation.'

'I bet it did!' hissed Drabble. 'Look, Wilson, this is *my* case—'

'I am aware of that, which is why I came to you with this information about the missing mummy.'

Drabble subsided, almost mollified, but not quite.

'So you're suggesting that the murderer killed the nightwatchman, and then stole the mummy.'

'That would seem to be the logical sequence.' Daniel nodded. 'Although that's just my opinion. I could be wrong.'

'Yes, you could be,' grunted Drabble. He fell silent, then added grudgingly, 'Although the business of the chloroform would back that up.' He looked inquisitively at Daniel. 'But why steal the mummy? And why just the one? If it's about the money he could get for them, why not take others?'

'I don't know,' admitted Daniel.

Drabble took up a copy of the *Cambridge Gazette* that had been lying under some other papers on his desk, and showed the front page to Daniel. 'Did you see this?' he asked.

'Yes,' said Daniel.

'What do you make of it?'

'According to Miss Fenton, it's a rehash of a story by Arthur Conan Doyle about a murderous mummy that's been reanimated by someone with a grudge against certain people.'

'A story?' repeated Drabble.

Daniel nodded. 'Apparently it appeared in an American magazine called *Harper's*.'

'So she doesn't think there's anything in it?' said Drabble. 'That this story's made up?'

'That's about the size of it,' said Daniel. 'I was wondering if you think there might be any merit in talking to the people who live near the Fitzwilliam, in case they saw anything during the night, such as people removing an object from the building.'

'The missing mummy?'

'It's just a thought,' said Daniel.

'Yes, I had the same thought.' Drabble nodded. 'I shall be putting men on to it. Knocking at doors.'

'And if there's anything that I can do—' began Daniel.

'Thank you, I'm sure we can manage,' snapped Drabble. 'We do know what we're doing here.'

'Yes, of course,' said Daniel.

As Abigail left the Fitzwilliam for home, she made a promise to herself. For some reason she'd backed away from offering to show Daniel around the city, and she couldn't understand why. He didn't seem predatory, like so many men she'd met. Far from it. He was polite, intelligent, thoughtful, and quite possibly the kind of man she'd like to spend some time with. She would ask if he would like her to show him around Cambridge when they met on Monday. Just an invitation from one colleague to another with no ulterior motive. A chance to find out more about him.

CHAPTER FIFTEEN

Daniel knocked again at the door of Harry Elder's house, louder this time as there had been no reply to his first knocks.

Still no response. So, Sunday morning, and neither Harry Elder nor his wife were at home. Had the wedding in Thetford been a cover after all? Had the murderer been Harry Elder all along?

Daniel was just about to turn and walk off, when the door of the neighbouring house opened and a shirt-sleeved man appeared.

'If you're after Harry Elder, he's at chapel,' he said.

'He's back, then?' asked Daniel.

The man nodded. 'Early this morning. Him and his missus. They were hardly back before they were off in their Sunday best. Every Sunday morning without fail, him and the family. Chapel. Very devout.'

'Thank you,' said Daniel.

As he walked back towards the city centre he felt relieved. He believed himself to be a good judge of character most of the time, although his judgement had let him down a few times in the past. Usually, he reflected wryly, with women.

As he neared the city centre, he heard the sound of raised voices, both men's and women's. Of course, the public meeting Miss Fenton's sister had sent the handbill about to Dr Keen.

He wondered if Abigail would be in attendance. Yesterday, after the abortive call at the offices of the *Gazette*, he'd been tempted to ask her again if she would care to show him the sights of the city, but he'd stopped at the memory of the last time he'd asked.

He wondered what the key was to getting her to trust him enough to perhaps socialise with him. There was no doubt in his heart and mind that he was attracted to her, and he felt frustrated by the fact that he couldn't allow himself to be at ease with her. But there was a definite shield around her.

It's often the way, he thought ruefully. The women he took a shine to didn't seem interested in him. On the other hand, there were women who seemed keen to throw themselves at him, but for whom he – in his turn – chose to keep at arm's length.

Sometimes he thought the issue lay with him being a policeman; some women enjoyed the frisson of excitement at being in the company of a man who faced death and danger, while others – like Abigail Fenton – seemed suspicious of policemen as agents of a repressive establishment. And although he was no longer in the force, to most people who met him – men or women – he would always be Abberline's right-hand man, a policeman.

He entered the open square where the public meeting was being held. A middle-aged woman was standing on a soapbox, attempting to make herself heard by means of a megaphone, but her voice was virtually inaudible as she was shouted down by a gang of men, yelling things such as 'Get back home and look after your husband!' and 'Votes for all men first!'

About a dozen women stood beside the woman on the soapbox, holding placards aloft with slogans, mostly saying 'Votes for Women', one with the more erudite 'Women's Right to Suffrage', and another, Daniel was pleased to note, that read 'Votes for All'.

The woman on the soapbox was struggling very hard to make herself heard, but without success, and the woman holding the placard with 'Votes for All' stepped forward towards the gang of shouting men and obviously remonstrated with them about their jeering and was urging them to quieten down. In response, one of the men snatched at her placard and tried to take it from her, but the woman held gamely on. The man, his face a mask of anger, suddenly threw the woman violently to the cobbled ground.

A feeling of rage filling him, Daniel rushed forward and grabbed hold of the man and threw him to the ground face first, falling down on him and twisting his arm behind his back to restrain him.

This seemed to be the signal for the other men to launch their attacks on the women with the placards, and Daniel was aware of a melee breaking out around him, the women giving as good as they got, slamming their placards onto the heads of the attacking men.

The sound of police whistles cut through the shouting, and the next moment the square was filled with uniformed officers. The immediate result was that the men ran off as fast as they could, leaving the women clinging onto their battered placards.

Daniel released the man he'd been holding, who pushed himself to his feet and bolted, then turned his attention to the woman the man had knocked to the ground. She was in her late twenties, blonde, and looking very flustered. Her bonnet had been knocked askew.

Daniel helped her to her feet.

'Are you alright?' he asked. 'No injuries?'

'No, thank you,' said the woman. She smiled. 'Thanks to you. I dread to think what might have happened if you hadn't intervened.'

'Bella!'

Daniel turned at the familiar voice, and saw Abigail hurrying towards them.

'Really, Bella, I warned you this might happen!' she snapped angrily.

'I can assure you I'm unharmed,' responded Bella.

'Thanks to the intervention of a *man*,' snapped Abigail pointedly. She turned to Daniel and said, 'Thank you, Mr Wilson, for rescuing my sister.'

Bella looked at Abigail, and then at Daniel, in surprise, before saying, 'You two know one another?'

'Mr Wilson is the private enquiry agent who is investigating the deaths at the Fitzwilliam,' said Abigail curtly. 'With my assistance.'

'I am sure that your sister was very capable of managing the situation,' said Daniel, doing his best to avert the argument between the two sisters that he saw looming.

'Thank you, Mr Wilson.' Bella smiled. 'And I am sure I would have been up to the situation, but I do express my very grateful thanks to you for your intervention.'

She held out her hand to Daniel. He took it and shook it gently, murmuring, 'My pleasure.'

'How is the investigation going?' asked Bella.

'It is proceeding,' said Daniel.

'As you know well enough, as I have told you so,' rebuked Abigail.

'That is not strictly true, Abi,' said Bella. 'After the initial reports of the deaths, you have been quite reticent on the subject.'

'Because there has been nothing to report,' snapped back Abigail.

'Is that correct, Mr Wilson?' asked Bella.

Daniel hesitated, aware that whatever he said would be wrong. 'There has been nothing of substance to report, Miss Fenton—'

'Bella, please,' Bella interrupted. 'After all, you saved me from the raging mob, so I'm sure that merits first-name terms.'

Daniel nodded. 'There has as yet been nothing of substance to report, but we are following lines of enquiry which I hope will lead us in the right direction.'

'How exciting!' Bella smiled. 'Perhaps you could come to tea with us and share these lines of enquiry. What do you say, Abi?' Before Abigail could speak, Bella continued with, 'Or, as you are a stranger in Cambridge, perhaps we could show you around the city.'

Abigail stared at her sister, unable to stop her mouth falling open. Bella had stolen her words! A sense of rage filled her as Bella prattled on. 'Parts of it can be like a maze if you don't know your way around, and it's very easy to get lost.'

Daniel offered an apologetic smile and said, 'I would love to, Miss Bella, but at this moment I'm on my way to follow a lead.'

'Which lead?' snapped Abigail, still feeling the fury at Bella having stolen her own plans to show Daniel the city from under her.

'I'm going to talk to Harry Elder,' said Daniel. 'You remember, I mentioned that to you.'

'Yes, of course.' Abigail forced a smile she did not feel to try and reassure Daniel her anger was not with him.

'I will, of course, report back to you on my discussion with him when I see you tomorrow at the Fitzwilliam and we go in search of Mr Blades. I suggest late morning, if that's acceptable to you. That will give me time to make enquiries at the cartage company and for you to continue your work cataloguing. Which might be politic, in case Sir William has questions of you about the collection that the board may raise.'

'Yes, I had already reached that conclusion on my own,' said Abigail, her tone curt.

Damn, thought Daniel. *I seem to have a talent for offending her.*

'Tomorrow, late morning,' he said.

After Daniel had made his polite farewell, doffing his hat and departing, Abigail turned to Bella, full of indignation.

'My God, Bella, could you have been any more forward? I'm surprised you didn't throw yourself into his arms.'

'My dear Abi, I was just being polite. The man had come to my rescue.'

'From the raging mob?' said Abigail sarcastically. 'It was one man, one ruffian.'

'Who threw me to the ground,' snapped Bella. 'What next? A boot to the head? We all know of suffragists who have been physically abused for expressing their opinions.'

'Yes, well, I agree his intervention was timely . . .' admitted Abigail.

'More than timely,' corrected Bella. She gave a warm smile. 'I believe he is a hero.'

CHAPTER SIXTEEN

This time, the door of the terraced house in Petworth Street was opened at the first knock, and Harry Elder, still wearing his Sunday best, looked out warily at Daniel.

'I apologise for disturbing you on the Lord's Day, Mr Elder . . .'

Elder nodded, and Daniel spotted a look of quiet appreciation in the man's eyes. *Good, I've said the right thing.*

'. . . but I'm afraid Mr Ransome has been killed.'

'Yes, I know,' said Elder. 'It was in yesterday's paper in Thetford.'

'As I say, I'm sorry to disturb you today, but the sooner I can gather information the more likely we are to find out why these things have happened.'

'I understand,' said Elder. 'Do come in. We'll go into the parlour.'

Daniel followed him into the house, and Elder opened a door and ushered him in.

'I'll just tell my wife we have a visitor,' he said.

He showed Daniel into the parlour while he disappeared towards the back of the house.

The room reminded Daniel of his own parents' parlour, a room only ever used for certain occasions, such as Christmas or after funerals. The furniture was even the same as in his parents' parlour: a dark oak sideboard, a small dark oak table and four sturdy upright chairs. The only difference here was the lack of brightly coloured china ornaments, possibly a side effect of Harry Elder's renunciation of ostentatious adornments that seemed to go with religions at the Nonconformist end of the scale.

Elder returned and gestured for Daniel to take a seat.

'I appreciate the consideration you expressed for the Lord's Day, Mr Wilson. Are you a man of faith?'

'Most of us have faith, Mr Elder.'

'Some have the wrong faith, and some have none,' said Elder gruffly. 'A man's faith tells a lot about that person. Whether, for example, he's a blind slave to idolatry, or Godless. I am always interested to know where a man stands before the Lord.'

Quickly, Daniel weighed up the situation. Chapel, Elder's neighbour had said. Which meant most likely Methodist or Baptist. Nonconformist, certainly. And his sharp words about idolatry and Godlessness meant he would have little time for Catholics, as shown in his reluctance to attend the wedding in Thetford; nor High Church of England, and none at all for atheists or agnostic doubters like Daniel.

'I was raised in a Quaker house,' said Daniel. It was a true answer, even if Daniel had moved away from any organised form of religion once he grew to adulthood.

Again, the nod of appreciation from Elder.

'My reason for calling is because I'd like to ask you some questions about Joseph Ransome.'

At the thought of being questioned about Ransome, rather than just general enquiries, Daniel saw the man's body stiffen and a look of wariness enter his face.

'On the night he died, did you notice anything unusual about him when he reported to change shifts?'

'Unusual?'

'His manner.'

Elder shook his head. 'No. He appeared the same as always.'

'Was he married, do you know?'

'A widower,' said Elder.

'Did he have any children? I'm asking because I intend to see the family, and I don't want to say anything that might upset them.'

Elder gave a sort of growl, then said, 'He had a sister. She lives in Sandy Lane. Though I don't think she had much to do with him.'

'How about you, Mr Elder?' asked Daniel, doing his best to make the question sound casual. There was something very wary in Elder's manner and he didn't want him to clam up.

'How about me, what?' grunted Elder.

'Did you have much to do with Mr Ransome?'

Elder shook his head. 'Apart from meeting when we changed over shifts, no. We didn't socialise.'

'And how did you get on with him?'

'Like I said, we didn't see each other except when we changed shift.'

'Of course. But what was your impression of him? As a person?'

Again, Elder noticeably stiffened. 'I didn't have any impression of him,' he said tersely.

Daniel nodded in understanding, then he said, 'Mr Elder, your colleague has been murdered—'

'I'm aware of that,' said Elder, curtly.

'—and I've been tasked with finding out who did it, and why. Which means looking into his character for a possible motive for why someone would want to kill him. You strike me as a decent and honest man.'

'I am, sir!' said Elder.

'And I get the impression that there was something about Mr Ransome of which you didn't approve.'

Daniel studied the man, saw the turmoil and torment in his eyes.

'There may be something there, something in his character . . .'

'He was ungodly and immoral!' burst out Elder.

'Yes, I had a suspicion of that,' said Daniel quietly.

'You did, sir?' said Elder, surprised.

Daniel nodded. The truth was, he'd had no such suspicion at all, but Elder's manner had alerted him to the fact that there was something wrong in the relationship between the two men, and it was just a case of finding out what that was.

'In what way was he immoral?' he asked.

Elder hesitated, his face going through various contortions, before he finally burst out, 'The women!'

'The women?'

'He brought women in, sir, at night. For immoral purposes.'

'I see. Did he tell you this? Boast about it?'

'Only after I realised what was going on.'

'And how did that realisation come to pass?'

'It was one night when I was on first shift. There was a knock at the door at the back. It was eleven o'clock at night and I thought it might be Ransome calling for some reason. But it was a woman.' His lip curled in anger at the memory. 'A loose woman, smelling of drink. She asked where Joe was. I told her it wasn't Joe's shift, and she laughed and said she always knew she'd get it wrong one day.

'I demanded to know what she meant, and she told me that Ransome had invited her to the museum for a bit of sport, as she put it. I told her there was no sport to be had, and for her to be on her way.'

'Did you challenge Ransome about it?'

'I did indeed! He just laughed, and then boasted about the women he had coming round. Said they liked the thrill of it, being in that place with all those dead bodies. It made 'em excited.'

He shook his head, angry.

'I was disgusted. I warned him I'd report him, but he laughed again, said I wouldn't because I was too decent to squeal on someone. That's what he said, and there was a sneer in his voice as he said the word "decent".

'If you ask me, Mr Wilson, Joseph Ransome received his just deserts.'

CHAPTER SEVENTEEN

Abigail added to her increasing list of artefacts, but her attention kept being drawn back to the conversation she and Bella had had the evening before, inspired by the events at the suffrage meeting.

'You were so rude to him, Abigail.'

It had been Daniel Wilson that Bella had been talking about.

'What do you mean, "rude"?' demanded Abigail.

'The curt way you spoke to him when he talked to you about meeting tomorrow at the Fitzwilliam. You almost bit his head off. Honestly, Abi, when you treat people like that, I wonder that they will work with you. I do declare, if I were Mr Wilson I would be reluctant to be in your company, treating him with such contempt as you do.'

'I do not treat him with contempt!' exploded Abigail. 'It

is my opinion that Mr Wilson is a fine gentleman: intelligent, courteous, thoughtful—'

'And brave,' cut in Bella. 'I do hope he takes us up on our proposal to show him Cambridge.'

'Takes *you* up on *your* proposal,' Abigail corrected her sternly.

'Very well,' said Bella. 'Then if you do not wish to join us, it will be my pleasure to show Mr Wilson the city. At least he will see there is one in this family that considers him worthy of decent treatment.'

I do not treat him with contempt, Abigail told herself fiercely. *That is just Bella's slanted view. I was angry with* her, *not him.*

But perhaps I allowed my anger to pass into my attitude towards him, she thought unhappily. But that was because Bella had stolen a march on her with her invitation. And without even consulting her!

Now I cannot say anything to him because it could be misconstrued.

She heard the sound of footsteps from the doorway, and turned expecting to find Sir William; but instead a tall young man, neatly dressed, sunburnt and with longish curling brown hair, was looking at her.

'Miss Abigail Fenton?'

'Yes.'

'I'm Edward Hardwicke. Just returned from Egypt.'

Abigail felt a sense of awe as she gazed at him; this was the man who'd sent all these wonderful antiquities that she was handling.

'Mr Hardwicke!'

'Sir William said I might find you here . . .'

She moved towards him, her hand outstretched for him to take. 'This is such a pleasure, Mr Hardwicke . . .'

'Edward, please.'

'Edward. And please, do call me Abigail.'

'Thank you.'

'I have to say, cataloguing the items you've sent from Egypt has been one of this job's particular delights. Such wonderful finds!'

'With more to come.' Edward smiled. 'I only arrived back in England yesterday, ahead of the next consignment.' His face looked saddened as he said, 'I've just heard about the recent tragedies here. The unknown man found in the sarcophagus, and the nightwatchman. Sir William said that it was you who found both of them.'

'Yes,' said Abigail.

'That must have been terribly traumatic for you.'

'Everyone keeps telling me that, but I insist that I am not unfamiliar with sudden and violent death. I have spent time in countries where human life is considered cheap, and been exposed to those consequences.'

'I assume you're talking of Egypt,' said Hardwicke.

'Amongst others. I was also in Palestine and Cyrenaica.'

'Yes, I was there, too.' Hardwicke smiled. 'A very different way of life to that in our own dear Britain. I must tell you, Sir William was full of praise for you, your scholarship and intelligence, and now I've met you, I can see why. Forgive my presumption, Miss Fenton . . .'

'Abigail.'

'Abigail . . . but Sir William has just asked if I would take part in a debate that's happening here on Friday on the pyramid inch theory.'

Abigail nodded. 'Sir Geoffrey Morgan and Professor Horst Waldheim.'

'Yes. Well, it seems that Sir Geoffrey has unfortunately had to pull out – a recurrence of an old illness – so Sir William has asked me if I'd take part in his place. It's short notice, but I said I'd be delighted to. I owe the Fitzwilliam a lot.'

'I'm sure not as much as the Fitzwilliam owes you,' said Abigail.

Hardwicke smiled, pleased at the compliment, then said, 'Anyway, I wondered if you would consider coming to the debate as my guest?'

'Me?' Abigail was stunned both by the suddenness of his invitation, and the fact that he was making it at all. To her!

'Well, I feel I owe it to you for the invaluable work you've been doing cataloguing my finds.'

Abigail studied him, his face, his stance, looking for some sign of mockery or condescension that she had encountered in some other field archaeologists, but found none. He just appeared to be a sincere, intelligent, courteous – and handsome, there was no doubt about that – young man, with a passion for the same subject as her: the ancient world.

'Mr Hardwicke . . .'

'Edward.'

'Edward, I would be honoured.'

He smiled. 'Excellent. I would be most interested to get your view on the debate after it's finished. I know Professor Waldheim's work, and his views on Piazzi Smyth and the pyramid inch certainly differ from mine, so I would be grateful if you could let me know afterwards if I acquitted myself well enough against him.'

CHAPTER EIGHTEEN

Peebles and Co., Cartage, were located outside the city centre in a yard not far from the railway station, with a strong smell of horse manure emanating from the stables somewhere at the back of the small two-storey building that housed the offices. One solitary wagon was parked in the yard, a flat-bed with its large wheels painted red and yellow, with a large metal sign on the side of the wagon bearing the logo PEEBLES AND CO., THE CARTER YOU CAN TRUST. Daniel assumed the other wagons were out making their deliveries.

Daniel followed the directions from a sign at the bottom of a metal staircase bearing the legend OFFICE, and an arrow pointing upwards.

A large man with cropped hair but a voluminous moustache, sitting barely contained in a swivel armchair, looked up as Daniel entered the office.

'Mr Peebles?' enquired Daniel.

The man gave an unhappy sigh.

'Alas, Mr Peebles is no longer with us. He departed from this earth some four years ago, when I took over the business.' He stood up and held out his hand. 'Josiah Trussell.' As Daniel shook his hand, Trussell added, 'I kept the name because Peebles has such a good reputation in the cartage business, it would have been foolish to change it.' He gestured at the empty chair across from his desk, and he and Daniel sat down.

'So, do I assume you want something removed, Mr . . . ?'

'Wilson,' said Daniel. He took a card from his wallet and handed it to Trussell.

'A private enquiry agent,' muttered Trussell, and he regarded Daniel with wariness.

'I've been asked by Sir William Mackenzie at the Fitzwilliam to look into recent tragic events there.'

At the mention of Sir William's name, Trussell relaxed slightly, as Daniel had hoped he would.

'I understand that your company recently transported some artefacts to the museum?'

Trussell chuckled. 'Ah-ha! The mummy!' he chortled. 'I saw it in the paper.' He leant forward, smiling as he added, 'Take my word for it, squire, when that thing was delivered to the Fitzwilliam it gave no indication of being alive.'

'Yes, that's what they say at the Fitzwilliam.' Daniel nodded.

'No knocking from the inside of the box.' And he laughed again. 'Someone's telling a real corker of a story to the papers. Their idea of a joke, I suppose.'

'Indeed,' agreed Daniel. 'But I'd be grateful if you could clarify a couple of things.'

'You're surely not giving this story credence!' burst out

Trussell, looking at Daniel with an air of bewilderment.

'No, absolutely not,' Daniel assured him. 'It's just to clear up one or two questions. For example, from which port was the last consignment collected?'

'Tilbury,' said Trussell.

'You're sure?' asked Daniel.

'Absolutely. The last three consignments for the Fitzwilliam have all come through Tilbury,' said Trussell.

'And do you know who your carter collected it from?'

Trussell frowned. 'The agents, I guess,' he said.

'Do you happen to have a name?' asked Daniel.

Trussell got up, went to a filing cabinet and pulled out a paper file. He opened it and took out some papers, which he returned to the desk with and passed across to Daniel.

'Here you are, squire,' he said.

Daniel looked at the piece of paper headed 'Collection Note'. It had been crumpled and then smoothed out, but the dates on it were clear enough. It showed the delivery being collected from the ship on the Sunday, then delivered to the Fitzwilliam on the Monday, which tied in with the delivery note that Abigail had shown to him. There were two signatures on the document, one a barely legible scrawl, the other an X.

'The X is Jim Hoy's,' explained Trussell. 'He can write, but can't be bothered.'

'The other signature?' asked Daniel.

Trussell shook his head. 'No idea.'

'Would it be possible to talk to the carter who made the delivery?'

'Why?'

'I'm interested in finding out about the man they collected the artefacts from. Mr Hoy may not be able to tell me his name, but a description of him would be enormously helpful.'

Trussell thought it over. 'Well, seeing as it's for the Fitzwilliam, and they're important clients . . .'

'I will make sure to tell Sir William how very helpful you've been,' Daniel assured him.

Trussell nodded. 'At the moment Jim and Bob are away on a long-distance job.'

'Bob?'

'Bob Hoy. Jim's son. He's like his apprentice. They're taking a load to Birmingham.'

'When do you expect them back?'

'Three days. Maybe four,' said Trussell.

'Would you ask them to get in touch with me when they return?' asked Daniel. 'I'll make it worth their while.' He pointed at the card he'd given Trussell. 'On the back is the address of where I'm staying while I'm in Cambridge, or they can contact me at the Fitzwilliam.'

CHAPTER NINETEEN

It was approaching noon when Daniel arrived at the Fitzwilliam to collect Abigail for their visit to the offices of the *Gazette*.

'How is your sister today?' he asked. 'Has she recovered from her encounter with that ruffian yesterday?'

'It was a push, that was all,' said Abigail. 'Bella has a habit of dramatising things that happen to her. I blame it on the fact she reads far too many romantic novels.'

'Still, she was assaulted,' said Daniel. 'That sort of thing is very unpleasant.'

'True,' agreed Abigail. 'But I must warn you, Mr Wilson, that my sister is prone to exaggeration in many areas. She can be fanciful.'

'Is this a warning to me?' asked Daniel, amused.

'Certainly not!' said Abigail. Then, aware of what Bella had said about her curt manner towards Daniel, she allowed herself a smile. 'I just thought it worth mentioning so that you might prefer to take things she says with a pinch of salt.'

'Such as her offer to show me the city?'

'No, I'm sure she means well in that respect. It's just that sometimes she expresses passions which seem genuine, but soon evaporate.'

Intriguing, thought Daniel. *Is she warning me off getting involved with her sister?* Deciding to change the subject, he said, 'I spoke to Harry Elder at length yesterday, and gained some valuable insights into the character of Joseph Ransome.'

With some slight toning down of what Elder had told him, he appraised Abigail of Ransome's exploits during his night shifts at the Fitzwilliam. Abigail, predictably, exploded with outrage at the revelation.

'That is appalling! A desecration! To use those priceless ancient artefacts as an . . . aphrodisiac!'

'The question is, is it connected with his murder? Could it be the result of jealousy?'

'A jealous husband or lover of one of the women?' asked Abigail.

'Or perhaps one of the women themselves,' said Daniel. 'We know that Ransome had women, plural. Could one of them have felt that he'd betrayed her? Perhaps he'd persuaded her that she was the only one, and when she discovered the truth . . .'

'Which could explain the chloroform,' said Abigail thoughtfully. 'She knew she wouldn't be able to strangle him unless he was already unconscious.' She looked quizzically at Daniel. 'Do you think that's a likely scenario?'

'I don't know,' said Daniel. 'It's a possibility, but personally, I doubt it. The business of the bandage from the mummy doesn't fit.'

'I don't see why not,' said Abigail. 'It sounds as if he was exciting them by showing them the mummies, so they'd have access to a bandage.'

'But why use it to direct attention towards the idea that a reanimated mummy did the killing? And if, as you say, that was inspired by the Arthur Conan Doyle story, I think it unlikely that one of Ransome's loose women would have read it, especially as it was published in an American magazine. And remember the phrase in the *Gazette* that this theory about the deaths being the result of a reanimated mummy came from – and I quote – "an eminent Egyptologist". Which is why we are on our way to see Mr Blades.

'But I also think that this business of Ransome letting women in at night answers the question of how the mystery man, and his murderer, gained access to the museum.'

'You think that Ransome let them in?'

'It certainly seems easier than visioning them clambering up and down drainpipes and over the roof.'

'But why would he do that?'

'Money. Harry Elder seems of the opinion that Ransome had very low moral standards. It wouldn't surprise me at all to find he'd let the victim and his murderer in for an exchange of cash, not anticipating it would result in murder, of course. They may even have come in together. In the end, it got Ransome killed.'

'Because he knew the identity of the murderer?'

'Exactly. My guess is he tried to blackmail the murderer, possibly arranged to meet him or her at the Fitzwilliam during the night to be paid off, and the murderer killed him.'

'So where does this mysterious Egyptologist fit into it?'

'He or she could be our murderer,' said Daniel.

* * *

A different man was on duty at the reception desk at the *Gazette*, this one younger and apparently more eager to please. When Daniel and Abigail presented their cards to the young man, instead of receiving obstacles to their visit as Daniel had expected, the young man invited them to follow him from the reception area and into the main room where the next edition of the newspaper was being prepared.

They followed the young man through a crush of tightly packed desks that overflowed with paper in apparently ramshackle style. Some pieces of paper had been stuck on dangerous-looking metal spikes on the desks. Others just spilt this way and that, while clerks and copyists sat and scrawled on them, their ink-filled pens scuttling across the papers, crossing out words and squeezing others in, at enormous speed. The smell of ink and paper filled the air, making a heady mix. And everyone seemed so intent, so busy.

The young man stopped by a desk where a man in his late twenties, with long locks of thin blonde hair and fingers stained black with ink, was frowning at a piece of prose, his pen poised above it.

'Mr Blades,' said the young man. 'Visitors for you.' And he laid the cards on the desk before heading back to his station at the reception desk.

Hector Blades looked up enquiringly at Daniel and Abigail.

'Visitors, eh. What can I do for you, Mr . . . ?' He picked up Daniel's card. 'Daniel Wilson, private enquiry agent,' he read, frowning. Then his expression brightened as he remembered. 'You were Abberline's assistant! The Ripper!'

Daniel nodded. 'Correct.'

'And the Cleveland Street scandal!' Blades chuckled. 'What I would have given to have had the inside story on that one! Paid off, eh!' And he laughed again.

Abigail looked at Daniel, puzzled, and noticed that the expression on his face had become grim.

'If you are alleging what I think you are,' snapped Daniel, 'I would correct you.'

'Oh, come on!' Blades smirked. 'Prince Albert Victor, second in line to the throne, and no charges brought?'

'Chief Inspector Abberline and I presented our report,' said Daniel curtly. 'The decision not to press charges against certain individuals was nothing to do with us. We had no influence on the prosecution.'

'Not so good for the telegraph boys, was it,' said Blades. Then he shrugged. 'Though they got light sentences, as I recall.'

'Fascinating though this remembrance is,' cut in Abigail impatiently, 'we are here on a more current and local issue.'

Blades picked up her card.

'Abigail Fenton, archaeologist, care of the Fitzwilliam.' He smiled. 'Let me guess. You're here about the mummy.'

'In a way,' she said. 'We're here to ask the name of the eminent Egyptologist who gave you the theory.'

He smiled and shook his head. 'Sorry. That's confidential.'

'Why?' demanded Abigail.

'We never reveal our sources,' said Blades.

'But this is a murder investigation,' said Daniel.

'Even if you were a proper copper – and, with respect, Mr Wilson, you ain't any more – I still wouldn't tell you. Never revealing our sources is one of the first rules of investigative journalism. If we did, no one would ever tell us anything.'

'And if you were threatened with prison for refusing to reveal the name?' asked Abigail.

Blades grinned.

'I would go to prison, and gladly. Because it would enhance

my reputation as The Man Who Keeps a Secret.' He smiled at them. 'I'm thinking of adopting that as my byline.' He looked around to make sure no one was near enough to overhear him, then leant forward and whispered, 'However, because I do have a sense of public duty, there may be room for manoeuvre in this particular case.'

'What sort of room for manoeuvre?' asked Daniel.

'You're conducting your own investigation into the murders?' asked Blades.

'On behalf of the Fitzwilliam,' Daniel clarified.

Blades nodded. 'Now, at the moment, I'm not getting a lot of information from Inspector Drabble, who's in charge of this case. He seems to disapprove of the press. Maybe that's because we've had cause to point out a few of his errors in the past.' And he gave his throaty chuckle again. 'Drabble arrested the editor, Mr Purslane, a year ago on a morality charge, before he realised who he was. No charges were actually pressed, but it got Mr Purslane in deep trouble with his missus, and Mr Purslane has got a long memory and bears grudges.'

'So, since then, you've given Inspector Drabble some stick in your pages.'

'Only when he deserves it,' said Blades.

'So, as a result, no police cooperation. Which seems rather short-sighted, as an editorial policy,' commented Daniel.

'Maybe, but Mr Purslane did suffer very deeply when Inspector Drabble informed Mrs Purslane of the charges being considered against her husband. Mrs Purslane has got a very ferocious temper. So, let us say that if you can furnish me with inside information of your investigations, exclusive to me, perhaps I might see my way clear to tipping you the wink on who my Egyptology expert is.'

'We are employed by the Fitzwilliam,' Daniel reminded him. 'Any information we gather must first be reported to them.'

'Sir William Mackenzie,' said Blades. He shook his head. 'No, that won't work for me. Sir William has got personal contacts with the big London papers. I want first dibs. I want them London papers to come asking *me* for tips. That's where my future lies. The Big Time.'

'We will ask Sir William—' began Daniel, but again Blades shook his head, firmer this time.

'No good. Sir William's not the kind of bloke who'd agree to it. And, even if he did, who's to say he'd stick to his side of the bargain.'

'Sir William is an honourable man!' snapped Abigail.

Blades shook his head again.

'Too risky. Look, what I'm offering is a fair trade. You give me something I ain't got, ahead of anyone else getting it, and I'll see about dropping you that name. What do you say?'

Daniel saw that Abigail was about to snap something curt at Blades, and before she did he said, 'We'll think about it. Thank you for your time, Mr Blades.'

CHAPTER TWENTY

'What an odious creature!' snorted Abigail as they walked away from the *Gazette* offices.

'I agree,' said Daniel. 'You see what I mean about not wanting to let them run the story about the photograph of the mystery dead man, rather than put it in as an advert. Mr Blades would certainly make it a colourful tale, and quite likely inaccurate.'

'But you are prepared to do that deal with him?'

'No,' said Daniel. 'I was prepared to let him think I might. I believe our duty is to report his offer to Sir William, and see what he says. Don't you agree that knowing the identity of the person who started this murderous mummy rumour could be quite crucial? I get the feeling whoever did it is connected with these murders in some way.'

'Yes.' Abigail nodded. She turned to Daniel and asked

suddenly, 'What was this Cleveland Street business that dreadful man was talking about?'

'You don't remember it?' asked Daniel. 'Five years ago. It was in the papers, some more sensational than others.'

'Five years ago I was in Egypt,' said Abigail. 'I would have not had time, nor the interest, in newspaper stories of a sensational nature.'

Daniel explained: 'My boss, Chief Inspector Abberline, received orders to investigate allegations of a homosexual brothel operating at Cleveland Street in Fitzrovia in London. Apparently a complaint had been lodged that suggested telegraph messenger boys who worked for the post office were also working as prostitutes at Cleveland Street. We investigated, and discovered that the Cleveland Street brothel had a very illustrious clientele. Among others, Lord Arthur Somerset, an equerry to the Prince of Wales, was a client, and stories were circulating that Lord Somerset had introduced Prince Albert Victor, the eldest son of the Prince of Wales, and thus second in line to the throne, to the place.

'The bush telegraph works very quickly, and once word of our investigation became known, most of the principals, including some very distinguished men, fled the country. The only ones who were arrested were the male prostitutes themselves . . .'

'The telegraph boys?'

Daniel nodded. 'They were given light sentences. But, because none of the clients was prosecuted, this led to rumours and allegations that there had been a government cover-up to protect prominent people.'

'Blades said you'd been paid off.'

'That was another rumour, that Fred and I had been bribed to let the clients slip away. Absolute rot! There was no one more honest than Fred Abberline. And I assure you I never took a penny in all my years on the force.'

'I believe you, Mr Wilson,' said Abigail. 'So now, what is our next move regarding this case?'

'I thought I'd return to talk to Mr Elder,' said Daniel. 'See if he can enlighten me further on Ransome's nocturnal activities.'

'Disgusting!' said Abigail. 'I shall be aware of such desecration the whole time I'm cataloguing the latest arrivals.'

'Perhaps it would have been better if I hadn't said anything to you,' suggested Daniel.

She shook her head. 'No, if I'm to be your partner in this investigation, I need to know everything. For my part, I need to return to the Fitzwilliam and press on with the cataloguing. I think that Sir William feels the process is not going fast enough.'

'I'm sure he'll make allowances in the circumstances.'

'I'm afraid Sir William can be very single-minded when it comes to the Fitzwilliam's reputation and fortunes,' said Abigail. 'Perhaps you would like to call at our house later, to update me.' She gave an arch smile as she added, 'I'm sure my sister would be pleased to see you.'

Daniel wondered how to respond. Abigail's tone suggested her disapproval of her sister's apparent interest in Daniel. He opted for a polite smile and murmured, 'I will certainly call later. What time would suit you?'

'I normally arrive home about six.'

'Then just after six.' Daniel nodded.

She took one of her cards from her bag and wrote on the back of it. 'This is our address.' She gave him the card. 'I look forward to seeing you later.'

Daniel watched her walk away with a feeling of confusion. He couldn't make Abigail Fenton out. Sometimes she seemed cold and aloof, and at other times he sensed a hint of warmth towards him. And her dig at her sister seemed to hint at jealousy, if indeed her sister – Bella – was interested in him; although he felt that Bella was the kind of outgoing person who expressed herself like that to everyone. Indeed, Abigail had said as much.

Still keen to get his bearings in Cambridge, in addition to Bella's offer to show him around, Daniel took a few turnings of minor lanes and found himself in Fitzroy Street, where a sign saying 'W. Heffer & Sons Booksellers and Stationers' caught his eye. He recalled a phrase of Professor Hughes' at breakfast: 'If you need any information about Cambridge while you are here, I recommend Heffers. They are so much more knowledgeable than most booksellers.'

Well, this enquiry will challenge their knowledge, he thought as he entered.

The young man at the counter looked up as he approached.

'Yes, sir?' he asked. 'Can I help you?'

'I hope you can,' said Daniel. 'I'm trying to find a copy of a story by Arthur Conan Doyle, called "Lot No. 249".'

The young man nodded. 'Indeed, sir, although I'm afraid that particular story hasn't yet been issued in book form, we do have a copy of the edition of *Harper's Magazine* in which it was published.'

Daniel couldn't help but stare at the young man, who had so casually offered this information. At the very least, Daniel had anticipated having to give the bookshop assistant more information about the story, including the publication in *Harper's*.

'I could let you have the magazine to look at,' continued the young man, adding apologetically, 'but unfortunately I can't let you take it out of the shop as it's the only copy we have, and we use it for reference. *Harper's* is an American magazine, you see, and we get our copy on subscription.'

'Of course,' said Daniel. 'I would very much appreciate the opportunity to look at it.'

'If you'll just wait here I'll go and get our copy,' said the young man.

As he headed for a back room, Daniel called him back.

'I'm sorry,' said Daniel, 'but I can't let this go without complimenting you. An acquaintance of mine told me that the people at Heffers are especially knowledgeable, but I never expected this. It's such a rare story, not even a known book, but a story in a foreign magazine, and yet you didn't even need to check on it. I am intrigued how you have trained your mind to get such instant recall of even the smallest trivia such as this story.'

The young man smiled. 'Thank you for the compliment, sir, but you give me more credit than I deserve. The reason I recall it is because you're the second person to ask after that story in the last few days.'

'Oh? Who was the first?'

'A gentleman.'

'Did he give a name?'

The assistant shook his head. 'I'm afraid not. Is it important?'

Daniel produced his card and handed it to the man.

'I'm investigating the recent deaths at the Fitzwilliam on their behalf,' he said. 'And this story of Arthur Conan Doyle's seems to figure in it, in an odd way. So I'd be quite interested in finding out who this gentleman was. Have you seen him before?'

'No, I'm afraid not. We're familiar with our regular customers, but he was new to me.'

'What sort of man was he?'

'An educated man, I'd hazard. In his forties, I think.'

'Any noticeable features? Anything that might make him easily recognisable?'

'Not really. Although he did have a very luxuriant moustache. Rather in the style of W. S. Gilbert, curling back towards his sideburns.'

'English?'

'Yes.' The man smiled. 'Actually, the most noticeable thing about him was his suit.'

'Oh?'

'It was of a light green colour, designed in rather large checks. Even the waistcoat. Rather ostentatious, I thought. And now, sir, I'll go and get you the story.'

CHAPTER TWENTY-ONE

Daniel headed to his lodgings, his mind still full of the Arthur Conan Doyle story he'd just read. A tale of the supernatural, a far cry from Doyle's Sherlock Holmes tales, and so well told that the supernatural element, the mummy being brought back to life to wreak vengeance, seemed entirely possible.

Careful, he told himself. To say such a thing to Abigail would only bring down more scorn on his head. But the main factor was that the plot of the story was the same as the story that Blades had told in the *Gazette*. There had to be a connection with the murders.

Mrs Loxley was out when he arrived, but there was a large envelope addressed to him waiting on the hall table. He opened it, and took out the photograph of the unknown dead man, along with a note from Dr Keen. There was no doubt that Dr

Keen had done an exceptional job. Some photographs Daniel had seen were blurred, or failed to look like the person being photographed. He'd only seen the dead man on the table in the basement of Gonville and Caius, but up close, the sepia depiction of the man's face was perfect.

Daniel set off immediately for the offices of the *Gazette*, where he handed the photograph and his prepared wording to the clerk in the Announcements and Advertisements Office.

'It's too late for today's late edition,' said the girl at the desk. 'That's already at the presses, but it'll go in tomorrow's early edition.'

Daniel thanked her and assured her that was very acceptable, and then headed for Harry Elder's house. By now it was mid-afternoon, so Daniel felt that Elder should be up and refreshed. Most night-workers he'd known slept during the hours of morning, surfacing shortly after noon.

Harry Elder didn't seem particularly pleased to see him, but Daniel felt that Elder was a man who did not like his regular routine to be disrupted by anything.

'I'm sorry to trouble you again, Mr Elder,' said Daniel when they were once more seated in his front parlour. 'But I need more information about Joe Ransome's activities.'

'Activities!' snorted Elder in disgust.

'It's only by asking questions that we can hope to get to the bottom of this, and hopefully prevent similar tragedies occurring. And the next victim may not be of disreputable character, like Ransome, but someone law-abiding. An innocent bystander, for example.'

Elder nodded, mollified by this argument.

'What do you want to know?' he asked.

'For one thing, I'm interested to discover which particular pub Ransome frequented.'

'The Lamb and Flag in Jessop Street,' said Elder, his mouth tight in disapproval.

'Did you ever accompany him there?' asked Daniel.

'Certainly not!' snapped Elder. 'I am a teetotaller. The only reason I know this was his favourite haunt was because he spoke of it, and suggested I should go with him for "some sport", as he put it. I soon disabused him of my desire to do any such thing.'

'I assume this Lamb and Flag is not a very reputable establishment?'

'You assume correctly,' said Elder with a snort of disgust.

'As I'm a stranger in Cambridge, I wonder if you can suggest someone who might be able to give me information about it. Accurate information, that is. Of course, I could go to the police . . .'

'The police!' said Elder with derision. Then he corrected himself. 'No, that's not fair. Generally, they're good. But there are some beat officers who aren't averse to looking the other way, if it suits them. Or their pockets.'

Daniel waited, feeling there was more to come, and after a thoughtful interval Elder said, 'There is someone, a member of my church, Neville Padstow, a very decent and honest man. He recently retired from the local force. He's not a man to tell tales . . .'

'I only want to know about the Lamb and Flag, not about any activities of his former colleagues in the police,' Daniel assured him.

'Very well,' said Elder. 'If you'll wait here, I'll go and see if he's available.'

'I'll come with you, if you prefer,' offered Daniel.

'There's no need,' said Elder. 'Padstow only lives round the corner, and he's a very private man not used to visitors.' He hesitated, then added, 'His wife suffers from nerves. A visit from a stranger might upset her. If I can ask you to wait here.'

'Of course,' said Daniel.

Neville Padstow was a large, serious-looking man in his early sixties. Clean-shaven, with close-cropped grey hair, he shook hands with Daniel after Elder had made the introductions, then sat down on one of the upright chairs, while Elder seated himself on another.

'You were Abberline's man,' said Padstow.

'I was,' said Daniel.

'It's a pity you both retired,' he said. 'The force needs honest men.'

'The same could be said of you, Mr Padstow,' Daniel returned the compliment.

'Me, I'm old. After years of pounding the pavements, I was ready to go.' He regarded Daniel solemnly. 'Harry said you wanted to know about the Lamb and Flag.'

'Yes. Was it on your beat?'

Padstow gave him a grim look. 'If it had been, I'd have cleaned it up. Or done my best to.'

'A cesspit of vice?' suggested Daniel.

'Along with suspected stolen goods,' grunted Padstow.

'You never mentioned it to your superiors?' asked Daniel.

'I dropped a few hints, but I was told that it was opportune to leave the situation as it was.'

'The landlord was passing information on,' Daniel guessed.

'When it suited him,' said Padstow.

'We had the same situation in certain places in London,' said Daniel. 'Our chiefs adopted the same attitude when some of us raised concerns. That while they stayed open, we were able to keep an eye on them and the people who operated out of them. And, in turn, they gave us useful intelligence on people we might be looking for.'

'In my opinion it's the thin end of the wedge,' said Padstow in disapproval. 'Soon other places start wanting the same leeway, the same blind eye turned to their illegal activities, and that one bad apple turns into a whole barrelful.'

Daniel nodded. 'I agree with you, but we are not in charge. We just have to follow orders. Or leave.'

'Is that why you left, Mr Wilson?'

Daniel hesitated, then answered blandly, 'The time was right for me to move on. Returning to the Lamb and Flag, who is the landlord?'

'Officially, a man called Herbert Crane. But the person who really runs what goes on there is his wife, Lillian. At least, she calls herself his wife and uses his name, but whether they're actually married is debatable.'

'And what is the best time to find Lillian there?'

'She sleeps most of the morning, is up at about noon and behind the bar at two. And she's there till about two in the morning.'

As Daniel listened to Padstow, a very different Cambridge was revealed to him than the one he'd so far seen: the colleges, the museum, the centuries of historical grandeur, respectable and professional people in respectable houses. From Padstow's description of the place and the tales he told of its patrons, the Lamb and Flag, and the area where it was to be found, was a den of iniquity, a cesspit, a sink of evil. To Daniel, it felt like coming home; these were the kind of places he'd earned his stripes as a uniformed copper, then as a detective, in London: the rookeries of Seven Dials, Whitechapel, Stepney, the slums where few coppers ventured on their own after dark.

But he was no longer a copper. And he needed to get to the bottom of this before the trail for the murderer went cold. He'd go to the Lamb and Flag tonight.

Aware that Harry Elder would be needing to get ready for his shift at the museum shortly, Daniel thanked Padstow and Elder for their assistance.

'Might I ask, Mr Elder, what's happening about your shifts now that Ransome is no longer around?'

'Bill Potts, the man you met the other night when you went to the Fitzwilliam, is going to take Ransome's place. I'm taking the early shift this evening, with him coming on at one, same as usual.'

'I'm glad you found a suitable replacement so quickly,' said Daniel.

'He would always have been my choice of colleague to share shifts with, but Ransome was already at the Fitzwilliam when I started, so there was no way in for him.'

'You could have complained about Ransome when you discovered what sort of person he was,' said Daniel.

Elder shook his head. 'I'm not in the habit of getting people the sack, Mr Wilson, whoever they are.'

Daniel thanked Elder and Padstow again, then left them together. As he left Elder's house, the door of the neighbouring house opened and the man he'd seen the day before gestured at him. 'Oi! Psst!'

Daniel approached him, curious, and the man beckoned him in, shutting the door.

'Copper, ain't you, right?' he asked.

'Private investigator,' said Daniel.

The man grinned broadly.

'I knew it! I can always tell a copper!' He nodded towards Elder's house. 'So, what's he done?'

'Nothing,' said Daniel.

'Oh come on!' appealed the man. 'We live next door to him. If he's a danger to anyone, we ought to know.'

'Why would he be a danger to anyone?' asked Daniel.

'Because of what happened before.'

'And what did happen before?' asked Daniel patiently.

The man looked at Daniel, weighing him up, then said, 'Yeah, you're new here, ain't you. Well, it was about a year ago. Some poor bloke had got a bit too much drink in him and was making a bit of a row in the street. It was the cussing that did it. It brought old Harry out and he gave the bloke a ticking off about using foul language among respectable people. Well, ordinarily the bloke would have just shut up and gone off, but because he'd taken quite a bit of drink he got very bold and told Harry what he could do with his respectable people. Hypocrites, he called them. And then he moved on to Harry's church. I don't know what they'd done to upset him, but he laced into them proper. And not just the church, but God and everyone else to do with it, and the next minute Harry's punching him and throwing him about. It was like he'd gone mad. We all came out because we thought Harry was gonna kill the bloke.'

'Were the police called?'

The man nodded. 'They turned up and took Harry in on a charge of assault.'

'What happened? Was he jailed?'

'No. The bloke he beat up didn't want to press charges. And Harry's sister turned up and appealed to the coppers to give him another chance, him being so religious and law-abiding and all

123

that.' He winked. 'I got the idea that a couple of the coppers at the station were in the same chapel as Harry, so maybe that helped.

'Anyway, he got let off with a caution. But the thing is, if he's done it once, he can do it again. And he works at the place where these people have been getting killed. So who's to say what may have been going on. This last bloke who died there, he was a nightwatchman, weren't he, same as Harry.'

'Have you mentioned any of this to the police?' asked Daniel.

'Yeah.' The man nodded. 'In passing to Constable Harris, the local beat bobby. I mean, I'm thinking of the safety of me and my family, if he is dangerous like that. But Harris just laughed. Said I was letting my imagination run away with me.' He leant in and added in an undertone to Daniel, 'I think Harris is one of them who goes to the same chapel as Harry, so they're covering up.'

Daniel nodded in appreciation. 'Thank you, Mr . . .'

'Smith,' said the man. 'Ben Smith.'

'Thank you, Mr Smith. Do you happen to know the name of the man that Harry Elder beat so badly?'

'Charley Pile,' said Smith. 'He used to live at a lodging house about six doors down, but he left after what happened.' He shrugged. 'Mind, he'd been given notice before that, because of his drinking. He used to make a fuss inside the house and disturb the others.'

'Where did he move to?'

Smith shook his head. 'No idea. He was just a wanderer, really. He hadn't been in the house that long before he upset Harry. No one knew where he came from.'

'You mentioned a sister of Mr Elder?'

Smith nodded again. 'Esther Sims. Good woman. Respectable. Not as churchified as Harry. She works at a chemist in the town. Allisons.'

An interesting new aspect to the case, mused Daniel as he left Smith's house. Harry Elder, a man with a temper who reacted with violence to mockery of his religion. With a sister who worked at a chemist, so he would have access to chloroform through her.

Was it possible that Harry Elder's anger at Joe Ransome's licentious lifestyle had built up to such a degree that it had finally erupted into murder?

CHAPTER TWENTY-TWO

It was Bella who opened the door to Daniel's knock and she greeted him effusively, taking his hands in hers.

'I'm so glad you decided to come! Do come in!'

She led him by the hand, only releasing him when she seemed to realise what she'd done. She flushed in embarrassment.

'I do apologise!' she said. 'I don't usually accost men in this way, but after what happened yesterday . . .'

'I do understand, Miss Bella,' said Daniel with a gentle smile.

'Abi! It's Mr Wilson,' Bella called.

Daniel followed her into a comfortable sitting room and found Abigail stood studying the *Gazette*, a grim expression on her face.

'Have you seen this?' she demanded.

'Mr Blades with more tales of murdering mummies?' enquired Daniel.

She held the newspaper towards him so he could read the headline: MURDERING MUMMY: WILSON OF THE YARD CALLED IN.

'It's the late edition,' she said. 'It's an outrage!'

'And inaccurate. I am no longer Wilson of the Yard.'

'Nowhere in this article is my name mentioned, despite the fact that we informed Mr Blades that we are both involved in this investigation.'

'I think you should be grateful he hasn't mentioned you, Abi,' said Bella. 'I certainly wouldn't like to be associated publicly with something as unsavoury as a murder.'

'That's not the issue!' snapped Abigail.

'But it does back up my point about putting the notice about the photograph of the dead man in ourselves, rather than entrusting it to someone like Mr Blades,' said Daniel.

'Yes.' Abigail nodded. 'Do you know when that is likely to be?'

'The picture will be appearing in tomorrow's early edition,' Daniel told her. 'Is there anything in the paper about what happened at yesterday's suffrage meeting?'

'There is!' exclaimed Bella.

'Hardly,' sniffed Abigail. 'A few sentences, and very dismissive.' She searched the pages until she found it, and read aloud, '"Scuffles broke out at a Votes for Women meeting being held in the city centre on Sunday. There were no injuries thanks to prompt intervention by the police. Doubts have been expressed at the wisdom of allowing such meetings to be held in public places for fears of injuries to innocent passers-by."'

'Doubts!' snorted Bella angrily. 'Treating us as if we are a disorganised rabble! I would have hoped the article would at least have discussed the issue.'

'That depends on the political tastes of the editor and owner,' observed Daniel. 'If they approved of the idea of votes for all, including women, they would have given a fuller account of the reasons behind the meeting. From what little they have said, and putting the blame for events on the meeting itself rather than the men who attacked it, they are discrediting the cause. So, regretfully, I doubt if you will get any support for your campaign from the local paper.'

Bella scowled. 'How typical of this society!' Then she smiled. 'But, as long as we have men like yourself to support us, I feel we shall prevail. Mr Wilson, would you care to have supper with us? I'm sure that Mrs Standish will be able to prepare another place.'

'Thank you for the invitation,' said Daniel, 'but Mrs Loxley will be expecting me for supper, and I'd hate to upset her preparations. Also, I have a visit to make this evening.'

'Oh? Who to?' asked Bella.

Daniel hesitated, then said, 'It's to do with the case, and if I get any returns from it I'll be happy to let you know.' He looked at the clock on the mantelpiece. 'But now, I must go, I'm afraid.'

'I'll see you to the door,' said Abigail quickly, cutting in before Bella could offer.

She waited until they were at the door and out of Bella's earshot before she said quietly, in annoyance, 'I thought we were meant to be partners in this case.'

'Indeed, I view us as that.'

'Then why are you being secretive about this visit you have to make tonight?'

Daniel shot a quick glance along the passage to check whether Bella was listening, then lowered his voice to say, 'I will be happy to tell you, but I am concerned that your sister's . . . enthusiasm . . . may mean her passing information on to friends of hers, or colleagues at the library. Not deliberately, of course, but in my experience, it's important to control the information given out for fear of alerting the culprit to our actions.'

'Yes, I see,' said Abigail.

'In fact, I'm going to a pub that Joseph Ransome used to frequent called the Lamb and Flag, where I hope to gain information about what went on during his night shifts.'

'I think we know what went on,' said Abigail curtly.

'I'm pretty sure there were other things as well. As I've said, possibly the way the first man who died gained entry to the museum.'

'Yes,' said Abigail. 'Thank you for that, Mr Wilson. Perhaps you could let me know if you find anything.'

'Indeed,' said Daniel. 'I'll report my findings – if any – to you at the Fitzwilliam tomorrow.'

After Daniel had left, Abigail returned to the sitting room to find Bella standing, full of indignation and glaring accusingly at her.

'What was all that whispering?' she demanded.

'It was of no importance,' said Abigail.

'For something of no importance, you spent a long time there,' snapped Bella.

'Hardly,' said Abigail.

'But you were whispering together,' persisted Bella. 'Were you talking about me?'

'Really, Bella!' exclaimed Abigail. 'Not everything is about you. I have never known anyone so self-obsessed.'

'Then was it because you are interested in Mr Wilson?' demanded Bella.

'I am interested in him as a person, but if you mean am I romantically inclined towards him, the answer is no.'

'Is he interested in you?'

'I have no idea. I doubt it. I feel our relationship is purely that of two minds working together to solve this case.'

But even as she said it, something inside her said that it wasn't strictly true. There was something special about Daniel Wilson, something that attracted her to him.

But, she told herself firmly, *nothing can come of it because we are two people from very different worlds. I am an academic, an archaeologist, looking to foreign parts and ancient history in my pursuit of my interests. Daniel Wilson is a policeman deeply rooted in the modern world, and especially rooted in everything that is cruel and inhuman in his search for criminals.*

If there was a man that might interest her, then a man such as Edward Hardwicke was more likely: an Egyptologist like her, an archaeologist, with an enquiring mind, and young, handsome and ambitious.

And he'd asked *her* to accompany him to the debate.

CHAPTER TWENTY-THREE

After the impression he'd been given by both Elder and Padstow, Daniel expected the area where the Lamb and Flag was to be found to be similar to the rookeries of London: narrow lanes where the houses on opposite sides of a street almost leant against one another; filth-strewn pavements and thoroughfares hidden in thick pea-souper fog, making them ideal for muggings. Instead, although the street where the pub was located may have been viewed as a cesspit of iniquity through Cambridge eyes, from a London perspective it was just down-at-heel. Similarly, the Lamb and Flag itself might have roused apprehension in the law-abiding citizens of Cambridge, but to someone who'd survived vicious attacks in the rookeries of Seven Dials and Whitechapel, it was almost genteel.

Yes, it was rough and ready, but the gas lamps were on, giving good lighting, unlike some of the dark drinking dens Daniel had experienced. The clientele also seemed to have done their best to dress up: most of the men wearing ties, and the women in heavy coats with scarves.

The air was thick with the smoke of cigarettes and pipes, mixing with the scent of stale beer and cheap gin. Most of the people here seemed to be regulars, as Daniel ascertained from the suspicious looks he received when he walked in. Their eyes stayed on him as he walked to the bar, but no one moved to block his path, as often happened in London drinking dens.

The tall, thin man behind the bar, his sparse strands of hair scraped back over his scalp, regarded him warily and, instead of asking Daniel what he would like, waited for him to speak.

'Is it possible to speak to Mrs Crane?' asked Daniel.

'Who?' said the man.

'Mrs Lillian Crane,' said Daniel. 'I was told I'd find her here.'

'Were you,' growled the man. 'Who by?'

'That's alright, Herbert, I can handle this,' said a woman's voice.

A large woman in her fifties had appeared from a door set behind the bar. Her make-up had been applied thickly and topped with what looked to Daniel like a silver wig. She shuffled along and faced Daniel across the bar.

'Copper?' she asked.

'Possibly,' said Daniel.

'That's no answer,' she said. 'So either you're not a copper, or you're from the Smoke. You're not local, anyway.'

'No, I'm not,' said Daniel.

Suddenly, she smiled. 'I know who you are! You're that private detective from London the Fitzwilliam brought in. Wilson.'

Daniel nodded. 'Indeed. My name is Daniel Wilson. I assume Joe Ransome told you about me.'

Her smile vanished. 'Who?'

Daniel gave her a gentle smile. 'Oh really, Mrs Crane,' he sighed. 'Why do you think I'm here?'

'I don't know,' she said warily. Then she added aggressively, 'All I do know is you've got no jurisdiction here. You ain't a copper no more. And even if you were, the London bobbies can't operate here.'

'Actually, they can,' said Daniel. 'When it comes to murder, Scotland Yard has authority over the local force. Which means, although I'm no longer on the force, I have very close contacts with very superior figures there, and a word dropped in certain quarters could mean a big investigation of your premises. Scotland Yard swarming all over you.' He leant in and added in a low voice, 'And all your influence with the local force won't be able to prevent that. You may be able to move certain items from the premises before they arrive, but the word will spread, and a lot of your clientele will vanish. Especially those with whom you do valuable business.'

Lillian Crane studied him carefully, then said, 'You'd better come in the back. We'll talk there.' She lifted the bar flap for him to join her, saying to Herbert, 'I'm gonna be tied up for a bit. If anyone needs me, you take care of it.'

Daniel followed Lillian through the door into a back storeroom, piled with wooden crates marked with the names of various sorts of alcohol. She sat down on one crate, and gestured for Daniel to sit on another.

'I thought you might be dropping in,' she said, 'after Joe telling me about you. So I did some asking around. They say you don't take anything. No cash, nor presents.'

'No, I don't,' said Daniel.

She shrugged.

'Worth asking,' she said. 'So, what do you wanna know?'

'About Joe Ransome's women,' said Daniel. 'I understand he used to invite some of them to the Fitzwilliam to inspect the bodies.'

She laughed.

'Inspect the bodies!' she chuckled. 'That's a good one! He inspected them, alright!' And she laughed again, a throaty phlegm-filled laugh.

'I'd like to talk to whoever went to see him there on the night he was killed.'

Immediately, her laughter was switched off and she looked at him suspiciously.

'I don't know if there was anyone with him that night,' she said. 'And even if there was, she wouldn't have had anything to do with his killing.'

'I'm sure you're right.' Daniel nodded. 'But she would be able to tell me what time she was there, which will help me pin down the time of death.'

Lillian weighed it up.

'I'll have to ask around,' she said.

'Fair enough,' said Daniel.

'I won't have anything until tomorrow,' she said. 'If it's who I think it is, she won't be here until later tonight.'

'And who do you think it is?'

She shook her head again.

'No, not yet,' she said. 'I might be wrong, and I ain't gonna drop someone in it if it wasn't them. Come round tomorrow and I'll see what I've got.'

'I'll be here just after one tomorrow afternoon,' he said. 'One word of caution,' he added. 'If you give me the name of someone and I discover that she's skipped before I can talk to her . . .'

'Yes, alright,' she growled. 'I'll make sure she stays.'

'Thank you,' said Daniel.

CHAPTER TWENTY-FOUR

Once again there was no sign of the mysterious Mr Barron at breakfast, just Daniel and Professor Hughes.

'I saw you at the Fitzwilliam yesterday,' said Hughes suddenly, in between mouthfuls of egg and bacon.

'Yes, indeed,' said Daniel.

'Might I enquire what your area of scholarship is?'

Daniel gave a rueful smile. 'No scholarship, I'm afraid. I'm investigating the deaths there.'

'Deaths?'

'Yes.'

'Where?'

'At the Fitzwilliam.'

Hughes frowned. 'Have there been deaths there?'

Daniel looked at him, surprised. 'Yes. Two. It's been in the newspapers.'

'I don't keep up with contemporary events,' said Hughes dismissively. 'My area of scholarship is the Civil War and the Interregnum. I'm currently writing a book on the subject, and I'm here because Cambridge was at the absolute heart of the struggle. Much of my research so far has been at Sidney Sussex College here. Cromwell was a student there, you know. In fact, his skull is buried beneath the college's ante-chapel.'

Daniel nodded politely as Hughes enlarged on his favoured topic of the Civil War, wondering how soon he could appropriately make an excuse to leave without appearing rude. It had never failed to astonish him how some people became so completely immersed in their own area of interest that they were able to completely ignore what was happening around them, even if that involved murder, public strife, or a horrific train crash.

Abigail was adding to her inventory of artefacts at the Fitzwilliam, and wondering whether Edward Hardwicke might call in as he had the day before, when the sound of footsteps caught her attention. To her disappointment, it wasn't Edward Hardwicke but Inspector Drabble, and he was brandishing a copy of the *Cambridge Gazette*.

'Where's Wilson?' he demanded.

'Mr Wilson is not here,' said Abigail. 'Is there anything I can do?'

Drabble scowled, hesitated, then thrust the newspaper at her.

'Your name's in here as well,' he said. 'So I guess you're also responsible for this . . . this outrage!'

'And what outrage would that be, Inspector?' asked Abigail.

'Interfering with a police investigation is a criminal offence!' barked Drabble.

'Would you explain to me how we have interfered with an investigation?'

Drabble tapped the photograph of the dead man. 'This asks people to contact you or Mr Wilson if they have any information about this man.'

'Yes, it does.'

'Not the police!'

Abigail looked at him levelly. 'If the police felt that line of enquiry was important, I'm sure they would have done something similar. As it was, you dismissed the death of this man as an accident.'

'That was before the second body was found!'

'Then you now agree that the first death was murder?'

Drabble swallowed.

'That decision is yet to be taken,' he said.

'But you obviously had no interest in trying to find out the identity of the dead man,' said Abigail. 'Otherwise you would have done the same.'

'We have been conducting our own investigation into this man,' said Drabble defensively.

'And what have you discovered?' asked Abigail.

Drabble fell silent.

'As I thought,' said Abigail. 'Nothing. Well, rest assured, Inspector, if Mr Wilson and I find out who this man is, we will inform you. Hardly interfering with the investigation, I would have thought.'

After breakfast, Daniel made his way back to Heffers bookshop in the hope that the stranger who'd worn the noticeable suit of large green check material and had enquired about 'Lot No. 249' might have made a return call, and the helpful assistant from Daniel's previous visit might have been able to find out some details about him. But it was not the case; there had been no further sightings of the man in the green suit.

Daniel made his way to the Fitzwilliam, and as he did so he felt a sense of pleasure at the thought of seeing Abigail Fenton again. He knew it was ridiculous to feel this way when she'd given no indication that her attitude towards him was anything other than involvement in the case, but he felt that there could be something there. A softening of that austere exterior now and then. Or was it his imagination?

If she is particularly pleased to see me, she hides it well, thought Daniel as Abigail turned at the sound of his gentle cough, an initial look of expectation on her face replaced instantly by what he was sure was a look of disappointment.

Who had she been expecting? Dr Keen, perhaps?

'Good morning, Miss Fenton,' he said. 'I've come to report on my visit to the Lamb and Flag, as promised.'

'Were you able to get any light on Mr Ransome's activities?'

'I hope to do so later. I've arranged to talk to the woman who was here the night that Ransome was killed.'

'And she has agreed to talk to you?' Abigail frowned.

'I've been promised that she will,' said Daniel. 'However, I haven't spoken to her yet, nor even been told who she is. But the landlady at the Lamb and Flag has promised she will be there for me this afternoon.'

'The Lamb and Flag has a bad reputation,' said Abigail. 'I recall overhearing Mr Elder talking about it to someone in disparaging terms. Can you be sure this isn't a trap you are walking into?'

'If it was, I feel sure they would have suggested an evening visit, when it's dark. I'm fairly sure I shall be safe.'

'Very well,' she said. 'I'm sure you know what you're doing.'

'Hey!' The shout made them turn. It was Hector Blades,

obviously angry, and holding a copy of the newspaper. 'What's this?' he demanded.

'It looks suspiciously like a newspaper,' said Daniel.

'You know what I mean!' snapped Blades. He opened the paper at the photograph of the dead man and showed it to them.

'It's an advertisement we placed,' said Daniel.

'But why didn't you come to me with it?' demanded Blades. 'It's my story. You know that. I could have given you a lot more space in the paper for it.'

'I wanted the wording to be unvarnished and honest,' said Daniel. 'Unlike your "Wilson of the Yard" story.'

Blades tapped the photograph.

'Who is he?' he asked.

'That's what we're hoping to find out,' said Abigail.

'He's the man you found in the sarcophagus, isn't he?'

'He is,' she said.

Blades looked annoyed.

'We should be working together on this,' he protested.

'I'd be more convinced of that if you told us the name of the person who gave you the story about the mummy,' said Daniel.

'I've told you, I'm sworn to secrecy,' said Blades.

'But prepared to divulge it in exchange for information.'

'For *interesting* information,' clarified Blades.

'Like the identity of this man, for example?' asked Abigail.

Blades hesitated.

'That depends who he is,' he grunted. 'He could be just a tramp who sneaked into the Fitzwilliam to get warm and got trapped in that sarcophagus thing. Inspector Drabble says it was an accident.'

'And you believe the inspector?' asked Daniel with a wry

140

smile. 'Especially in view of what you said about him the last time we met.'

Blades glared at Daniel.

'I reserve judgement,' he said primly. 'Let's wait and see what this advertisement of yours turns up.'

With that, he stormed off.

'Well, that visit was only to be expected, I suppose,' said Daniel.

'It was the second today,' said Abigail. 'Inspector Drabble was here earlier, venting much the same indignation.'

'Well, at least our advertisement has provoked two callers into coming,' said Daniel. 'Let's hope that more surface, and with more concrete information. Namely, who the dead man is.'

CHAPTER TWENTY-FIVE

This time, when Daniel entered the Lamb and Flag, Lillian Crane was sitting at a table in the main body of the pub with a young woman. Daniel was interested to note that even at this hour, early afternoon on a weekday, the pub was still busy. *So, it's a place of business as well as for drinking*, he decided. He wondered how much business was going on right now, then dismissed the thought; that wasn't why he was here.

He approached the table and nodded politely at Lillian Crane, then doffed his hat deferentially to the young lady.

'Good afternoon,' he said.

'This is him,' said Lillian. She got up and said to Daniel, 'Her name's Dolly. And buy her a drink, this ain't a charity shop.'

'It will be my pleasure,' said Daniel. 'And perhaps you and Herbert would have one, as well.'

'Now you mention it, we will,' said Lillian. 'Ports all round.'

'Thank you,' said Daniel.

'I'll send Herbert over with 'em.'

As Lillian walked heavily away to the bar, Daniel looked at the young woman. Not much more than a girl, on closer inspection. Late teens, he guessed, and nervous from the way she twisted her handkerchief between her hands and forced a nervous smile at him.

'Thank you for talking to me, Dolly,' said Daniel gently, 'and rest assured, you are not in trouble. I can assure you that nothing bad will happen as a result of you talking to me. I'm only interested in finding out as much as I can about Joe. It must have been a big shock for you when you learnt what had happened to him.'

'It was.' She nodded, and Daniel saw her eyes fill with tears which she wiped away. 'He was a bit of a rogue, was Joe, but there was no call for anyone to kill him. He liked his fun, but he never hurt no one.'

'Which is why it's important we know as much as we can about what happened that night in order that we can catch the person who killed him.'

'Will I have to talk to the police?'

Daniel hesitated. The truth was, if her story led to the killer then it was quite likely she'd find herself embroiled with Inspector Drabble. But he could tell from her tone as she asked the question that any involvement with the police was the last thing she wanted.

'I promise I won't mention your name,' he said. 'Now, would you mind telling me what happened that night, from the time that you arrived at the Fitzwilliam. What time was that, do you recall?'

'It was half past two in the morning,' said Dolly. 'I know that because there was a big clock on the wall outside the room where the bodies are kept.'

'The bodies?'

'The mummy things. The ones wrapped in bandages.'

'And is that where you and Joe . . . stayed?'

She nodded. 'I'd brought a bottle with me so we could have a drink – that was Joe's suggestion – then, after he'd showed me the bodies, we . . . well, we had a bit of sport.'

Daniel nodded.

'Then afterwards, we had a bit more drink, just being sociable.'

'And . . . that was it?' asked Daniel.

'Well, yeah,' said Dolly. 'I mean, we talked, of course.' She smiled as she remembered. 'Joe was full of this big thing he was doing.'

'What big thing?'

She winked. 'He had some dodge going.'

'What sort of dodge?' asked Daniel.

She hesitated, as if unsure whether to reveal Joe's obviously criminal scheme.

'Whatever you say can't come back on Joe now,' prompted Daniel gently. 'And it might even help nail his killer.'

She nodded. 'Yeah. Maybe it could. The thing was, he'd met this professor bloke and was selling him something worth a bit of money. Something to do with Oliver Cromwell.'

Immediately, Daniel was alert. 'Did he say a name for this professor?'

'No. Just that he was mad about Cromwell. Joe reckoned he'd pay good money to get his hands on something that belonged to Cromwell.'

'What was Joe going to sell him?'

'Joe didn't say.' She grinned. 'I got the impression he didn't actually have anything really; it was pretend. He'd told this professor that there was something that'd belonged to Cromwell in storage at the Fitzwilliam that he reckoned the museum had as good as forgotten about, and he'd agreed a price for it with this professor.'

Well, *this* was a new development, and no mistake. She could only be referring to Professor Hughes. So had Hughes turned up to collect this item, recognised it as a fake, and – furious – killed Ransome?

'Abigail.'

At the sound of that once so familiar voice, Abigail turned from the ornamental scarab she was inspecting, her heart beating with deep shock. Yes, it was him: Edgar Bruton, the man who'd taken her, claimed to have loved her, and then abandoned her. He looked at her now, a picture of remorse, a hangdog expression on his face.

'Edgar! What . . . what are you doing here? I thought you were in London.'

'I was until yesterday, but a friend sent me a copy of the local paper.' He produced a rolled-up copy of the *Gazette* from his pocket. 'And when I saw today's edition, I was even more worried.'

'About what?'

'About you, of course! My God, two murders!'

Abigail felt her rapidly beating heart settling down, and now she fixed him with a cold stare. This was the man who'd ruined her. This was the man who'd abandoned her, who'd broken her heart, destroyed her trust, and now he had the audacity to turn up and claim to be worried about her.

'I'm perfectly fine, thank you,' she said icily. 'You've no need to worry. Thank you for your concern, but you can safely return to London.'

He stared at her, bewildered by her reaction.

'Abigail, this is me!' he protested, his voice a bleat.

'I am fully aware it is you, Edgar. I had hoped that I wouldn't see you again, after the abominable way you treated me. But you are here. I now wish you to go.'

'But . . . I've come all the way from London. By train.'

'Do you wish me to refund your train fare?' asked Abigail.

Suddenly, his manner changed. The 'poor little boy lost' look that had become bewilderment now took a venomous turn.

'Is that meant to be funny?' he growled, and she was now aware of the menace in him. Menace she hadn't been aware of before. *I will not let him frighten me*, she decided grimly.

'There was absolutely nothing funny about what happened between us,' she said firmly.

The menacing posture vanished, as if he was a balloon that had just been punctured. He bowed his head, ashamed.

'I know,' he said. 'I admit it. I was weak.'

'No, I was weak. I let you take advantage of me. And then you abandoned me.'

'I didn't know what I was doing!' Edgar burst out. He moved towards her, appeal writ large on his face. 'Please, Abigail, I've come back because I want to be with you. Protect you.'

'From what?'

'From whoever's doing these murders, of course!'

'There's no need,' she said crisply. 'I'm perfectly capable of looking after myself. I faced far worse dangers when I was in Egypt.'

'Egypt!' he exclaimed scornfully. 'Always Egypt!'

She looked at him, her turn now to be bewildered.

'I don't understand,' she said. 'What is wrong with Egypt?'

'It took you away from me!' He moved towards her now, reaching out for her, and she backed away and moved swiftly behind a stone sarcophagus. He stopped and glared. 'Always damned Egypt! Why do you think I left?'

'Because you had used me and wanted to move on to pastures new,' said Abigail tersely.

'No, because I couldn't compete with your obsession with Egypt. I wanted a woman I could share things with . . .'

'Horse racing and playing cards were never my idea of entertainment,' said Abigail.

'You know what I mean!'

'Edgar, please don't pretend you wanted someone who was content to be just a wife. If you did then you misjudged me. I always intended to make my mark in the world of archaeology. What we had was an interlude, something that I hoped would continue and develop into – yes – into a proper marriage. But I never intended to abandon my interest or ambitions in archaeology.'

'And does this new man in your life give you satisfaction in that way?' Edgar demanded, and once again menace returned to his manner.

Abigail stared at him. 'What new man?'

Edgar looked at the newspaper and read out: '"Anyone with any information, please contact Daniel Wilson or Abigail Fenton at the Fitzwilliam Museum."'

'Mr Wilson is a private enquiry agent hired by the Fitzwilliam to look into the deaths,' said Abigail, tight-lipped. 'And he is more than capable of giving me protection, if any were needed.'

'And he's nothing more to you?' demanded Edgar.

'That is no business of yours,' snapped Abigail.

'So he *is* something to you!'

'Edgar, you will leave these premises immediately.'

He stood, hesitant, clenching and unclenching his fists. Then he burst out, 'He will not have you, Abigail. You are mine! Never forget that!'

CHAPTER TWENTY-SIX

Daniel headed for Mrs Loxley's house, his mind in a whirl. Professor Hughes! Was it possible that every morning Daniel had been sat breakfast with the murderer he'd been hunting?

One of the murderers, he corrected himself. If Hughes had killed Ransome in a rage over the fraudulent Cromwellian artefact, Daniel doubted if he'd also killed the unknown man in the sarcophagus.

But so many things didn't fit with Hughes being the killer of Ransome. The traces of chloroform, for one thing. Unless Hughes had left with the relic, found it to be a fake, and then returned later, armed with chloroform to overpower the younger and stronger Ransome.

Then there was Hughes' attitude, no traces of guilt or fear of discovery. Garrulous, an easy conversationalist – attributes

Daniel had experienced in some professional criminals, but not what he expected in a professor who'd just committed a murder completely out of character.

He needed to talk to Hughes; that would reveal the truth about him, he was sure. But when he arrived back at Mrs Loxley's he discovered that Professor Hughes had suddenly departed at very short notice.

'Did he say why he had to leave?' Daniel asked.

'He said he'd received a letter from his niece to tell him his sister was very ill and he had to go to her at once.'

'Did he say where this sister was?'

Mrs Loxley shook her head. 'I'm sorry, sir, I didn't think to ask. Why, sir?'

'I'd promised to let the professor have something, to do with Cromwell. Did he say if he'd be back?'

She shook her head again. 'No, sir. I asked him if he wanted the room kept, but he said no. But he paid me for the time he'd booked, so he was a gentleman on that front.'

'Yes indeed. Did he leave an address where he can be contacted? I recall when I arrived, I signed in the visitor's book.'

'Yes, of course,' said Mrs Loxley. 'He lives in Essex, I believe.'

Daniel followed her to the table in the hall where the visitor's book was displayed, and wrote down the address in Colchester that Professor Hughes had given as his home.

His sudden flight, following from what Daniel had heard from Dolly, seemed to confirm his guilt. The next thing was to get hold of the professor.

It was the first time Daniel had called at the central police station in Cambridge. Immediately, he was reminded of some of the London nicks he'd been attached to: the same expression of serious intent on the faces of the sergeants, the constables doing their best to keep out of sight of authority to avoid being roped in for extra duties, and the strong smell of sweat and tobacco.

Daniel was told that Inspector Drabble was in his office, and after a constable had been despatched to tell the inspector that a Mr Wilson was here to see him on a matter of urgency, Daniel was escorted to Drabble's small, cramped office at the rear of the station.

'Your message said it was urgent,' said Drabble suspiciously.

'Yes. I believe we may have a suspect for the murder of Joseph Ransome.'

'Oh? Who?'

'Professor Wynstan Hughes.'

'Who?' asked Drabble, looking puzzled.

'He's been in Cambridge writing a book about Oliver Cromwell,' said Daniel.

'And why would he want to murder a nightwatchman?'

'Because Joseph Ransome had promised to sell him a relic that was in the Fitzwilliam that belonged to Cromwell. But either this relic didn't actually exist, or it was a fake. Either way, it's possible that when Professor Hughes discovered he'd been duped, he fell into a rage and killed Ransome.'

Drabble shook his head. 'Frankly, Wilson, this sounds a bit like a made-up story. Have you got any evidence to back it up?'

'The word of someone who was consorting with Ransome, and he told them about his plan to dupe the professor. And also, Hughes was staying at the same boarding house as me: Mrs Loxley's. In conversation with him this morning, I told him I was investigating the deaths at the Fitzwilliam. During the day, I found out about this dubious scheme of Ransome's to fleece the professor. When I returned to the boarding house, intending to ask him about it, I discovered he'd left abruptly, claiming he'd been called away to visit a sick relative.'

'Maybe he had,' said Drabble.

'A bit of a coincidence, don't you think?' asked Daniel.

'Maybe,' mused Drabble thoughtfully. 'Who's the person who told you about Ransome's scheme to sell the professor this dodgy relic?'

'I'm afraid I promised that would be confidential. Unless it comes to an arrest, of course, in which case I'm sure I can persuade them to speak out, if only to get justice for Joe Ransome by bringing his killer to justice. If the professor is that killer.'

'There's lots of *ifs* there,' said Drabble doubtfully.

'But what else have we got?' asked Daniel. 'I think it's at least worth talking to him, asking him about Ransome, don't you?' When he saw that Drabble was still hesitating, he said, 'Of course, I can always go and see him myself, but I thought – as this was your investigation – I'd bring this to you first.'

Drabble thought it over, then nodded.

'Very well,' he said. 'I'll have him brought here, but you can do the questioning.'

'That's very kind of you, Inspector,' said Daniel.

'Kindness has got nothing to do with it,' grunted Drabble. 'These university types can be prickly, reporting you if they get upset by you poking into their business. I'll tell him you're the person accusing him, so if there's any comeback it'll be on you, not me.'

'Understood,' said Daniel.

'So, where will we find this professor?'

'Colchester,' said Daniel, and he handed Drabble the address he'd got from Mrs Loxley.

'It'll mean sending a constable all that way to bring him here,' complained Drabble.

'Or we could go there?' suggested Daniel.

Drabble shook his head. 'I like to talk to people on my own patch, where I know what's going on. And if he is our killer, it'll unsettle him being brought here.'

CHAPTER TWENTY-SEVEN

Abigail was hard at work cataloguing, when a familiar voice behind her saying a cheery, 'Good afternoon, Abigail,' made her turn, a welcoming smile on her lips.

'Edward! This is a pleasure.'

'I'm pleased to hear you say so; I feared you might think my unannounced arrival was an unwelcome interruption to your work.'

'As most of my current work consists of cataloguing your finds, I can assure you your presence is very welcome. Have you come to see how I'm doing with your items?'

'Well . . . yes, but incidentally. My official reason for coming to the Fitzwilliam today was a request from Sir William.'

'Oh?'

'It seems that when the debate was originally arranged,

Professor Waldheim had provided Sir William with a photograph of himself, which he had requested be displayed on the poster advertising the event. In the form of fair play, Sir William had acquired a photograph of Waldheim's original opponent, Sir Geoffrey Morgan, to also go on the poster, but with Sir Geoffrey's withdrawal, he asked me if I could provide him with a photograph of myself to go there in its place. I've just been delivering the photograph to Sir William, and I thought, while I was in the building, I'd pop down and see how things are going here.'

'They are going very well.' She sighed. 'Unfortunately, things are being held up as a result of the investigation into the two deaths.'

'Yes, Sir William tells me you are part of the investigating team.'

Abigail felt herself blushing with an embarrassed pleasure at being so described.

'Yes, that is true,' she said.

'And how is the investigation going?'

'There is a possible lead through a reporter on the local paper, a man by the name of Hector Blades.'

'What sort of lead?'

'He wrote in his newspaper a story about a murderous reanimated mummy, hinting that the mummy was the culprit. Blades claimed he was given the tip by – as he called it – an eminent Egyptologist, but I saw immediately it was the plot of a story by Arthur Conan Doyle called "Lot No. 249". We interviewed Mr Blades to try and ascertain the identity of this so-called eminent Egyptologist, but he was reluctant to identify him.'

'The confidentiality of the press.' Hardwicke nodded. 'I believe they are very strong on not revealing their sources.'

Abigail gave a snort of derision. 'That may not be the case with Mr Blades. He let us know that he was amenable to giving us the name, providing the price was right.'

The sound of footsteps in the doorway made them both turn, and on seeing Daniel enter, Abigail gave a broad smile.

'Why, this is very opportune! The very man to answer your question in more detail!' She gestured towards Hardwicke and said, 'Mr Wilson, this is Edward Hardwicke. Remember, I told you about him.'

Daniel nodded. 'The archaeologist.' The two men shook hands. 'A pleasure to meet you, Mr Hardwicke.'

'Mr Wilson is the person investigating the murders that took place here.'

'You're from the police?'

'No, I'm a private enquiry agent,' explained Daniel.

'Daniel worked with the famous Inspector Abberline,' added Abigail.

A moment of realisation struck Hardwicke, because he smiled. 'Of course! Now I remember. The Ripper case. Frederick Abberline and Daniel Wilson.' He turned to Abigail and added, 'It was in all the newspapers.'

'Different times, Mr Hardwicke,' said Daniel. 'Now, I'm happy to take private commissions.'

'Mr Hardwicke was just asking about the investigation and I was telling him about Hector Blades and his mysterious eminent Egyptologist, and the murderous reanimated mummy from Doyle's story.'

'Yes. Do you know the story, Mr Hardwicke?' asked Daniel.

Hardwicke shook his head.

'I'm sorry, I can't say that I do.' He smiled. 'But it does sound a lot of tosh.'

'I agree,' said Abigail. 'We've decided it's a smokescreen to conceal the identity of the real murderer.'

'And you think it could be this eminent Egyptologist that Mr Blades talked about?'

'If such a person even exists,' said Daniel. 'I believe that Mr Blades is perfectly capable of inventing so-called experts to add colour to his newspaper column.'

'So there are other avenues you are investigating?'

'Indeed.'

'Today, Mr Wilson was following a lead at the Lamb and Flag, a public house with a very low and dangerous reputation, weren't you, Mr Wilson,' said Abigail enthusiastically.

Daniel hesitated momentarily, then said apologetically, 'Alas, initially promising, but it seems to be a dead end.'

Abigail looked at him in surprise.

'But I thought . . .' she began.

'It's usually the way with investigations.' Daniel shrugged ruefully. 'A promising lead that leads nowhere. But we shall continue looking.'

'Of course, and I wish you well,' said Hardwicke. He looked at the clock and gave a smile. 'Actually, I have to return to see Sir William. I promised I would check if there was anything more he needed of me before the debate. Will you be coming, Mr Wilson?'

'The debate?' asked Daniel.

'I told you about it,' said Abigail. 'It's going to be the highlight of the Fitzwilliam's season. Mr Hardwicke is going to be debating with Professor Waldheim on . . .' She looked at Hardwicke. 'What will be the topic? Has it changed since Sir Geoffrey withdrew?'

'Still the same,' said Hardwicke. '"Piazzi Smyth and the

Pyramid Inch". Waldheim will be pushing Smyth's antiquated and now disproved theory, while I'll be pitching for Flinders Petrie.'

'It sounds like it will be highly entertaining,' said Daniel politely.

'And instructive!' said Abigail.

'Abigail – Miss Fenton – has kindly agreed to accompany me to the debate and evaluate my performance afterwards.' Hardwicke beamed.

As Daniel heard these words, he felt a pang of jealousy, but he forced himself to give a smile and say, 'I am sure Miss Fenton's assessments will be both invaluable and insightful.'

'I know you are to accompany me at the debate, but would it be alright if we met at the Fitzwilliam, rather than my collecting you from your home?' asked Hardwicke. 'It will give me a chance to run through my notes before I face Professor Waldheim. He's quite a ferocious advocate of Piazzi Smyth's theories, so I want to make sure I'm on solid ground.'

'Of course,' said Abigail.

She waited until Hardwicke had gone, before turning to Daniel and asking expectantly, 'What did you think of him?'

Truth to tell, not a lot, thought Daniel. In fact, he felt there was something suspicious about Hardwicke, but quite what he couldn't put his finger on.

Be careful, he warned himself. It could just be jealousy over the way her eyes sparkled when she looked at Hardwicke, her open admiration for him. It annoyed him.

'He seems very personable,' said Daniel.

She pursed her lips as she said disapprovingly, 'And yet I got the impression you didn't want to tell him anything about the investigation.'

'What makes you think that?'

'The way you responded when I asked how it had gone today at the Lamb and Flag. You said it was a dead end, but I'm sure that was not the case.'

'What gives you that impression?'

'Mr Wilson, I may have only known you for a short time, but I can read you like a book. When you first entered the Egyptian Room this afternoon, you had a look on your face that suggested you had information to impart, but that look vanished when you saw Mr Hardwicke was here.'

'I'm wary of imparting information to people I don't know,' said Daniel.

'You didn't know me when you invited me to work with you,' Abigail pointed out.

'That's true,' admitted Daniel, 'but I had a feeling about you. After all, you discovered the body. Both bodies. As far as I'm concerned, everyone else is suspect.'

'But surely not Mr Hardwicke!' burst out Abigail. 'That's ludicrous! He wasn't even in the country at the time of the murders. In fact, he only got back to England yesterday, when he came here to see if his artefacts had been received.'

'That may be true, but nevertheless, I'm reluctant to share information that may help us catch the killer – or killers – with someone I'm not sure of. As I said with regard to your sister, it's not her herself I'm wary of, but the people she may talk to and pass on that information unwittingly.'

'I still think you're being overcautious in relation to Mr Hardwicke,' said Abigail. She looked at him quizzically. 'You said killers, plural.'

'I did,' nodded Daniel. He told her what he'd learnt about Professor Hughes arranging to buy a stolen Civil War artefact from Ransome, and the fact of his unexpected departure from the boarding house when he discovered that Daniel was investigating the murders.

'We could be looking at two different murderers here. Say our mystery dead body was killed by person A, for reasons we still don't know. But say that Hughes is killer B. He paid Ransome money for something that he found was a fraud. If it was something that Ransome told him he'd got hold of illegally, he couldn't go to the police. So, in his rage, he kills him.'

'But why use the bandage?' asked Abigail. 'That suggests someone who wanted to put suspicion on a mummy being involved in some way, either as the killer – as in the Conan Doyle story – or at least as the weapon.'

'No, you're right. It doesn't fit,' said Daniel thoughtfully. 'It's too convoluted for a man who says he's only interested in the English Civil War. Egyptology isn't in his thinking. But why would he flee in this way if he's innocent?'

'Worried he might be charged with some kind of crime over the relic he was buying from Ransome, whatever it was?'

'Possible.' Daniel nodded. 'And then we have Harry Elder.'

Abigail looked at him, dubious. 'I thought you said Mr Elder was innocent.'

'So I believed, until I heard a story about him attacking another man because he insulted his religion. And it appears that Mr Elder's sister works at a local chemist, so he would have access to chloroform through her.'

'You think his rage against Ransome's low morals, and his sneering attitude, drove him to attack him?'

'I don't know,' admitted Daniel. 'It's feasible, but I can't see Mr Elder coming to work equipped with chloroform. It shows cold-blooded planning, and Mr Elder strikes me as a man who can be provoked, but who would respond immediately.' Then a thought struck him. 'Unless the chloroform wasn't forcibly administered on Mr Ransome!'

Abigail frowned, puzzled. 'Then how did it get onto his mouth and nose?'

Daniel hesitated, then said, 'I'm told that some people use narcotics to . . . er . . . increase their pleasure during lovemaking.'

She stared at him. 'You mean he may have taken it himself?'

'It's possible,' said Daniel. 'I'll need to talk to the young lady he was with on the night. If he did, she may have been aware of it. Possibly taken some herself.'

'How degenerate!' she said coldly.

Daniel shrugged.

'We are not all the same in our tastes and preferences,' he said.

'What it all comes down to is that we are no nearer to identifying the killer,' said Abigail. 'With that being the case, it puts both Mr Elder and Professor Hughes back in the picture. And there is still the possibility of it being a jealous lover related to Ransome's nocturnal assignations.'

'But I can't see that relating to the first death,' said Daniel. 'The man in the sarcophagus.'

'Neither can I,' she agreed. 'So we are no further forward.'

'Hopefully we'll find out more once I talk to Professor Hughes. Inspector Drabble is having him brought to Cambridge from Colchester for me to question him.'

'Why you?' she demanded. 'Why not me?'

'Inspector Drabble is reluctant to question the professor himself in case there are repercussions that adversely affect his reputation among the academic world here in Cambridge. As you are part of that same academic world . . .'

'Yes, I see.' She nodded. 'You're protecting my reputation.'

And not allowing you to upset the way I carry out questioning, thought Daniel, but aloud he said, 'Yes. If you don't mind.'

'Not at all,' said Abigail. 'I appreciate the consideration you've shown.' She cast her gaze around the artefacts that were crowding into the room and gave a sigh. 'I had better return to my cataloguing. I want to get as much done before Friday's debate. Will you be coming?'

I'd rather hit myself over the head with a hammer, thought Daniel at the idea of spending an evening listening to two Egyptologists yammering on about – what was it Hardwicke had said – The Pyramid Inch? What on earth was that? And who was Piazzi Smyth? But aloud he said, 'I will be delighted.'

'Perhaps you would like to meet me at my house and walk with me to the Fitzwilliam?' asked Abigail.

To deliver you to your precious Mr Hardwicke, thought Daniel bitterly. But he forced a smile and said, 'It will be my pleasure.'

CHAPTER TWENTY-EIGHT

When Daniel entered the Lamb and Flag the following day, Wednesday, there were only a few customers in the bar. Herbert Crane was behind the bar, wiping glasses, and he scowled at Daniel as he approached.

'Lillian's not in,' he said curtly.

'That's alright, I want to talk to Dolly.'

'Why?' demanded Herbert suspiciously.

'I have a question I want to ask her.'

'Didn't you bother her enough yesterday?' growled Herbert.

'The question's very simple,' said Daniel. 'When she was with Joe Ransome, did he ever use chloroform as a drug?'

'She wouldn't do something like that,' snapped Herbert. 'She's not stupid.'

'I'm asking if Ransome ever did,' said Daniel patiently.

'Why?' demanded Herbert.

Daniel looked at him levelly. 'Mr Crane, we can do this the easy, informal way, or I can ask Inspector Drabble to take Dolly in for questioning, and he can ask her.'

'You've given Dolly's name to the police!' growled Herbert, anger flashing in his eyes.

'No,' replied Daniel. 'And I'd like to keep it that way. So, would you pass on the message to Dolly that I need the answer about Ransome and chloroform, or any other drugs he might have used, as quickly as possible.' He took a piece of paper and a pencil from his pocket and wrote down the address of Mrs Loxley's boarding house. 'She can find me or leave a message for me at the Fitzwilliam, or here.'

He passed the piece of paper and then nodded goodbye to Herbert. He could feel the man's angry glare on his back all the way to the door.

Where to now? thought Daniel. There was nothing more he could do about Professor Hughes until Drabble brought him in. Assuming that the professor had returned to Colchester and not really been called to see his ill sister.

He would return to Mrs Loxley's and see if there had been any results from the photograph of the dead man in the *Gazette*.

He could dig deeper into Harry Elder, talk to Harry's sister who worked at the chemist and ask her about chloroform, but Daniel had a feeling that Harry Elder was not their killer. It was almost a sixth sense about people he'd picked up during his years in the police, an intuition about whether someone was guilty or not, despite whatever the physical evidence suggested. It was as if some people gave off an aura that Daniel picked up, whatever their outward demeanour. So often innocent people appeared shifty or suspicious because of nerves when finding themselves in a situation that was alien to them. And equally, others who appeared open and honest could do that because they were well practised in the art of deceit. But to Daniel, after years of looking into people's eyes, and their hearts, he felt he could see beneath the surface.

Like Edward Hardwicke, for example. He seemed so right, so open and upstanding, but Daniel had a feeling about him. There was something wrong there.

Or was it simply jealousy on his part?

Daniel was attracted to Abigail, and every now and then he felt that attraction may be mutual. But then this Edward Hardwicke appeared, and it was obvious that Abigail had eyes only for him.

It was understandable, of course. They were both immersed in ancient Egypt, both working archaeologists, both obviously highly intelligent and ambitious in their sphere, both single.

What could he offer Abigail, by comparison? A former policeman, now a private enquiry agent, whose sole ambition was to protect the vulnerable from criminals. A laudable aim, but hardly a match for unearthing precious remains from ancient sites in far-flung exotic places.

Lost in thought this way, he was unprepared for the attack on him as he pushed open the gate to Mrs Loxley's front garden, although an inner sixth sense alerted him to something close behind him. He started to turn, but before he could do so something smashed into the back of his head and he felt himself falling and crashing to the pavement.

CHAPTER TWENTY-NINE

Instinctively, he threw his hands up to protect his already throbbing head. He felt an agonising pain surge through him as a boot thudded into his ribs, then a man's voice snarled at him, 'Leave her alone!'

A woman's scream cut through his pain, then he heard Mrs Loxley's panic-stricken voice shouting, 'Leave him alone! Police! Help! Murder!'

There was the sound of boots clattering hastily away, and then Mrs Loxley was kneeling beside him, lifting his head up and cradling it in her lap.

'Be careful, his neck might be broken,' said a man's voice.

'No, just my head,' Daniel heard himself say, his voice thick and slurred to his ears.

'Can you stand?' asked the man.

'Martha! Martha!' called Mrs Loxley urgently.

As Daniel pushed himself up into a sitting position he saw the young housemaid come running out of the house.

'Martha, go and get Doctor Bunyan. And then find a policeman and bring him back here.'

'Yes, mum.' Martha nodded, and she hurried off.

'Let's get you indoors,' said the man, and he helped haul Daniel to his feet, then put his arm around him to support him.

'Can you walk?'

Daniel was about to nod, but the pain in his head stopped him.

'Yes,' he whispered. 'I'm sure I'll be alright.'

'Let's wait and see what the doctor says,' said the man.

Between them, the man and Mrs Loxley guided Daniel down the path and into the house.

'Into the parlour,' said Mrs Loxley.

They settled Daniel down into an armchair.

'Thank heavens Mr Barron was here,' said Mrs Loxley.

So this is the mysterious Mr Barron, thought Daniel. He forced a smile at the man, a portly figure in his fifties.

'Thank you, Mr Barron. And you, Mrs Loxley. I dread to think what might have happened if you hadn't shouted at him.'

'I was dusting in the front parlour when I looked out of the window and saw that man attack you,' said Mrs Loxley.

'Did you get a look at his face?' asked Daniel.

She shook her head. 'He had a scarf pulled up around his face.'

'Hair colour?' asked Daniel. 'Long? Short?'

Again, she shook her head. 'He had a hat on. One of those woolly ones that sailors wear, and it was pulled right down.'

'Clothes?' asked Daniel. 'Well-dressed? Rough?'

'I'm not sure,' admitted Mrs Loxley.

'Neither,' said Barron. 'Not well-dressed, but not a down-and-out either. Jacket and trousers. But working men's boots, by the look of them.'

'Yes, that's what it felt like,' muttered Daniel, aware of the pain in his ribs. He was sure that one of them was cracked.

Dr Bunyan arrived, his single-horse carriage pulling up outside Mrs Loxley's house.

'Your maid's gone to find a policeman,' he said as he came in, toting his bulky surgeon's bag.

'You've received a blow on the head,' he announced. 'The skin's broken at the back. I'll have to shave around it and sew it up.' He then helped Daniel remove his jacket, shirt and undervest, the procedure a slow one because of the pain in his ribs.

Dr Bunyan did an inspection, probing with his fingers – a gentle touch, Daniel was relieved to find – and stethoscope.

'A cracked rib?' asked Daniel.

'Yes.' Bunyan nodded. 'But fortunately not completely fractured, otherwise it could have punctured your lung. But your lungs sound alright. You'll survive. I'll put some ointment and a bandage on your ribs first, then I'll sew your scalp. It's a pity you weren't wearing a hat; it would have softened the blow.'

'I shall be wearing one from now on,' Daniel told him. 'Rather than walk around with the back of my head shaved for all to see and causing comment.'

As the doctor was putting the stitches in the back of Daniel's scalp, Martha arrived with a police constable.

'If you can wait to question him until I've finished,' said Bunyan.

'Perhaps you'd care for a cup of tea while you're waiting,' Mrs Loxley suggested to the policeman. 'I saw what happened so I can tell you, and so can Mr Barron.'

While Mrs Loxley and Mr Barron talked to the constable in the kitchen, Dr Bunyan put the finishing touches to patching Daniel up. Stitches completed, and a bandage wrapped around his ribs, Daniel put his clothes back on, relieved to feel that it didn't seem such an effort as removing them.

'Thank you, Doctor,' he said. 'How much do I owe you?'

'I'll send you my bill,' said Bunyan. As he put his equipment back in his case, he said, 'You're the detective who's investigating the deaths at the Fitzwilliam?'

'I am,' said Daniel.

'Do you think this attack on you is related to that?'

'It must be,' said Daniel. 'I can't think of anyone I've upset over anything else during the short time I've spent in Cambridge. Am I alright to start moving?'

'I'd rest for the remainder of the day,' advised Bunyan. 'Just in case there might be concussion, and to let your body recover from the cracked rib.'

After the doctor had left, the constable joined Daniel to ask his questions. Daniel admitted that he couldn't help much with a description of his attacker, but the constable assured him he'd already got a description from Mrs Loxley and Mr Barron.

'Can I suggest you make sure that Inspector Drabble knows about this attack,' said Daniel. 'It may be connected with a case he's working on.'

The constable promised he'd make sure Inspector Drabble had a report about the incident, then left.

After he'd gone, Daniel's thoughts turned to Abigail. Daniel was sure the attack was the result of his asking for Dolly during his most recent visit to the Lamb and Flag, in which case he'd be seeking out Herbert Crane. But just in case it was related to the overall investigation, he needed to warn Abigail to be on her guard.

CHAPTER THIRTY

Mrs Loxley's young housemaid, Martha, was sent to the Fitzwilliam with a note from Daniel for Miss Abigail Fenton, with instructions that if she wasn't there to deliver it to her home address. As it turned out, Martha caught Abigail just as she was on the point of leaving work.

Abigail opened the note and felt a frisson of alarm as she read: *Have been attacked. No need to be alarmed, a doctor has stitched me up, but it is advisable I see you. Please can you come and see me at Mrs Loxley's.*

Attacked! Who by? Then she remembered her encounter with Edgar, and his threats against Daniel, and her alarm was replaced with a feeling of anger, and of humiliation. If it was possible that Edgar had carried out this attack, she would have to tell Daniel why.

A short time later, Abigail was seated in Mrs Loxley's front parlour opposite Daniel, having first examined the surgical stitches in the shaved area of his scalp.

'The doctor did a good job,' she said. 'It looks like a nasty gash.'

'I expect you saw a lot worse in Egypt,' said Daniel.

She had been about to say that indeed she had, when she stopped herself.

'You are making fun of me,' she said accusingly.

'Only in a gentle way, to show you that I'm not badly affected. The reason I asked you to come is to warn you.'

'You think I might be attacked, too?'

'I hope not. I'm fairly sure this is a result of my poking around at the Lamb and Flag today. Providing you avoid doing that, or anything like it, you should be alright. But I've sent a message to Inspector Drabble about the attack, so I think it worth you talking to him, especially if you feel anyone is following you at any time.'

'I can take care of myself,' she said.

'I thought I could as well,' said Daniel ruefully.

'Why do you think the attack relates to today's visit to the Lamb and Flag?' asked Abigail.

'Because when he attacked me, he growled "Leave her alone." I've only questioned two women in relation to this case: Lillian Crane, the landlady of the Lamb and Flag, and the woman called Dolly, who spent time with Joseph Ransome at the Fitzwilliam on the night he died. So, the man who attacked me has to be connected with one or both of them and is protecting them.'

'There is another possibility,' said Abigail awkwardly.

Daniel caught the note of hesitation in her voice, and looked at her quizzically. She looked towards the door to make sure she couldn't be overheard, then dropped her eyes and said, 'Some

172

time ago I formed a . . . friendship with a gentleman. It did not end well.'

Did you abandon him, or he you? wondered Daniel, watching her, aware of her efforts to try and remain emotionally detached as she told the tale, but failing.

'I thought I would not see him again, but yesterday he arrived at the Fitzwilliam. He said he'd come because he'd read about the events in the newspapers, and was worried about me. He offered his protection.'

'Thoughtful of him,' commented Daniel carefully.

'Yes.' Abigail nodded. 'However, I informed him that would not be necessary. I told him that the Fitzwilliam had employed a private investigator, a man of renown and resource, and he was more than capable of protecting me.'

'I'm flattered.' Daniel smiled.

Abigail didn't return his smile. 'I'm afraid he appeared to interpret my words to mean that there was more between us than just a professional association. Obviously, I did my best to dissuade him that was the case . . .'

'Obviously,' said Daniel

'But . . .' She sighed.

'He is jealous,' said Daniel.

'Yes.'

'Is he a man capable of violence?'

'I had not thought so before, but his last words before he left were certainly threatening.'

'To you?'

'Possibly. Or to you.'

'This man's name?'

'Edgar Bruton.'

'And where would I find him?'

173

'I don't know,' Abigail admitted. 'When I knew him he lodged with a cousin of his. The cousin's name is Ernest Bruton.'

'With your permission, I shall go and see this Ernest Bruton and see if I can track down your gentleman friend.'

'He is no friend of mine!' she said firmly. 'And he is no gentleman.' Then, concerned, she asked, 'But say he attacks you again. You have a cracked rib. You'll be no match for him.'

'Yes, I will,' Daniel assured her grimly. 'Next time, I will be watching out.'

CHAPTER THIRTY-ONE

That evening, and the next morning at the Fitzwilliam, Abigail found it difficult to concentrate on her work in hand. Her mind kept turning to Edgar. Was it he who'd attacked Daniel? Should she have elected to call on Edgar's cousin, Ernest, to face Edgar, rather than letting Daniel do it? But if she did, Edgar would simply deny being the attacker. It would also drive his jealousy of Daniel even more, even though there was nothing for him to be jealous of.

She wondered how Daniel viewed her, now that she'd told him about her relationship with Edgar. As a fallen woman? No, Daniel wasn't that kind of bigoted, judgemental person.

It was odd; she and Daniel came from such different backgrounds with such different life experiences that they should have nothing in common, yet she felt very much at ease with him.

Most of the time, she corrected herself abruptly. There were still many things that irritated her about him.

Well . . . perhaps not many. Some.

As she was sure there were things about her that upset or irritated Daniel. Was she really rude and curt to him, as Bella had said?

Her thoughts were interrupted by the appearance of a middle-aged woman, respectable in appearance, holding a copy of the *Gazette*.

'Am I addressing Miss Abigail Fenton?' she asked.

'You are,' said Abigail.

'The man at the desk said I'd find you here,' said the woman. 'My name's Mrs Edwina Bristow.' She opened the newspaper to show the photograph of the dead man. 'This says for anyone who recognises this man to come and see you or Mr Daniel Wilson.'

'I'm afraid Mr Wilson's out at the moment. But do I gather that you know this man?'

'Yes, I do,' said Mrs Bristow. 'I've got a small cottage that I let out. Very respectable. Visiting lecturers who might want somewhere nice to stay for a month or so. That sort of thing.'

'And this gentleman took it to rent?'

'Yes. He arrived about a week and a half ago, the Monday before last. An Egyptian gentleman. Very cultured. Spoke really good English. He said he'd just arrived from Egypt on business, and needed somewhere to stay for a couple of weeks.'

'What was his name?'

'Dr Ahmet Madi.'

'Did he say what he was a doctor of?'

Mrs Bristow looked puzzled.

'A doctor's a doctor,' she said. 'They cure people.'

'Not all,' said Abigail. 'Some people are doctors of theology, or literature. Different strands of learning.'

'Oh. I never knew that. I just thought he was the normal sort of doctor. Anyway, because the fortnight's nearly up, I went round to see if he wanted to carry on renting, but he was gone, and so was all his stuff.' She gestured at the photo in the paper. 'This is him, but in this photo he looks dead. Was he the man they found here? The mystery man?'

'Yes,' said Abigail. 'Have you got anyone else in the cottage?'

'No, there hasn't been time yet. I wanted to see what had happened to him first, in case he wanted to stay on. But when I saw all his stuff was gone . . .'

'Would you mind if I came with you to look at the cottage? In case he might have left something behind.'

'He didn't,' said the woman. 'He had a small suitcase with him when he arrived, but that's gone. There's no clothes, nothing.'

'He might have left a scribble on a piece of paper,' said Abigail. 'Something small.'

'I didn't see anything,' said Mrs Bristow.

'Please, I promise I won't mess things up,' said Abigail. 'And it won't take long.'

The one thing that Abigail hadn't mentioned about Ernest Bruton was that he was a minister of the church. Daniel wasn't sure which church, and the grim look on Bruton's face as he stood on the top step of his large house and scowled down at Daniel didn't appear to be welcoming to those kind of questions. The clerical collar he wore so proudly said it all, as did his pugnacious stance. A fire and brimstone preacher, Daniel guessed, the sort who would call down the wrath of the Lord on sinners. And that included his cousin, Edgar Bruton, Daniel thought, because this pugnacious posture, chest thrust out, chin forward, a scowl that involved not just his mouth and eyes but seemed to even include his ears, had come about when Daniel had said he was calling to enquire after the whereabouts of Edgar Bruton.

'You are a bailiff?!' thundered Bruton, and once again Daniel reflected he was right in his fire-and-brimstone assessment. This man would be a terrifying accuser of his parishioners.

'No, sir,' said Daniel. 'My name is Daniel Wilson and I have been hired by Sir William Mackenzie at the Fitzwilliam Museum to make enquiries about certain incidents that have happened there.'

'Thefts?' The emphasis that he gave to that one brief word, extending it beyond the single vowel and giving it a feeling of disgust, disgrace and utter degradation, spoke volumes of Ernest Bruton's powers as an orator.

'No, sir, but sadly there have been some tragic deaths there recently which the Fitzwilliam have asked me to look into.'

For the first time, Bruton seemed taken aback. 'Deaths? And you suspect that Edgar might be involved?'

'Not with the deaths, sir, but there have been associated activities which we are looking into.'

'And why do you come to my door?' demanded Bruton.

'Because I was given information that Mr Edgar Bruton lodged with you while he was in Cambridge.'

'He did, sir! He was a wastrel and a drunkard, yet when he appealed to me for shelter I did what the Good Lord would have done: I gave him succour. I invited him into my own home. *This* home!' Bruton's voice rose a tone as he suddenly roared out, 'And how did he repay me?!'

Not well, Daniel guessed. Bruton's next words verified his assumption.

'He defiled this house, sir! He made advances to our serving maid. He even did the same to our cook, a respectable lady of advancing years! And he stole from me! The man is a degenerate, a loathsome creature, a serpent, a Judas . . .'

'I assume you asked him to leave?' enquired Daniel, doing his best to avert a lengthy list of metaphors describing Edgar Bruton.

'No, sir, I *ordered* him to leave!' thundered Bruton. 'And never to darken my door again!'

'When was this?'

'Three months ago.'

'And you have not seen him since?'

The scowl on Bruton's face grew darker. 'On the contrary, sir. You can imagine my surprise – nay, shock – on being told by my maid that he was here not yesterday lunchtime, asking to see me.'

'Yesterday?'

'Indeed, sir! I came out to see him, as I am here on this step to see you, today, thinking that perhaps he had come to repent and apologise and open his heart to me. But NO!'

The 'no' was so loud that Daniel wondered if it would alarm the neighbours and bring them to their doors, but then he reflected that they must be used to such explosions.

'The blackguard had come to ask if he could borrow money from me! Borrow! Ha! The wretch!'

'Did he say why he needed the money, sir?'

'I did not give him a chance to unload a pack of lies for the reason. It would have entailed some false story of illness. The truth is that my cousin has always run up debts, usually related to unsavoury activities such as gambling, or unsuitable women.'

'So you did not give him the money.'

'I certainly did not! And then he had the temerity to ask if he could lodge with me at my house for the night, after all that had gone before. I tell you, sir, if it wasn't for the fact that I am a man of God, I would have smote him there and then, as our Good Lord smote the money-lenders and chased them from the temple.'

'So he had nowhere to stay in Cambridge?'

'That's how it would appear, and I wasn't surprised – he has used up his goodwill as he abused people's good intentions towards him. He pleaded that no one here in Cambridge would give him shelter and all he asked for was a bed for the night. I told him he could not stay here, but – as a Christian – I would not let him spend the night shivering on the streets of Cambridge.'

'So where did you send him?'

'I did not send him, sir, I took him. To the railway station.'

'The railway station?'

'I told him that Cambridge was no place for such a person as him. I have a good reputation in this city, and to have that loathsome creature here and known to be related to me is intolerable. I told him I would buy him a single ticket to that cesspit of vice and corruption that seems to suit him so well: London. And there may he look to God to guide his steps in the right direction in future.'

'And what time of day was this, sir?'

'He caught the 1.20. I remember because I checked the time on the station clock with my watch as the train drew out.'

'And Edgar was on that train?'

'Absolutely, sir. With my instructions for him not to return until he has found salvation.'

So, thought Daniel as he left Ernest Bruton's house, *it was not Edgar Bruton who attacked me yesterday afternoon. It was also unlikely that he would have had the money to hire someone to do his dirty work.*

Which brings us back to someone protecting Lillian Crane and Dolly.

CHAPTER THIRTY-TWO

The inspection of the small cottage didn't take long. It was on its own at the end of a lane on the outskirts of Cambridge and consisted of a living room and a small kitchen, with a bedroom upstairs. Outside was a wooden privy.

'There are no neighbours nearby?' asked Abigail.

'No,' answered Mrs Bristow. 'It's very private, which is one of its attractions.'

So, no neighbours who might have seen any comings or goings at the cottage, thought Abigail.

The furniture was basic: a table and three chairs along with an armchair in the main room; a range in the kitchen fired with coal and wood for cooking and hot water; a single bed and a bedside table in the bedroom.

The shelves were empty. There were no books, no pieces of

paper, no sign of anyone having been at the cottage.

'Would you mind if I returned with Mr Wilson?' asked Abigail. 'He's a former detective with Scotland Yard and he might be more expert in seeing things that I may be missing.'

'Providing he doesn't start messing things up and taking things apart. I know what the police are like when they're looking for something.'

'I can assure you that Mr Wilson is not like that,' said Abigail. 'As you'll see when you meet him. You can watch him the whole time he's here.'

Mrs Bristow looked doubtful.

'Yes, well, I can't do that today,' she said. 'I promised my sister I'd go and see her.' She hesitated, then said, 'If you really think he can be trusted, I could leave you the key and you can show him over, and drop the key in to me later.'

'That would be excellent!' said Abigail.

Mrs Bristow dipped a hand into her pocket and pulled out a small card, which she gave to Abigail.

'This is my address.'

'Thank you,' said Abigail. 'I'll see the key is returned to you this afternoon.'

'Good,' said Mrs Bristow. 'The sooner I can start cleaning the place, the sooner I can let it.'

Abigail found Daniel waiting for her when she returned to the Egyptian Room at the Fitzwilliam. He had a piece of paper and pencil in hand, and, as he explained, was just about to leave a note for her on the desk in her office.

'It was not Edgar Bruton who attacked me,' he told her.

'You're sure?'

'Yes. His cousin, Ernest, told me that he escorted Edgar onto the London train yesterday lunchtime, so it could not have been him who was my assailant. So I shall be returning to the Lamb and Flag to seek out the real attacker.'

'You know who it is?'

'I suspect it was a man called Herbert Crane, the husband of the pub's landlady.'

'He was protecting her?'

Daniel shook his head. 'No. I feel he was protecting the woman I questioned, Dolly. I saw the way he looked at her. I believe he is in love with her.'

'Will you have him charged?'

'No,' said Daniel. 'Providing he gives me the information I'm after. I'm off there now.'

'Before you do, I've found out who the mysterious dead man was, and where he was staying,' said Abigail.

She reported to him what Mrs Bristow had told her, and her visit to inspect the cottage.

'She left me with the key. I thought it would be a good idea if you took a look to see if it affords any clues. You are more expert in these matters than I.'

'This is excellent!' said Daniel. 'This is the best lead we've had so far!'

'I don't know if it will help us find his killer,' said Abigail.

'It moves us a major step nearer,' said Daniel. 'Now we know who he is and where he was staying, we can build a trail on his movements and find out who he came into contact with.'

'I don't think that will be easy,' said Abigail. 'There was nothing of his left in the cottage, and the cottage itself is quite isolated. No neighbours to report on anything.'

'I'm sure you're right,' said Daniel. 'But you never know what might be revealed.'

Daniel stood in the small living room, having just completed his inspection of the cottage with Abigail.

'Well?' she asked.

He shook his head. 'You're right, there's nothing left to give us any clue to him or what he was here for. But that alone is valuable information.'

'Because someone came in after he was killed and took everything away?'

'Exactly,' said Daniel.

'The person who killed him?' suggested Abigail.

'Possibly, but that would mean they knew where he was staying. The other possibility is that Dr Madi had a companion.'

'Mrs Bristow didn't mention anyone else staying with him at the cottage.' She gestured at the sparse and empty rooms. 'And there's no hint of anyone else being here.'

'Let's see what the outside may tell us,' said Daniel.

'Outside?' queried Abigail. 'There's nothing except a privy.'

Daniel smiled at her. 'Am I really having this conversation with an experienced archaeologist, who spends her life discovering what the soil might hide?'

He led the way out to the back of the cottage, and approached the privy slowly, scanning the ground carefully.

'There,' he said.

In between the back door and the privy could be seen the imprints of two sets of footwear: the marks of neat shoes, and those of a larger pair of studded boots.

'Two people,' said Daniel. 'These prints were made during

rain, and once the rain stopped the impressions remained when the ground dried.'

'The last time it rained in Cambridge was the Monday and Tuesday, just before I found the body in the sarcophagus.'

'So we have two people here on that Monday and Tuesday, one wearing shoes and one wearing boots. I think the imprint of the shoes look similar to the shoes Dr Madi was wearing, but I think we ought to return to Dr Keen and check. So the boots are those of his companion.'

'Why his companion?' asked Abigail. 'Why not his killer?'

'If that was the case, why wait to kill him at the Fitzwilliam? Why not kill him at the cottage? Much easier.'

He went back into the cottage and returned with a sheet of newspaper and a pair of scissors, with which he proceeded to carefully cut out silhouettes of the shapes of the boots, and the shoes.

'There,' he said, standing up. 'Now we hope that Dr Keen is still available.'

CHAPTER THIRTY-THREE

Dr Keen studied the pieces of cut newspaper Daniel handed to him.

'Prints of shoes,' he said.

'Yes,' said Daniel. 'Thanks to the photograph you took, we've been able to identify the dead man.'

'He was a Dr Ahmet Madi,' said Abigail. 'Egyptian.'

Dr Keen smiled.

'So the little exercise we had here in Sherlock Holmes deductive reasoning was right,' he said.

'It would seem so,' said Daniel. 'Our next task is to find out if he had a companion.' He pointed at the pieces of newspaper. 'I feel sure that the smaller one will match the shoes Dr Madi was wearing when he came in. We're hoping the other might lead us to his mysterious companion.'

'Working men's boots, by the look of it,' murmured Keen. 'It's not going to be easy to identify who they belonged to.'

'Checking it against Dr Madi's shoes and making sure the boots weren't his will be a step forward,' said Daniel.

Keen nodded and went out, returning shortly afterwards with the shoes they'd taken from Dr Madi. They put the soles of the shoes against the newspaper cut-outs.

'Yes, the shoes are definitely his. The boots are much larger and belong to a bigger man.'

'Do you think it could be a local man?' asked Abigail. 'That would explain why there's been no trace of him at the cottage.'

'But if Dr Madi knew someone local, then surely he'd have stayed with him rather than rented the cottage.' Daniel frowned. Suddenly, he burst out angrily, 'I am a fool!'

As Abigail and Keen looked at him in surprise, he said to Abigail, 'Mrs Bristow said she was contacted by Dr Madi on the Monday, right?'

'Yes,' nodded Abigail. 'He moved into the cottage that same day.'

'And on Wednesday morning you found him dead in the sarcophagus at the Fitzwilliam, after he was killed some time during Tuesday night.'

'Yes,' said Abigail.

'I'd bet money that he arrived on the Sunday, the same day the latest consignment of Egyptian artefacts for the Fitzwilliam arrived at Tilbury!'

'You think he was on the ship that brought them?'

'I do! He and his companion. And if we check the passenger list I'm sure we'll find their names on it. I need to go to Tilbury to check the list.'

'When?' asked Abigail, wary.

'The sooner the better,' replied Daniel. 'I can leave for Tilbury in the morning and be back on Saturday.' As he saw the look of disappointment flood her face, he stopped himself. Of course, his promise to escort her to the debate the following evening. Even if it was to take her to meet another man. 'No, it would be better if I went on the weekend,' he said, and smiled. 'I don't want to miss the debate tomorrow.'

His heart swelled inside his chest as he saw the look of disappointment vanish, replaced by a warm smile. *Maybe there is a chance for me*, he thought.

'I shall be coming to the debate as well,' said Dr Keen. 'I must say, it sounds as if it's going to be quite a lively contest. Professor Waldheim can be quite a fierce character and he doesn't like being challenged, especially by younger people.'

'He's an old-fashioned reactionary,' said Abigail, showing her temper. 'I read an article he wrote in one of the journals about the reasons the pyramids were built, and he was harking back to theories that had been discredited years ago.'

So, thought Daniel, *a heated contest with the rivals at each other's throats, the intellectual equivalent of a prizefight.* Perhaps the evening wouldn't be boring, after all.

'Mr Wilson?'

They turned and saw that a police constable had appeared.

'Yes?' said Daniel.

'They said at the Fitzwilliam I might find you here,' he said, and he took a piece of paper from his pocket and handed it to Daniel.

'From Inspector Drabble,' he said.

Daniel read it, then passed it to Abigail.

'Professor Hughes has arrived and is in custody,' she read aloud.

'And he wants me to question him,' said Daniel.

'Professor Hughes?' questioned Keen.

'I'll leave Miss Fenton to explain where he fits in, while I go and talk to him,' said Daniel. 'I'll see you tomorrow, Doctor. And thank you again for the photograph – without it we'd still be in the dark.'

CHAPTER THIRTY-FOUR

Drabble was waiting expectantly in his office when Daniel arrived.

'My man found you,' he said. 'Good. I was worried you might be off somewhere, and the sooner we can get this business of Professor Hughes dealt with the better.'

He rose, but Daniel gestured for him to sit down again, and settled himself into the empty chair across the desk.

'Before we talk to Hughes, we've found out the identity of the dead man in the sarcophagus.'

'Oh?'

'His name is Dr Ahmet Madi.'

'A doctor?'

'Not a medical one. A doctor of history, I assume.'

'Another academic,' grumbled Drabble.

'Our guess is he arrived from Egypt just two days before he

was killed. We think he may have arrived on the same ship that brought the latest consignment of artefacts for the Fitzwilliam last Monday, but we won't know for sure until we check the passenger list.'

'Where did the ship arrive?'

'Tilbury, in Essex, on the day before, the Sunday.'

'It could be a wild goose chase,' said Drabble doubtfully.

'It could, but the evidence points to it. Madi took on the rent of the cottage on Monday, the day after the delivery arrived at Tilbury from Egypt. The carters who brought the delivery from Tilbury arrived in Cambridge on Monday. I don't know how frequently ships from Egypt arrive in England, but it seems quite a big coincidence.'

'It's worth a try.' Drabble nodded. 'Right, I'll send a note to Tilbury police asking them to get hold of the passenger list and send it over.'

Daniel stared at Drabble, stunned.

'You'd do that?' he asked.

Drabble looked back at him, obviously offended. 'As you say, it seems like a strong lead, and that's my job as a policeman.'

'Yes, but . . .' began Daniel. Then he shut up. He was about to remind Drabble of how antagonistic he'd been towards Daniel at first, how competitive, and that this offer seemed out of character. But then he reflected that of late the inspector seemed to have mellowed towards him. The fact that Drabble had brought Hughes in showed that he seemed to be open to Daniel's opinions on the case.

'Thank you,' said Daniel.

'So what are we looking for on this passenger list?' asked Drabble.

'Dr Ahmet Madi,' said Daniel, 'and other names, in the

hope we might be able to find out if he came with anyone else.'

'You think he might?' asked Drabble.

'We're sure of it. We went to the address where Madi was staying, and it had been cleaned out. Everything taken. That suggests an accomplice who took everything to stop anyone finding out about the doctor, and what he was after.'

'Or the killer did it?' suggested Drabble.

'He arrived on Monday and was killed on Tuesday night,' said Daniel. 'We're not sure if that would have given the killer time to find out where he was staying.' He passed Drabble a piece of paper with the address of the cottage. 'This is where Madi was living.'

'Thank you,' said Drabble. 'You say "we". I assume you're talking about Miss Fenton?'

'Yes,' said Daniel.

'So she really is part of this investigation?' asked Drabble. 'She's not just involved to keep the Fitzwilliam happy?'

'She is definitely part of it,' said Daniel. 'In fact, it was she who first learnt of the address where Dr Madi was staying.'

Drabble scowled.

'I'm not sure I approve,' he said. 'Frankly, police work is no job for women.'

'I can think of many men who are unsuited to it,' said Daniel blandly. 'And, sadly, some of them are in the force.'

'What's that supposed to mean?' demanded Drabble.

'Nothing.' Daniel shrugged. 'Just an observation. Shall we talk to Professor Hughes?'

As the two men rose and headed out of the office towards the interview room, Drabble said, 'I understand you were attacked and badly beaten the other day?'

'Yes,' said Daniel.

'But you look alright to me.'

'A cracked rib and a gash on the back of my head,' said Daniel. 'I've had worse.'

'Any idea who it was?'

'A pretty good one.'

'Want me to arrest them?'

'No, but thank you,' replied Daniel. 'If it's who I think it is, I'll be able to get more out of them in unofficial ways.'

'I don't want any vigilante stuff,' warned Drabble.

'There won't be,' Daniel promised him.

Drabble stopped in the corridor by a door, opened it, and walked in, Daniel following.

The room was windowless, light coming from the gas lamps. Professor Hughes was sitting at a table. A uniformed constable stood against the wall just behind him. Two chairs were on the opposite side of the table to Hughes.

The professor didn't stand up or show any sign of welcome as Daniel and Drabble entered the room. Instead, he glared angrily at them.

'Professor Hughes, this is Daniel Wilson,' said Drabble. 'He's the one who's made the allegations against you, so I'm allowing him in his role as a police officer to carry out the questioning, while I supervise. If you feel he has overstepped the mark in any way I will intervene on your behalf.'

So, Drabble is making very sure he protects himself, thought Daniel.

'I do consider he has overstepped the mark!' snapped Hughes. 'Ordering me to be escorted back to Cambridge by a police constable, like a common criminal!'

'Hardly a common criminal, Professor,' said Daniel gently, sitting himself down across the table from Hughes. 'Might I ask why you told Mrs Loxley that you had been summoned to see a sick relative?'

'Because I had,' said Hughes.

'Could you let us have the name of this sick relative?' asked Daniel. 'Just in order to confirm it. It was your sister who was ill, I believe.'

Hughes' mouth clamped shut.

'I am saying nothing more,' he said.

Daniel nodded in sympathetic understanding.

'As is your right,' he said. 'However, the thing is, Professor, we are not here to accuse you, but to protect you.'

'Protect me?' echoed Hughes, frowning.

'Your reputation.' Daniel nodded. 'As an esteemed author and expert on Cromwell and the Civil War.'

Hughes frowned even more, puzzled at this. 'I don't understand.'

'Someone reported to me that you had made a deal to purchase something from Joseph Ransome, a nightwatchman at the Fitzwilliam Museum. A relic connected to Oliver Cromwell.'

'Nonsense!' exploded Hughes.

Again, Daniel gave a sympathetic nod. 'The problem is, Professor, that this person approached me and said they were going to sell this story to the newspapers. And, following the recent murder of Joseph Ransome at the Fitzwilliam, you can see why the newspapers would be interested.'

Hughes stared at Daniel, shocked. 'What . . . But . . . This must be stopped!'

'I agree,' said Daniel. 'But there's little we can do to stop it without knowing the facts.'

'I shall sue any newspaper that prints such a libel!' said Hughes, trembling.

'I'm sure you shall, but alas, by that time the story will be out there for the public, casting doubts on your reputation as an honest scholar. Because, according to this person, the item you were going to purchase from Joseph Ransome had been stolen from the Fitzwilliam collection.'

Hughes looked at Daniel, and now Daniel saw a look of panic in the professor's eyes. *Got him!* he thought.

'I'm guessing you didn't know that this particular item was stolen, sir,' said Daniel.

Hughes swallowed, then said faintly, 'No.' Then suddenly he went on the defensive in the same aggressive manner as before. 'And because of that, no paper can publish such a lie without risking a very expensive lawsuit!' And he sat up straight, a smirk of triumph on his face.

'I agree, sir,' said Daniel. 'But that is not what they will be printing about you. As I understand it, they will be writing to infer that you had a part to play in the murder of Joseph Ransome because you discovered that he had fooled you over this item. You thought you were buying something in good faith, but when you found out that it was irregular, you lost your temper with him.'

'That's a lie!' Hughes burst out, and the look of panic had returned to his face.

'I'm sure it is.' Daniel nodded. 'But the papers are clever, to avoid a lawsuit they will hint at the connection between you and Joseph Ransome over this item, while at the same time giving good mention to the fact that Ransome was murdered. It's called trial by newspaper.

'You can imagine the effect on your good reputation, and especially its effect on the book you are currently writing on Cromwell. With that kind of scandal, it's possible that most reputable publishers may be averse to being associated with it.'

Hughes sat and looked at Daniel. His face had gone ashen.

'There must be something you can do about this,' he whispered.

'I'm sure there is, but before we can decide the best course of action to take to protect you, we need to know exactly what happened between you and Joseph Ransome, and how this transaction went. Then we can counter these accusations and put pressure on the press to spike the story.'

'Spike?' queried Hughes.

'Cancel it,' explained Daniel. 'They put it on a spike on the editor's desk, and it's taken away and destroyed.'

'And that's what will happen to this?'

'Once we know the full story.'

CHAPTER THIRTY-FIVE

'What was the relic that Ransome said he had for sale?' asked Daniel.

'A leather cap he claimed belonged to Oliver Cromwell,' said Hughes. 'He said it wasn't on show at the Fitzwilliam, but was kept in a store, along with other articles that were waiting to be displayed.'

'And how did he make this offer to you?'

'He approached me late one afternoon, at the Fitzwilliam. I'd been doing some research there, and he said he worked at the Fitzwilliam as a nightwatchman. He said he'd noticed my interest in the Civil War exhibits and wondered if I might be interested in getting hold of something that had belonged to Oliver Cromwell.

'I must have shown my excitement. The truth is that such items are rare. After the Restoration, many of Cromwell's possessions were destroyed in retribution for the execution of Charles I. As I'm sure you know, Cromwell's body was exhumed and hung in chains, even though it was falling apart. His head was put in a cage and hung outside Westminster Hall in London. So the opportunity to actually lay hands on something of Cromwell's was too good to resist.'

'You believed that it was genuine?'

'I did,' said Hughes. 'But that was before I actually viewed it.'

'And when you did get the chance to look at it, did you still think it was genuine?' asked Daniel.

'I never got that chance,' said Hughes. 'Ransome said he would deliver it to me at Mrs Loxley's on the Saturday, but he never arrived. And then I read about his murder in the newspaper.'

'When I mentioned that to you, you claimed you didn't know about it,' said Daniel.

'I lied,' admitted Hughes, shamefaced. 'The truth was I was worried that the investigations into his death might turn up something about the leather cap, and me.'

'So you never went to see Ransome at the Fitzwilliam on the night he died?'

'No. It's not my practice to roam the streets in the early hours.'

'Why did you vanish so suddenly?' asked Daniel. 'That story you told Mrs Loxley about your sister being gravely ill . . .'

'Another lie,' said Hughes, looking more ashamed than ever. 'I panicked. When I realised you were a detective investigating what had happened to Ransome, I decided to get out quickly.'

Daniel nodded. 'I'm fairly sure that Inspector Drabble and I can protect you, now that we know the whole story,' he said.

Hughes stared at him, a light of hope appearing in his expression. 'You mean I can go? Return home?'

Daniel gave a thoughtful frown. 'Can I suggest, Professor, that for the moment you return to Mrs Loxley's. After all, you've paid up, and I'm sure she'd be delighted to welcome you back. That way, I can keep you informed of developments, and you'll be able to resume your researches again.'

'Won't she find it suspicious my coming back like this?'

'Not at all, sir. You can tell her your sister wasn't as ill as you'd been led to believe.'

Drabble and Daniel accompanied the relieved professor to the street and each shook his hand, with Daniel promising to keep him abreast of any developments.

'Very clever,' Drabble commented, albeit reluctantly, as they walked back into the station. 'Getting him to cough up that business over the relic.'

'It was just a question of probing at his weak spot,' said Daniel. 'I'm sure you do the same, Inspector, when faced with a difficult situation.'

'Of course.' Drabble nodded.

'Sir!' A constable had appeared, hurrying towards them. 'We've got another dead body!'

'Another!' groaned Drabble. 'Not at the Fitzwilliam?'

'No, sir, at Magdalene Bridge.'

Or, as the constable said it, Maudlin Bridge. That was another thing about Cambridge, Daniel reflected. So many places seemed to be pronounced differently to how they were spelt.

'It was in the Cam,' continued the constable. 'Someone discovered it as they were punting.'

'Well, what's that got to do with us?' demanded Drabble. 'Suicide or accident. Happens all the time.'

'Yes, sir, but this body seems to be Hector Blades.'

'That reporter!'

'Yes, sir. And it looks like his head's been bashed in.'

CHAPTER THIRTY-SIX

A crowd had gathered on the bridge, and there were also people in punts on the far bank of the river, eager to get a glimpse of what was going on.

'Damned circus!' grumbled Drabble as Daniel followed him across the grass to the river's edge. A tarpaulin had been thrown over a shape on the grass and Daniel saw a boot poking out from beneath it. Two constables were standing by the tarpaulin, and as Drabble and Daniel reached it they peeled one end of the tarpaulin back to reveal the upper part of the body.

It was Hector Blades, weed from the river still caught in his hair and tangled in the collar of his jacket. There was a gash at one side of his forehead.

Drabble crouched down to examine it, Daniel joining him.

'What do you think?' asked Drabble.

'At this stage, I'm not sure,' said Daniel. 'It could be the result of a blow before he died, or he could have been bashed against something. What's the current like here?'

'Depends on the amount of rain we've had,' said Drabble. 'Lots of rain, the river runs faster.'

'There hasn't been that much rain lately,' Daniel commented. 'But then, anything else could have caused it. The edge of a punt coming into contact with him as he was floating.'

Drabble nodded. 'I wouldn't rule out suicide,' he muttered. 'By all accounts Blades was a heavy gambler, deep in debt.'

'You know him well?'

'No, not personally, but I've been interested in him since he started bad-mouthing me and the Cambridge police in his rag of a paper.'

'What sort of people did he owe money to?'

'All sorts. His tailor, and he was always running it close with his rent. That sort of thing gets to a man after a while.'

'It depends on the man,' commented Daniel. 'Some seem to have no conscience about money they owe other people.'

'Yes, well, that was certainly true of Blades,' said Drabble.

'But some people who are owed money can get very upset,' continued Daniel. 'And I'm not talking about his tailor or his landlord. His gambling, for example. Bookies don't take kindly to being stiffed for their money.'

'Yes, it's possible,' said Drabble. 'Give him a roughing up to try and get some cash out of him, and in the event he falls in the river.'

'Do you know who he owed money to? Any particular rough type of bookie?'

'I might,' said Drabble. 'Anyway, we might as well get Dr Keen to take a look at the body. He seems to have an eye for working out how people die.' He gave a sigh. 'It's all this science stuff these days.' He stood up and turned to the constables. 'Get it loaded onto a wagon and take it to Gonville and Caius, for the attention of Dr Keen. I'll go on ahead and make the arrangements with him.' He turned to Daniel. 'Would you like to come with me, Mr Wilson, seeing as how you now know Dr Keen?'

'Thank you, Inspector. I appreciate the invitation, but there's something else I need to look into.'

'Oh? What?'

'The person who attacked me.'

'You said you thought you knew who it was,' said Drabble.

'Yes.'

'And you're going to see them?'

'Yes.'

'D'you think that's wise? Like I said before, I don't want any vigilante stuff. And you've already had one bashing. The next one could be worse.' He hesitated, then offered, 'If you like, I can send a constable along with you. For your protection.'

Daniel gave him a grateful smile.

'Thank you, Inspector. I really appreciate that offer, but unless I'm very wrong, I don't think I'm in any great danger.'

Drabble shrugged. 'Have it your own way.' He looked down at the dead body of Blades. 'But I'm sure Blades here felt the same way. As did the nightwatchman at the Fitzwilliam. And the bloke in the sarcophagus.'

'Point taken, Inspector, and I'll be very careful.'

'Very well.' Drabble nodded. 'And, if you're right, you'll tell me who it was?'

'If it turns out to be related to the murders,' said Daniel.

'Surely he did it to stop you investigating them,' said Drabble.

'Yes, but I don't think that was the whole reason,' said Daniel.

'Well, you'll find out soon enough if you're right,' said Drabble. 'But take a warning: if you ain't, it could be your body we'll be fishing out of the Cam.'

CHAPTER THIRTY-SEVEN

There was no sign of Lillian Crane or Dolly as Daniel walked into the Lamb and Flag, but Herbert Crane was in his usual place behind the bar. He scowled as Daniel walked up to him.

'We need to talk,' said Daniel.

'I've got nothing to say,' muttered Herbert.

'We can talk privately outside, or I can call your wife from the back and we can talk in front of her about you and Dolly.'

It was as if he'd punched Herbert, who swallowed and cast a nervous look towards the door in the wall behind the bar.

'I've got nothing to hide!' he whispered in an attempt at bluster.

'That's fine. Then I'll just call Lillian out. I assume that mirror behind the bar is two-way glass and she's watching us, even though she can't hear us.'

Daniel raised his arm as if to signal a secret watcher, and Herbert grabbed Daniel's arm and pulled it down.

'How do I know you won't beat me up?' he demanded hoarsely.

'You have my word,' said Daniel.

Herbert hesitated, then said, 'I can't leave and go outside. She'll get suspicious.'

'You left before, when you followed me and attacked me.'

Herbert stood, a man torn apart. Then he gestured to an empty table away from the few drinkers in the bar.

'Over there,' he said.

He lifted the flap of the bar, and he and Daniel walked to the table and sat. Herbert kept casting nervous glances towards the door behind the bar.

'I'll make it quick,' said Daniel. 'You're in love with Dolly. I saw that in the way you looked at her. I'm guessing she doesn't know?'

'No,' muttered Herbert.

'You attacked me to protect her,' Daniel continued. When Herbert didn't answer, just looked down, unable to meet his gaze, Daniel added, 'I'm not going to have you arrested, or beat you up. But only if you get me the answer to the question I asked you about Joe Ransome using chloroform as a drug.'

'He didn't,' mumbled Herbert. 'Dolly was in here last night, and I asked her.' His head went up and he looked defiantly at Daniel. 'Not because of you, but because I was worried about her and what she might have been led into by Ransome.'

'And?'

Herbert shook his head. 'She said he didn't use drugs with her, they just drank.'

Daniel nodded. 'Good. That's all I needed to know. Except one other thing: you hated Joe Ransome because he was with Dolly.'

'He used her!' burst out Herbert. 'She thought he loved her, but he didn't.'

'But you did. So, did you kill him?'

Herbert stared at Daniel, shocked.

'No. No. Never,' he burbled. 'On my life!' He swallowed again. 'I'm sorry I hurt you, but I was worried about her. You asking questions might drive her away from here, and I couldn't bear that.' He paused, then asked nervously, 'You gonna hurt me?'

'I've already said I wouldn't,' said Daniel. 'But if I find you've lied to me, I'll tell your wife, and she'll hurt you a lot worse than I could.'

There was an envelope waiting for Daniel when he arrived back at Mrs Loxley's.

'It's from Miss Fenton,' said Mrs Loxley. 'She came to see how you were.'

The note from Abigail said much the same, with the addition of an invitation for him to call on her that evening so they could exchange information. She added, *Bella will be out this evening at one of her meetings, so we will have privacy to talk.*

Abigail greeted him with a look of concern when she opened the door to him.

'I'm still not sure you should have been so busy today,' she said. 'There is always the risk of concussion after a nasty bang on the head, even the day after.'

'Thank you, but I've been fine,' he assured her.

'We'll go into the parlour,' she said. 'I'll get Mrs Standish to bring tea for us. Would you like some cake? I believe we have some fruit cake.'

'No thank you, tea will be fine,' said Daniel.

Abigail hurried off to order tea from Mrs Standish, then joined Daniel in the parlour.

'How did it go with Professor Hughes?' she asked.

'I'm fairly sure the professor is innocent of the murders. His only crime was gullibility, allowing himself to be duped by Ransome over a leather cap that he claimed had belonged to Oliver Cromwell. Hughes fled at the thought that I might discover his involvement with Ransome.'

'He admitted as much?'

'He did.' Then, his face adopting a more sombre expression, he told her, 'I have other news. Hector Blades is dead.'

She stared at him, shocked. 'Dead?'

'While I was with Inspector Drabble, a report came of a body being found in the Cam by Magdalene Bridge. Inspector Drabble asked me to accompany him. It was Blades. He looked like he'd been beaten.'

'So . . . it's murder?'

'It looks like it. Unless he fell in and received the injuries from a passing punt.'

'How horrible! Who . . . who would do such a thing?'

'Inspector Drabble seems to think it may be connected with Blades' lifestyle. Apparently he was a heavy gambler and had run up large debts to some dubious people. But there is always the possibility that he may have been killed to stop him revealing the identity of his so-called Egyptology expert.'

She sat, taking this in, and didn't immediately seem aware of Mrs Standish coming in bearing a tray laden with a pot of tea, a jug of milk and cups and saucers.

'Tea, Miss Abigail,' she said, putting the tray down on the table.

'Thank you,' said Abigail absently.

'There is another thing to report,' said Daniel, as Abigail set to pour the tea. 'I'm fairly confident that Ransome did not use the chloroform on himself.'

'How did you discover that?' she asked.

'I had a discussion with the barman at the Lamb and Flag. It was he who attacked me yesterday.'

'You should have him arrested!' burst out Abigail.

'No, it's better to keep him where he is,' said Daniel. 'He'll be a useful informant.'

'Can he be trusted?'

'Not a bit,' said Daniel. 'But he's afraid of his wife finding out that he's in love with the woman Ransome spent part of the night with at the Fitzwilliam.'

'My God, it sounds like the plot of one of the trashy romantic novels Bella reads,' said Abigail in disgust.

'I'm afraid that real life often seems like a romantic novel for many people,' said Daniel wryly.

'Are you referring to my admission about my friendship with Edgar Bruton?' she asked, her tone icy.

'Not at all,' said Daniel. 'And I apologise if you felt that was my intention. I just meant that I've worked on many cases of murder and serious assault, and a great many seem to have resulted from an affair of the heart, or a tangled romantic life.'

'Which could still be the case over the death of Mr Ransome,' mused Abigail. 'Do you think the barman at the Lamb and Flag could be the guilty one?'

'No,' said Daniel.

'Then we are no further forward.' Abigail sighed.

'On the contrary, we have moved forward,' said Daniel. 'I feel we can eliminate Professor Hughes and the barman from our list of suspects. We also now know the identity of the first man,

Dr Madi, and I feel that once we have the passenger list of the boat he arrived in England on, we might be able to identify his mysterious companion who cleared out the cottage after he died.'

'There will be hundreds of names,' said Abigail.

'I believe we're looking for another Egyptian, and I'm keeping my fingers crossed his name will be near that of Dr Madi on the list, if – as I hope – they booked together. Fortunately, Inspector Drabble seems to be on side with the idea. In fact, he's taken on the responsibility of getting hold of the passenger list from the shipping company's offices at Tilbury. Hopefully, we should have it this weekend.'

She sipped at her tea, then gave him a look that was part question, part heartfelt appeal.

'How did you manage to do this for so long?' she asked.

'Do what?' asked Daniel, puzzled.

'Investigate crimes.'

He smiled. 'I don't think there's much difference between what we both do. You don't only catalogue, you enquire: where did this object come from? How did this mummified body meet their end?'

'Yes, but mine involve long-departed people. Yours is full of questions involving those who live – the relatives and friends of someone who's been murdered, who suffer terrible anguish – and they look to you to provide them with the answers to their pain.'

'Which is why I came into the force,' said Daniel. 'Someone needs to be there for them, and not just in a sympathetic way, but practically working to give them help to deal with what they are suffering.'

'Some clergymen would say they are doing the same thing,' said Abigail.

'It's very different,' said Daniel. 'They're trying to maintain people's faith in God. I'm trying to maintain their faith in the law, and justice.'

'But you're both on the side of the angels,' said Abigail.

Daniel laughed. 'If angels exist,' he said, 'which, as an agnostic, I have doubts about. Although I accept the idea of humans as ministering or protecting angels, in a non-figurative sense. The difference is that some of us have to deal with the Devil to get the just result.'

She smiled at him and said, 'I didn't realise you could be so loquacious. You put out the image of the pedestrian policeman, but you are not at all. You are a deep-thinking philosopher, taking in theology as well as the new sciences of psychology.'

'Or, "sound and fury signifying nothing",' said Daniel, returning her smile.

'Who also quotes Shakespeare. You are a surprising man, Mr Wilson, with hidden depths.'

And so are you, too, Miss Fenton, Daniel wanted to say. But instead, he said, 'I had better go. Mrs Loxley will have my supper ready for me, and she does tut discreetly but disapprovingly if it's allowed to congeal.'

He stood up and put his hat on. Abigail also rose to her feet.

'You're quite sure you're not in pain?' she asked. 'Not just from your head, but your ribs.'

'I will be fine,' said Daniel. 'I shall rest tomorrow, unless something comes up that needs looking into. And I shall call tomorrow early evening to escort you to the debate at the Fitzwilliam.'

CHAPTER THIRTY-EIGHT

'I assume you'll be at the Fitzwilliam today, Abi?' asked Bella, taking a pause from munching on a piece of buttered toast as the two sisters ate their breakfast.

'Of course,' said Abigail. 'Sir William has asked me to take responsibility for preparing the room for the debate. It is to be in the larger of the Egyptian rooms, so I shall be working with the porters and stewards to clear the main room, but leaving enough artefacts around to create the right atmosphere and hopefully stimulate the topics that will be raised.'

'Will that include mummies?' asked Bella. 'In view of the recent reports, I'm sure the mummies will add a certain frisson to the occasion, with people wondering if one of them will suddenly rise up and launch an attack on the gathering.'

'Don't be ridiculous!' snapped Abigail. 'In fact, there'll be no room in where the debate is to be held to have mummy cases on display. We are expecting quite a large crowd, so most of the space will be taken up with chairs.'

'And who will be chairing the debate?' asked Bella. 'You?'

'Good heavens, no! That will be Sir William.' She gave a wry frown. 'I doubt if Professor Waldheim would be pleased if a woman was to chair the debate; he's been quite forthright in some of his views on the nature of women, especially in the sciences.' She smiled. 'I think he's a likely candidate for some of your leaflets on rights for women.'

'You think I should bring some with me when I come this evening?' asked Bella.

'Absolutely not!' said Abigail. 'The Fitzwilliam is not a political arena.' Then she looked at her sister, puzzled. 'I did not realise you were planning to come to the debate. You haven't mentioned it.'

'My dear, that's because I've hardly seen you. You're either at the Fitzwilliam or traipsing all over Cambridge in search of this murderer. But tonight, we can go together.'

Abigail hesitated momentarily, then said, 'Yes we can. I've asked Mr Wilson to accompany me to the Fitzwilliam . . .' Seeing the look of look of anger that clouded her sister's face, and before Bella could say anything, Abigail added hastily, 'Where I am to meet Mr Hardwicke, who has asked me to be his companion for the occasion to discuss how the debate went.'

Bella's face brightened. 'So Mr Wilson is purely coming to accompany you.'

'Yes.'

'Then he can accompany us both!' Bella beamed.

As Abigail walked to the Fitzwilliam, her mind was filled with Bella's reaction to Daniel Wilson, and despite herself she had to admit to feelings of jealousy. Not that she had anything to feel jealous about: Mr Wilson had made no advances towards her, and although she did feel an attraction to him she wasn't sure how well they might be suited. But of one thing she was sure: Bella was totally unsuitable for Mr Wilson. For all Bella's pretensions at intellectual pursuits, Daniel Wilson was far too intelligent for her. And too polite to say so. *And because he's an honourable man, if he's not careful, Bella will ensnare him,* she thought angrily.

Honourable. Caring. Intelligent. Thoughtful. And brave.

How had he managed to stay single for so long? Or, was he single? He seemed to be alone, but had there been someone in his life? A wife, or fiancée, now dead, for whom he still grieved?

She shook her head. Enough of this wild speculation.

As she arrived at the Fitzwilliam she saw that Edward Hardwicke was on the entrance steps, talking to one of the porters. He stopped as soon as he saw her and smiled in greeting.

Such a nice smile! she thought.

'Good morning, Miss Fenton – Abigail,' said Hardwicke. 'I came to offer my services, if I can be of assistance in preparing the room for the debate. Plus, I have to see Sir William about the form for the evening, so I thought it would be two birds with one stone.'

'That's very kind of you, Edward,' said Abigail. She walked into the museum, Hardwicke following her. 'But fortunately, I have enough assistance in preparing the room. And I would think you would need the time to marshal your opinions in preparation for whatever Professor Waldheim may unleash at you.'

'I believe I'm prepared for him,' said Hardwicke. 'By the way, any news on the case?'

'Actually, yes,' said Abigail. 'We discovered the identity of the man who was found in the sarcophagus.'

'Oh?'

'His name was Dr Ahmet Madi. An Egyptian. He was staying in a cottage on the outskirts of Cambridge.'

'How strange! What was he doing here, do you have any idea?'

'No. I wondered if you'd come across him while you were in Egypt?'

'Me? No.' He laughed. 'We had our own medic with the team.'

'I don't think he was that sort of doctor,' said Abigail.

'What makes you say that?'

'When we examined the body, we worked out that his hands showed all the signs of an academic. Ink-stains on his fingers, that sort of thing.'

'You examined the body?'

Abigail looked uncomfortable. 'Well, not exactly *examined* it. We went along to see Dr Keen, who did the post-mortem, and he let us look at it.'

'We?'

'Mr Wilson and I.'

'Ah. The detective.'

'Yes. Anyway, the evidence suggested an academic, so we think he might have been a doctor of archaeology. That would explain his presence here.'

'But does it?' queried Edward. 'If he was a genuine doctor of archaeology interested in what you have here, he'd have come during the day, made his presence known. The suggestion, as I understand it, is that he crept in during the night.'

'Yes,' agreed Abigail. 'It looks that way.'

'That suggests a burglar more than an academic,' said Edward.

'Yes, it does,' said Abigail thoughtfully. 'I'm intending to ask Sir William if he's ever heard the name. He has a lot of contacts with the Egyptian end, and if this man was an academic, at least we'd know one way or another.'

'Yes, true.' Edward nodded. 'Although I know at the moment Sir William is very tied up with the debate. As I said, he's asked me to see him to finalise details.' He smiled. 'Tell you what, why don't I mention it to him? That way you can get your answer quicker.'

'Would you?' said Abigail. 'Why, that's lovely of you.'

'Anything I can do to help,' said Edward. 'What was his name again? Madi?'

'Dr Ahmet Madi.'

Edward nodded. 'Leave it to me. I'll let you know what Sir William says.'

CHAPTER THIRTY-NINE

That evening found Daniel sitting between Abigail and Bella in the front row of the audience in the larger of the Egyptian rooms at the Fitzwilliam. Dr Keen was sitting on the other side of Bella. The room was packed, leaving very little space for displays of ancient artefacts, so most of those that Abigail had carefully positioned had had to be removed to the inner room.

Professor Waldheim and Edward Hardwicke sat on two chairs at one side of the room, on either side of Sir William Mackenzie, who stood at a lectern. Waldheim was a big man in every respect, tall and with a bulging paunch that suggested a man of hearty appetites for good food and wine. With his thick, unruly hair, and particularly his spectacularly bushy beard, he reminded Daniel of paintings he'd seen of zealous Old Testament prophets.

As Daniel looked around at the audience, he found to his

surprise that there was just as much an air of excited anticipation amongst them as there would have been at a boxing match in some of the dingier halls in East London.

Sir William introduced the two speakers, and the subject of the debate, which concerned something called the pyramid inch. As the debate got under way, with Professor Waldheim opening, it seemed to Daniel that the pyramid inch was a measure, one twenty-fifth of a sacred cubit, which some pyramidologists claimed to have been used in ancient times to work out the proportions for the pyramids to be built. There was a chart on the wall behind Professor Waldheim which he pointed at frequently whenever he quoted from one of the names on the chart – those who had first proposed, and then developed this theory of the pyramid inch. The names meant nothing to Daniel, but he could tell from the pompous way that Waldheim spoke their names that he, and the rest of the audience, were meant to be impressed by this roll call of pyramid inchers: Professor John Greaves (1602–1652), John Taylor (1781–1864), and finally Charles Piazzi Smyth (born 1819). Isaac Newton also appeared on the professor's list of names. As far as Daniel could gather, the main thing in this theory was that the total length of the four sides of a pyramid would be 36,524 pyramid inches, a hundred times the number of days in a year, and the reason Newton's name appeared was because this was part of some larger universal scheme of things which even had religious implications involving the earth and the solar system.

Whether it was Professor Waldheim's heavy-handed style of delivering the theory (and Daniel was still unsure what the implications of the theory were), or just the repetition of numbers, Daniel had to force himself to keep his eyes open. Obviously, this sense of drowsiness was not shared by the majority of the other people in the room: Abigail, for one, sat forward on the edge of her seat as if spellbound, and he could see she was frequently champing at the bit to interrupt with a question.

Things livened up when it was Edward Hardwicke's turn to speak, mainly because he began by dismissing the theory of the pyramid inch as quasi-religious mumbo-jumbo based on a major error.

'The theory of the pyramid inch is based on one particular measurement, the height of the Great Pyramid at Giza. But Flinders Petrie . . .'

At the mention of the name of Flinders Petrie, there were catcalls and boos from a large section of the audience, and Sir William was forced to bang his gavel repeatedly on the lectern in front of him to restore order.

'But Flinders Petrie found,' continued Hardwicke, determined not to be put off, 'that when he measured the Great Pyramid in 1880, the pyramid was actually several feet smaller than previously believed. In other words, the pyramid inch is based on a serious miscalculation of measurement, and as such the theory is completely discredited!'

Once more this led to howls of anger from Professor Waldheim's supporters, and Sir William duly gave the professor the opportunity to come back and try and refute Hardwicke's point. The professor, however, merely launched into a personal attack on the character of Flinders Petrie and all those associated with him, accusing them of denigrating a great man in Piazzi Smyth, and the memory of all those who'd gone before him.

'The argument goes to your Mr Hardwicke, I think,' Daniel muttered to Abigail.

There then followed an invitation from Sir William for

questions from the floor, and Daniel wasn't at all surprised when Abigail was one of the first to raise her hand. Sir William pointed towards her and she rose.

'Professor Waldheim,' she began, 'can I ask . . . ?'

That was as far as she got.

'No, you cannot!' boomed the professor. 'I refuse to answer questions about science from a woman! Women have no brain! You have no intellect of any value!'

Before Daniel knew what he was doing, he was on his feet, shouting indignantly back at the professor, 'And you, sir, have no manners! And I would venture to suggest that Miss Abigail Fenton, who you have so unjustly abused, is possibly the most intelligent person in this room. And that includes yourself.'

At this, there were outbursts from all over the room, loud shouts of abuse directed at Daniel, while others echoed Daniel's sentiments and shouted at the professor, demanding an apology from him.

As Sir William tried to restore order, banging a gavel on the lectern, Bella leant into Abigail and whispered to her, 'Well! How does it feel, Abi, to have a knight in the form of Mr Wilson coming to *your* defence?'

Abigail, who felt she must have gone a bright red, shook her head and muttered back, 'I do no need anyone to come to my defence.' But as she looked at Daniel, who had retaken his seat, she felt an overwhelming burst of gratitude towards him. No one before had ever stood up for her. Everyone – her parents, her schoolfriends, her colleagues, certainly her sister – seemed to believe that there was no need to stand up for Abigail because 'she is self-sufficient'.

Part of her felt she should be angry at his intervention, made without her permission, but the spontaneity of it – the way he had leapt to his feet, the controlled anger in his voice on her behalf – made her want to hug him.

I'm being foolish, she rebuked herself.

As the hubbub in the room, subsided, Daniel leant towards her and said, 'My apologies for embarrassing you with my outburst, Miss Fenton.'

'There is no apology necessary,' Abigail murmured back. 'In fact, I am grateful for your intervention. Although you may have exaggerated the level of my intellect. There are many people in this room whose intellectual and archaeological achievements far exceed mine.'

'Perhaps, but I do not know them so I cannot pass judgement on their abilities,' said Daniel.

With the audience calmed down, Sir William obviously decided enough was enough and not to take the risk of another outburst, so he put the debate to the vote. The result was a narrow victory for Professor Waldheim's view.

'As expected,' said Abigail. 'Piazzi Smyth's supporters are here in force tonight.'

With the debate finished, Daniel saw the figure of Edward Hardwicke pushing his way through a crowd of well-wishers, all keen to congratulate him on his performance, towards them.

'Abigail!' He beamed. 'We lost, but I trust I put our case well enough to persuade even some of those here tonight on the virtue of Petrie's theories.'

'You did, indeed, Edward.' Abigail smiled.

Hardwicke turned towards Daniel and held out his hand. 'And allow me to shake your hand, Mr Wilson. Your defence of Miss Fenton was admirable. To be honest, I was about to say the same myself, but you beat me to it.'

'Yes, wasn't Mr Wilson wonderful!' enthused Bella. 'Like a Lancelot, or St George rising up against the dragon!'

'It certainly made for a lively debate,' said Dr Keen.

Suddenly, a flash of lurid green at the back of the room caught Daniel's eye. He turned, and saw a man heading towards the exit who fitted the description given by the assistant at Heffers to perfection. The luxurious side-whiskers in the style of W. S. Gilbert, but most of all his suit of the almost luminous pale green large-checked material.

'Excuse me,' he said. 'There's someone I need to talk to.' He turned to Abigail and Bella and said, 'My apologies, ladies, but I may be caught up. If I'm not back when you are ready to leave, perhaps Mr Hardwicke or Dr Keen would walk you home.'

'I would be delighted to.' Hardwicke smiled.

'As would I.' Keen nodded.

'Is this something to do with the case?' asked Abigail.

'It may well be,' said Daniel. 'Excuse me, but I must catch this person before they vanish. I'll see you tomorrow, Miss Fenton, and report. Will you be here?'

'Indeed,' she said.

Daniel nodded his farewell and hurried off. The man in the green suit had disappeared, but Daniel hoped he wouldn't have gone far. Unless he had a cab waiting for him outside.

CHAPTER FORTY

Daniel was in luck. The man had stopped at the gates of the Fitzwilliam and was looking along the line of cabs waiting in the road. Daniel reached him just as he was about to climb aboard one.

'Excuse me!' called Daniel.

The man stopped and turned to look at Daniel, curious. 'Yes?'

'I'd like to talk to you about "Lot No. 249".'

The man stared at Daniel, an expression of bewilderment on his face. 'I'm sorry, I don't understand.'

'"Lot No. 249". It's a short story by Arthur Conan Doyle. You went to Heffers bookshop to ask about it.'

The man shook his head. 'I'm afraid you must be confusing me with someone else.'

'I don't think so,' said Daniel. 'But there's a simple way to clear this up. If you would accompany me to the police station . . .'

'I will do no such thing!' said the man indignantly. 'Who the hell do you think you are?'

'My name is Daniel Wilson. I'm a private investigator. I've been hired by the Fitzwilliam to investigate the recent deaths there.'

'Which are nothing to do with me,' said the man firmly.

'Shall we see what Inspector Drabble thinks?' asked Daniel. 'If you won't talk to me, then I shall be forced to place you under citizen's arrest and hand you over to the police for questioning.'

'You have no authority to do that!' protested the man.

'On the contrary, I have every authority,' said Daniel. 'As a former detective inspector with Scotland Yard, I am well versed in the law. So, what's it to be? Me, or the police?'

Abigail was still filled with a sense of excitement at the evening's debate as she and Edward Hardwicke walked home, side by side. Bella and Dr Keen trailed behind them, also deep in their own very different conversation.

'How on earth can any supposedly intelligent person, with a practical experience of the pyramids, still insist on promoting Piazzi Smyth's outdated theories?' asked Abigail, exasperated.

'In fairness to Smyth, they aren't really his theories,' Hardwicke pointed out. 'He's just reiterating views that have been expressed for the past few hundred years.'

'Which have been discredited by Flinders Petrie's work!' Abigail pressed.

'True.' Hardwicke nodded, then smiled. 'I have to say, Professor Waldheim's face was a picture when your friend, Mr Wilson, stood up and attacked him. I don't think the professor is used to being taken to task so publicly.'

'Mr Wilson can be very old-fashioned with his view that

225

women need a man to protect them,' said Abigail.

'And would you have thought I was being old-fashioned if I'd said the same out loud?' asked Hardwicke. 'Because I was on the point of saying exactly that when Mr Wilson rose to his feet in your defence.'

'I'm not saying I wasn't grateful for his intervention,' said Abigail. 'All I'm saying is that I felt I could have countered the professor's statement on the ignorance of women on my own terms.'

'If you'd been given the chance,' said Hardwicke. 'Which, with the professor in a bullish mood, looked unlikely.' He frowned thoughtfully as he asked, 'Do you know who Mr Wilson was so eager to see when he rushed off?'

'I have no idea,' said Abigail.

'Do you think it's connected with the case?' asked Hardwicke.

'I expect so. I'm sure he'll report back to me tomorrow.'

'I'd be interested to find out,' said Hardwicke.

'You're interested in the case?'

'Inasmuch as it involves the Fitzwilliam, and – apparently – the articles I sent back from Egypt. I've never been involved in a murder mystery before.'

A few paces behind them, Bella nodded as Dr Keen talked, although she wasn't really paying attention. She was also thinking about Daniel Wilson's sudden departure from the room. She had been so sure that he would walk her home after the event, having spent the past few hours with her and Abigail – and with Abigail so obviously enraptured with Edward Hardwicke, there would have been every opportunity for her to invite him in after he'd walked them home. And she was sure he would not have been so churlish as to refuse. And afterwards . . .

Suddenly, she caught the word 'matrimony', and her attention turned to Dr Keen, who was looking earnestly at her as they walked.

'I beg your pardon?' she said, puzzled.

'I asked how you felt about matrimony?' said Dr Keen. 'I know at this moment I am really just starting out on my career as a doctor and my income is not as large as I would wish, but in the future . . .'

Bella stopped and stared at him.

'You are asking me to marry you?' she said, stunned.

'Yes,' said Dr Keen. 'If you'll have me.'

CHAPTER FORTY-ONE

The man's name was Algernon Cobb. He'd decided to opt for talking to Daniel, while still insisting his innocence of anything to do with the murders, and now the two men were sitting in a quiet corner of the bar at the Lion Hotel, not far from the Fitzwilliam. Cobb had elected for a large whisky, Daniel for a lemonade, determined to keep his head clear.

'"Lot No. 249",' prompted Daniel.

'I'm a theatre producer,' explained Cobb. 'I'm always alert for new ideas, especially ones that would be suitable for a small touring company. It so happened that I was in a bar here in Cambridge, reading in the newspaper the report of the murder of the nightwatchman at the Fitzwilliam, when this gentleman sitting at the next table suddenly burst out "My God, it's 'Lot No. 249'!"

'That sort of outburst is unusual, and especially when it's done by an American. That's not an accent you hear very often in Cambridge.'

'You're sure he was American?'

Cobb nodded. 'We got into conversation, and he told me he was from New York, over here on business. I asked him what he meant about "Lot No. 249", and he explained that the story in the paper was the same plot as this story of Arthur Conan Doyle's that he'd read in an American magazine called *Harper's*.'

'Did you get this man's name?' asked Daniel.

Cobb shook his head. 'I do know that he was leaving the next day, to return to America. So, alas, I can't produce him to back up my story. The thing was, I was intrigued by this story. A murderous Egyptian mummy, reanimated. Revenge. Murder. Terror. It's got it all!'

'So you went in search of the story?'

Cobb nodded. 'Heffers is the best bookshop around, so I thought if anyone would know about it and could get me a copy, they would. But it turns out it hasn't been published in book form yet, just as a short story in this magazine.'

'So you set about trying to get the rights to it, to turn it into a stage play.'

Cobb hesitated, then said reluctantly, 'Not exactly.'

Daniel regarded him quizzically.

'Not exactly?' he repeated.

'This whole thing about rights is complicated,' said Cobb. 'I mean, who really owns an idea.'

'I would assume the original writer,' said Daniel.

'Ah, that's where you're wrong,' said Cobb. 'So often it's the publisher. Or even someone else who was nothing to do with it. It's all about contracts. For example, did you know that for the first Sherlock Holmes story that Conan Doyle wrote, *A Study in Scarlet*, he sold all the rights to the publisher for £25. So no matter how many copies it sold, or if there were any translations or adaptations done of it, Conan Doyle got not one penny more for it. Now is that fair?'

'No,' agreed Daniel. 'But I'm sure that Mr Doyle had his reasons for accepting those terms.'

'Lack of money and an eagerness to see his work in print,' said Cobb. 'That's the fate of all new writers. They'll take any terms they're offered to see their words on the printed page. In my opinion, most of these publishers are vultures, living off the soul and spirit of the original creator, and I don't want to give them one brass farthing to add to their ill-gotten gains.'

'So you were planning to take the story and adapt it without permission?'

'Not exactly,' said Cobb again, his tone cautious.

'That's the second time you've used that phrase,' said Daniel. 'What do you mean?'

'Alright, this is how it is,' said Cobb. 'If I find a really good story that I know audiences will love, I look at it, at the very core of it, and see if some things can maybe be altered. Like, for example, "Lot No. 249" is set in Oxford. Why Oxford? Why not, say, Edinburgh. Or Paris. Then I look at the main characters. Have you read the story?'

'Yes,' said Daniel.

'So you'll know it centres on three students all at the same Oxford college,' continued Cobb, 'Abercrombie Smith, Edward Bellingham and William Monkhouse Lee. But say instead it's a lodging house in Paris, with two young men and a young woman they're both in love with. And one of them uses some ancient ritual to reanimate this mummy to get rid of his rival. See what I mean? It's a different story!'

'It's still the same story,' said Daniel.

'No it's not. The only thing they have in common is a reanimated mummy, and that's an old Egyptian myth, things coming back from the dead. There's no copyright on that. The thing is to check everything that's in the original, and make sure you avoid them. Hey presto, you've got a whole new story. And you've beaten the vulture publishers.'

'And also avoided paying anything to the original writer,' observed Daniel.

'Yes, well, that's the nature of the creative business.' Cobb shrugged. 'Look at Shakespeare. He stole most of his plots from Holinshed, but who today remembers Holinshed?'

CHAPTER FORTY-TWO

Bella sat at the breakfast table and beamed. *God*, thought Abigail, *she's positively* glowing*!*

'He said he's been thinking about asking me to marry him for ages, but he's never had the courage or the opportunity to ask. Until last night.'

'Marriage,' repeated Abigail. 'You and Dr Keen.'

'Yes!' squealed Bella. Then she gave a pout and added, 'And there's no need to say it in that tone of voice, Abi.'

'I wasn't aware I was saying it in any sort of tone of voice,' said Abigail.

'Well, you were. As if you doubted it. But he said it to you as well, just before he and Edward left.'

Yes, he had, thought Abigail. Dr Keen had looked suddenly very fragile as he stood at their doorstep and said, 'I have just asked Bella to marry me, Miss Fenton. And she has said yes. I hope we have your approval.'

I am not her parent! Abigail had wanted to shout at him. *I am not her old maid aunt. I am her sister!*

'And who knows, Abi, but the same may happen to you!' Bella smiled, and Abigail wanted to shout at her for the patronising way she said it.

'With whom?' demanded Abigail.

'Why, Mr Hardwicke, of course. I believe he is very taken with you. He would make a wonderful beau.'

Daniel had wondered how it would be at the boarding house, whether Hughes would make a point of avoiding him, but the opposite had been true. Hughes was obviously keen to find out what the situation was with 'the vultures of the press', as he called them. So as Daniel sat down to breakfast on Saturday morning, he found himself being interrogated by Hughes: who were the people who were after dragging his name through the mud? Was it just the local paper, the *Gazette*, or were they from the London papers?

Daniel did his best to reassure him that so far they had been able to keep the press under control, and if there were any developments the professor would be the first to know.

'But be assured, we will protect you and your good name,' Daniel told him.

'What about this reporter whose body they found in the Cam?' Daniel reflected it was interesting how Hughes had gone from someone who proclaimed he never read about current events in the papers to devouring every paragraph. 'Was he one of those who were planning to write about me?'

An interesting question, thought Daniel. Although he felt it

233

was extremely unlikely that Hughes could have been Blades' killer, he really didn't seem the type. The fact that both Daniel and Drabble still considered him a valid suspect for the murder of Ransome raised a question about the professor in relation to Blades' death. Had Blades contacted the professor about the murders, asking questions, which Hughes had interpreted as a threat? But how would Blades know about Hughes' involvement?

Aloud, he said, 'His name was Hector Blades. Did you know him?'

Hughes shook his head. 'No,' he said. 'I've not spoken to anyone at the newspapers, nor they to me. What happened to this man, Blades? An accident?'

'We're still looking into the cause of death,' said Daniel. 'It could have been an accident, although there are also indications that there might have been an assault.'

Hughes gave a darting look around to make sure that Mrs Loxley wasn't within earshot, then lowered his voice to hiss urgently, 'It wasn't me. Like I said, I didn't even know the man.'

Daniel gave him a reassuring smile. 'Don't worry, Professor, we never even considered that possibility.'

But I will now, he thought.

The appearance of Mrs Loxley beside their table caused Hughes to hastily turn his attention back to his breakfast.

'Excuse me, Mr Wilson, but there's someone to see you. Two men.'

'Oh?'

'From Peebles the carters.'

'Ah! Would you mind if we used your parlour again, Mrs Loxley?'

'I offered that, but they said they'd prefer to see you outside the house.' She hesitated, then muttered, 'It's their clothes, you see.'

Daniel saw as soon as he stepped outside the house. Two men, one older, the other obviously his son, stood on the doorstep, and although they may have cleaned themselves up for this visit, their outfits were very rough, with patches on the knees of their ragged trousers and their jackets. And their boots were of the heavy variety, metal-toe-capped with thick studded soles.

'Mr Wilson?' asked the older one.

'I am indeed,' said Daniel.

'Jim Hoy. This is my son, Bob.'

Daniel held out his hand and shook theirs.

'We won't come in on account of our boots,' explained Hoy. 'They'd ruin a good carpet.'

'There's a park just along the road,' suggested Daniel. 'We could find a bench and talk there, if that's acceptable.'

Hoy nodded. 'That suits us.'

As they made their way to the small park, Daniel asked, 'I'm interested in the delivery you made to the Fitzwilliam the Monday before last.'

'The one nearly two weeks ago?' queried Hoy, set on getting things right.

'That's the one. You picked up the consignment at Tilbury, is that right?'

Hoy nodded. 'Right,' he said. 'That's regular for me and Bob, that is. Tilbury up to the Fitzwilliam. Cos they know we're careful with 'em. We load 'em on the wagon gentle like, not throw 'em on like some people.'

'Who did you collect them from at Tilbury? Is there a storage facility there? A warehouse of some sort?'

Hoy shook his head. 'Stuff like this is precious. They like us to be there waiting when the ship arrives. I mean, the stevedores do the actual unloading of the ship, that's their job, but we're there waiting on the dockside with the wagon. Too much stuff goes missing if it goes in storage.'

'So how do you know what you're collecting?'

'We have a signed ticket that says "Delivery for Fitzwilliam Museum, Cambridge, to be collected". We show that to the clerk at the docks and he tells us where to wait with the wagon.'

By now they'd reached the small park. At this early hour there were very few people in it, so they were able to find a bench near the entrance.

'What happens then?' asked Daniel.

'The people who are handing the stuff over go to the clerk and he tells them where to find us. We show him our ticket, and then he takes us and our wagon to where the stuff is piled up on the dockside, waiting for us. We load it on the wagon and sign his docket, and that's it.'

'Can you remember who you saw when you collected this last consignment?'

Hoy thought about it. 'He never gave us his name, but he was a toff. Which is unusual.'

'A toff?'

Hoy nodded. 'Usually it's a gangmaster, or one of the leading hands, who deals with us. But this last time it was the bloke himself what found 'em. The artefacts, as you call 'em.'

'How do you know it was he who found them?'

'He told us so. "Take good care of these," he said. "I've spent a lot of time finding them in Egypt. I don't want anything to happen to them on the last leg." Of course, we assured him we've done this a lot and nothing's ever gone astray or damaged while it's in our care.'

'Can you describe this man?'

Hoy thought about it, then turned to his son. 'How would you picture him, Bob? You're better than me at this sort of thing.'

'Like dad says, a toff,' said Bob. 'Tallish. About your height. Thin. Dressed well. Longish hair. Had a good tan, but I guess that went with being in a place like Egypt.'

'How old?'

'Thirties, at a guess,' said Bob. He shrugged. 'Sorry I can't be more helpful.'

'Oh, you've been very helpful,' said Daniel. He took out his wallet and produced a ten shilling note, which he offered to the older man. 'For your trouble.'

Hoy snaffled it between his fingers with a nod of thanks.

'A pleasure,' he said.

'There's just one more thing I'd ask of you,' said Daniel. 'Would you accompany me to the Fitzwilliam Museum? There's something I'd like you to look at.'

Hoy looked doubtful. 'We don't normally go inside,' he said. 'Not in the front way. We go in the back door, and only just to deliver.'

'That'll be no problem,' said Daniel. 'What I'd like you to look at is outside.'

Intrigued, the two men followed Daniel to the Fitzwilliam, where he showed them the poster advertising the previous evening's debate, pinned up on the noticeboard just behind the railings.

'That's him!' said Bob, pointing at the photo of Hardwicke.

'You're sure?'

Bob nodded. 'It's a really good likeness.'

'And he was the man you picked up the consignment from at Tilbury the Sunday before last.'

'That's him.' Bob nodded, and he looked at his father, who'd been studying the picture of Hardwicke.

'Definitely,' said Hoy.

CHAPTER FORTY-THREE

It was all activity inside the Egyptian Room as Abigail supervised and directed the porters and stewards in the removal of the chairs from the previous evening, and the return of various exhibits.

'Good morning, Miss Fenton,' said Daniel. 'And my congratulations on an excellently organised evening.'

'The credit for the organisation of the event must go to Sir William,' said Abigail.

'True, but you created the ambience,' said Daniel. 'I must apologise for rushing off the way I did.'

'Did you manage to catch the person you wanted to talk to?'

'I did. It was a man called Algernon Cobb.'

She frowned. 'The name is unfamiliar to me. How is he connected?'

'I'm not sure he is any longer. I first heard of him at Heffers when I went in search of that story you told me about, "Lot No. 249". They told me that another man had also been asking after that same story, and the description they gave me was enough for me to be able to identify him last night.'

'But now you think he's not involved?'

'Not in the murders, at any rate.' He looked at the people at work in the room, and then said, 'Could we talk somewhere privately? Your office, perhaps?'

'You have information?'

'I do. But at this moment I'd rather it was kept between ourselves until I've verified it.'

She led the way to her office and once they were in, closed the door, and she and Daniel settled themselves on chairs.

'It seems that Mr Hardwicke lied about when he returned to England,' said Daniel.

Abigail stared at him, unsure of what he was telling her.

'I don't understand,' she said.

'He told you he came back last Sunday.'

'Yes,' she replied, still frowning.

'In fact he arrived at Tilbury with his latest delivery almost two weeks ago, the Sunday before last.'

Abigail stared at him, and he could see that she was shocked by this revelation. He saw her swallow and recover herself.

'I'm sure there must be a perfectly good reason for that,' she said.

'I'm sure.' Daniel nodded. 'But the point is that he was in England at the time the murders occurred. Not out of the country, as he claimed.'

Abigail looked at him, bewildered. 'Are you suggesting that because of that he may be involved in some way?' she demanded. 'That's ludicrous!'

'But why did he lie?' asked Daniel. 'You said he told you that he arrived in England after Joseph Ransome was killed.'

Abigail bridled, obviously uncomfortable. 'As I said, I'm sure there is some perfectly reasonable explanation.'

'Would you like to ask him what it is?' asked Daniel.

'I certainly will not!' snapped Abigail.

'Then I shall,' said Daniel. 'Do you have his address, or where he can be found?'

'No, I do not,' she said curtly.

'Then perhaps Sir William will be able to furnish me with the information.'

'Surely you are not going to make this ludicrous accusation about Mr Hardwicke to Sir William?!' demanded Abigail.

'Are you so sure it's ludicrous?' asked Daniel. 'All we know at the moment is that he lied about when he returned to England. I wish to know why. All I need is his address. Rest assured, I will not be telling Sir William why.'

He rose and went to the door.

She glared at him, tight-lipped. 'I cannot believe that someone like Mr Hardwicke can be involved in these murders.'

'That is where we differ. I keep an open mind. Everyone is a suspect.'

'Including me?' she challenged him.

'No,' he said.

He left and headed up the stairs to Sir William's office. Miss Sattery was at her desk and nodded in greeting as Daniel entered.

'I didn't expect you to be working on a Saturday, Miss Sattery,' he said.

'The day after the evening before,' she said. 'There is much to put together after last night's debate: ticket sale receipts, expenses for the speakers, overtime wages to be calculated.'

'Indeed,' said Daniel. 'Is Sir William in?'

'He is,' said Miss Sattery. 'He is preparing the official press release on last night's debate.'

'Would it be possible to disturb him for a few moments?'

She got up, went into the inner office and returned almost immediately.

'Sir William will be delighted to see you.'

Sir William did indeed seem delighted to see him, getting up from behind his desk and shaking his hand, then offering him a cigar as Daniel took the seat on the other side of the desk, Daniel politely declining the cigar.

'What an excellent evening!' Sir William beamed. 'I believe it will have helped put the Fitzwilliam on the map with the academic and archaeological communities in a good measure.'

'Indeed, Sir William,' said Daniel. 'A very lively debate.'

'Which you added to immensely.' Sir William chuckled. 'Your defence of Miss Fenton to Professor Waldheim was an absolute tonic! It was unfortunate I had to bring the discussion to heel at that point, but I did fear that fisticuffs might break out. We could have ended up with a duel!' He chuckled again.

'I thought your Mr Hardwicke acquitted himself very well indeed,' said Daniel.

'Yes, he's a very fine speaker,' said Sir William. 'And it's good to have new blood with new theories shaking things up. It brings new people into the Fitzwilliam to find out what all the fuss is about, which is a good thing.'

'Where did you find him?' asked Daniel. 'Through the university?'

'No,' said Sir William. 'In fact, most unusually, his background is in civil engineering. I believe he was involved in various projects in London, particularly around the railway stations.'

'Oh?'

'Yes. When a new railway line is to be built, the route has to be checked for possible remains. Churchyards, that sort of thing. I think he was involved in removing the remains from a cemetery near St Pancras Station, so they could put a new railway line in. I suppose that's where he developed his expertise at excavating ruins in a sensitive manner. Very necessary when handling precious relics from tombs in Egypt.'

'Which part of London did he come from?' asked Daniel. He gave a smile. 'It's just my curiosity. You'll find with Londoners we're always interested in where fellow Londoners come from. There's fierce rivalry between those from the north of the river and those south of the Thames.'

'I doubt if it's as fierce as the rivalry between Cambridge and Oxford,' chuckled Sir William. He stood up and went to a wooden filing cabinet. 'One moment – I believe I've got his application here, which will give us the answers.'

A short while later, Daniel was in possession of the background information he was after on Edward Hardwicke: his address in Cambridge, his former address in London, the names of his previous two employers, and the name of the college where he'd studied civil engineering.

'But you came to see me, Mr Wilson,' said Sir William. 'Do you have anything to report? Any new line of enquiry?'

'We have established the identity of the man found in the sarcophagus. He was an Egyptian academic, Dr Ahmet Madi. I don't know if the name is familiar to you, Sir William?'

Sir William shook his head, frowning.

'No,' he said. 'Most of my contacts in Egypt are administrators, senior curators, that sort of thing. The name of Dr Madi doesn't ring any bell.'

'We believe he arrived on the same day, and on the same ship, as the last consignment of artefacts from Egypt. At the moment I'm working with Inspector Drabble to go through the ship's passenger list.'

'You think the murderer might have been on the ship?'

'It's possible,' said Daniel. 'I also need to make some enquiries along that line in London, and I wondered if you would agree to my bringing in another private enquiry agent there to do some footwork in the capital.'

Sir William looked doubtful. 'I'm not sure about that,' he said. 'We hired you because of your known discretion when conducting an enquiry. Bringing in another who might not be as discreet . . .'

'I can assure you that the man I'm thinking of is as discreet as me,' said Daniel. 'Like me, he was part of Abberline's team of detectives at Scotland Yard. I worked with him for years, and would trust him with my life. He knows that in dealing with a private investigation, confidentiality is everything. However, there would be the additional cost.'

'But you think this man would be worth it?'

'I do,' said Daniel. 'And if I'm right, it would result in us reaching a conclusion on this case much quicker.'

'Very well.' Sir William nodded. 'When will you see him?'

'I'll go to London this evening and call on him first thing tomorrow. I shall be back in Cambridge tomorrow afternoon.'

CHAPTER FORTY-FOUR

When Daniel returned to the Egyptian Room, he found Edward Hardwicke there engaged in conversation with Abigail. Their conversation seemed amicable – *very amicable, almost playful,* thought Daniel bitterly – but as Abigail saw Daniel arrive her friendliness evaporated.

'If you'll excuse me, Mr Hardwicke, I believe that Mr Wilson wishes to ask you some questions.'

Hardwicke frowned, puzzled. He turned to Daniel and said, 'Questions?'

'Yes,' said Abigail. 'And I wish to state that I am having no part in it.'

She left, and Hardwicke continued to study Daniel with the same puzzled air.

'Do I gather that something has arisen that has upset you?' he asked.

'Intrigued me,' said Daniel. 'I believe you informed Miss Fenton that you arrived back in England three days after the nightwatchman, Joseph Ransome, was murdered.'

'Yes, that is correct,' said Edgar.

'The thing is, Mr Hardwicke, that I have received information that in fact you arrived back in England three days before the first body was discovered.'

Hardwicke frowned. 'May I ask from where you received this information?' he asked.

'From the carter who collected the consignment at Tilbury and brought it to the Fitzwilliam,' said Daniel. 'He and his son, who accompanied him, identified you as the man they collected it from.'

Hardwicke fell silent, his eyes studying Daniel's face. Finally, he said, 'Yes. That is true.'

'May I ask why you led Miss Fenton to believe otherwise?'

'Because I had an errand of a private nature to attend to before I travelled to Cambridge.'

'May I ask what that errand was?'

Hardwicke hesitated, then said, 'In view of the situation, I will tell you. While I was in Egypt I received a letter from the wife of a friend of mine, in which she sadly informed me that he had passed away suddenly. To be honest, he had taken his own life. I promised I would call on her as soon as I returned to England, to commiserate. And that is what I did.'

'For seven days?' asked Daniel.

'There were complications to be sorted out,' said Hardwicke. 'Legal situations. He and I had been involved in a business partnership, which had to be unravelled. All this took longer than I had anticipated, hence my delay in London.'

'Thank you,' said Daniel. 'Would you be able to furnish

me with the name of the lady in question? Or the legal people you instructed in unravelling the business while you were in London?'

'No, I would not,' said Hardwicke. 'There is an issue of someone's reputation at stake here, Mr Wilson. Their good name.'

'The lady you mention?' enquired Daniel.

'Indirectly,' said Hardwicke. 'It seems her husband had got into severe financial difficulties. There was talk of . . . mismanagement of funds. It was this, and the fear of the shame that would be heaped upon himself and his wife, that led him to take his own life.'

'I see,' said Daniel.

'I hope you do, Mr Wilson. He was a dear friend to me, and I have vowed to protect his good name, and that of his wife. For that reason their names will remain confidential. Now, if you have no further questions, I shall take my leave.'

Yes, I've got plenty of further questions, thought Daniel grimly as Hardwicke departed.

He wasn't surprised when Abigail appeared; he'd expected her to keep out of sight but within earshot to learn what Hardwicke would say in his defence. It was what he would have done.

'I assume you heard?' he said.

'Yes,' she said, her face tight-lipped with disapproval. 'I trust you are satisfied with his explanation.'

'Not really,' said Daniel. 'He gave no details of who he visited in London.'

'As far as I'm concerned, he doesn't need to go into details. He is protecting the reputation of a friend and his bereaved widow. I would have thought you would have understood that, and sympathised with it.'

'I would feel better about it if I had the details to back it up.'

'You suggest he is lying?'

'He lied about when he returned to England. That suggests he is capable of being economical with the truth.'

'He did that for a reason,' said Abigail curtly. 'And for a very *good* reason.'

'So he says,' said Daniel. 'But look at the facts dispassionately. It was an eminent Egyptologist who gave the story of the mummy to Blades. Hardwicke is an eminent Egyptologist.'

'But he was in London at that time.'

'So he says. But we have no way of checking that. It's just his word.'

She looked at him, angry. 'I believe you ought to examine yourself, Mr Wilson,' she said. 'It seems to me you have spent so long among thieves and criminals that you fail to realise that not all of society falls into that category. There are many people who seem respectable and loyal, and are just that.'

'There are also those who seem respectable and the pillars of society and high morals, yet the outward appearance conceals some of the vilest people I've ever encountered,' retorted Daniel. 'The Cleveland Street scandal I mentioned earlier was one such. For the moment, I reserve judgement on Mr Hardwicke. And now, I wish you good day.'

And with that, he left.

CHAPTER FORTY-FIVE

Drabble was in his office, leafing through a document as Daniel arrived at his office.

'Ah, Mr Wilson!' beamed Drabble. He tapped the papers on his desk. 'The passenger manifest's just arrived by special messenger. I was about to send a message to you.'

'Excellent,' said Daniel. He sat down next to the inspector. 'Have you found the name of Edward Hardwicke on it?'

'Hardwicke?' Drabble frowned. 'He's the man who was doing that debate at the Fitzwilliam last night, isn't he?'

'That's him,' said Daniel. 'I've discovered that he lied about when he got back to England. He said he only returned after Joe Ransome had been killed, but it turns out he actually got back a week before. So he was in the country when the murders happened. I'm expecting to find his name on the passenger list.'

'How would he have travelled? First class, second class? Steerage?'

'I would guess first class,' said Daniel.

Drabble turned to the first class list and ran his finger down the pages before saying triumphantly, 'Yes! Here he is! Mr Edward Hardwicke.' He looked quizzically at Daniel. 'So, he lied about when he was actually back in Britain. Think he's involved?'

'I questioned him about his whereabouts before he returned to Cambridge, and he said he was in London the whole time,' replied Daniel.

'Think he was?'

Daniel shook his head. 'There are lots of questions I've got about Mr Hardwicke.'

'Think I ought to pick him up? Officially?'

'No, not at the moment. If he turns out to be telling the truth, arresting him won't look good for the Fitzwilliam. He's their man, after all. But I'm off to do some checking on him. If I find anything, I'll let you know.'

'Well, I have some news for you,' said Drabble with a happy smile. 'We've got the bloke who did in Hector Blades. And it's not connected with the murders at the Fitzwilliam.'

'Oh?'

'His name's Billy Moss. He works for a bookie Blades owed money to. He took Blades to the river to shake him up and frighten him, but then claims things got out of hand. There was a fight, and he hit Blades, who fell into the water and sank. Moss can't swim. He took fright and ran.'

'How did you get on to him?'

'He got drunk in a pub last night and blurted it all out, and one of the drinkers there is one of our snouts. We've got Moss in the cells now. So that's one result.'

'Well done, Inspector,' complimented Daniel. 'Excellent work.'

'Just dogged police work,' said Drabble. He tapped the passenger lists. 'What's the name of that Egyptian again?'

'Dr Ahmet Madi.'

'Madi,' muttered Drabble. Once more, he ran his finger down the lists, and then said, 'Got him! In fact, there's two of 'em.'

'Two?'

'Dr Ahmet Madi and beneath that's the name Kemal Madi. Mind, that doesn't mean they're connected. Madi could be a name like Smith in England, lots of people could have it.'

'They obviously went on board together,' said Daniel. 'That suggests to me they were companions.'

'You think this Kemal Madi could be our killer?'

'I don't know. He could be family. From the evidence we found at the cottage that Madi stayed at, there were two men there. If the other man was this Kemal Madi, I doubt if he killed Dr Madi and dumped his body in the sarcophagus. He could have done it easier at the cottage. But he could be the killer of Joe Ransome.'

'Why?'

'We won't know that until we catch up with him.'

Drabble frowned. 'I'm still not sure where this Edward Hardwicke fits into things. By all accounts, he sent back artefacts to the Fitzwilliam, and then comes back to see them and talk about them at this debate. Yes, he lied about when he was back, but if he wasn't in Cambridge during that time and in London as he says, it's hard to put him in the frame. He's too respectable to go around bumping people off that way they were killed.'

'With respect, Inspector, if you remember the Ripper enquiry there were many suspects from the ranks of the ultra-respectable. Some of them very eminent: surgeons and such associated with the royal family.'

'Yes, but that was killing women. These were two fit men who would have had to be overpowered.'

'Mr Hardwicke has just come back from digging in Egypt. He may not look it, but I think he has the strength.'

'But why? Why would a man like that do something that could ruin his career, his reputation?'

'I don't know. That's why I'm going to London.'

'London?'

'He said that was where he stayed before the killings. I may be completely wrong, but I'd like to check.'

'How long will you be there?'

'Just overnight and tomorrow morning.'

'You won't find much out in that time.'

'I'm not intending to. I'm going to get an old friend of mine to do the poking around for me.'

'Who?'

'His name's George Pegg. He and I were on Abberline's team together. He's got a great nose for digging out the truth.'

'And say he finds this Edward Hardwicke is exactly what he says he is and is telling the truth?'

'Then that'll be one less thing to consider.'

'And one step backwards,' grunted Drabble.

But not as far as Abigail Fenton is concerned, thought Daniel.

CHAPTER FORTY-SIX

As he stepped out of the train onto the platform at King's Cross Station, the old familiar smells struck him. Soot. Coal. The air was heavy with it. The Smoke, people called London, and they were right.

He walked along Pancras Road to Crowndale Road, then up Royal College Street to Plender Street and his own little terraced house.

Home again.

The house was cold and damp, and the first thing he did was get a fire going in the range in the kitchen. He sat in his favourite wooden armchair and watched the fire start up as he opened the damper. He filled a kettle and put it on the range. It would take a while before it came to the boil, but it was satisfying to sit and watch it and know a cup of tea was on its way.

This kitchen was where he lived; this was where he kept his few books and papers. The parlour next to it was for entertaining, but as he never entertained, the room was always empty. It had a table and four chairs in it, and a sideboard. Unlike the parlours of the houses he'd seen in Cambridge, Abigail and Bella's, Mrs Loxley's and Harry Elder's, there were no adornments. No pictures on the walls, no decorative pottery objects on the sideboard, no flowers, nothing.

The same with his bedroom upstairs. There was a bed and a bedside table, and a chair.

He'd first rented the house fourteen years ago, when he joined Abberline's team. Fourteen years of living here, and to anyone coming in and seeing it they'd have thought he had yet to move in properly, or was about to move out.

The truth was the house was just a place to lay his head, and sit and think when he wanted somewhere private. He justified its sparseness by saying: *What's the point when I'm often away on an investigation?* as was the case with the Fitzwilliam murders.

As he sat watching the kettle, he wondered about this trip to London. Apart from the fact that Hardwicke had lied about when he returned to England, there was nothing to suggest he was involved in the murders. But the fact that the first victim had come to England on the same ship that brought Hardwicke and his Egyptian artefacts was too much of a coincidence to ignore.

Don't let your judgement be clouded, he warned himself. *Yes, you have feelings for Abigail, and she in turn has them for Hardwicke. But if you're going to dig into him, do it for the right reasons. Why are you looking into him? Is it just because you want him out of Abigail's life?*

No, he decided, as the kettle came to the boil. *It's my copper's nose. I can smell when something's not right. And Hardwicke smells. Or am I losing it?*

Next morning he made his way to George Pegg's house on the outskirts of Parliament Hill Fields. Like Daniel's, it was in a terrace, but much more welcoming, the flower box on the windowsill packed with brightly coloured blooms, and even a floral hanging basket by the door.

The door was opened at his knock by Effie Pegg, George's wife, who gave a broad smile as she saw who her caller was.

'Daniel! Well, this is a surprise! Long time no see.'

Daniel realised just how long it had been when he spotted Effie's tell-tale bump. Pregnant again, by the look of it.

'You're looking well, Effie,' said Daniel.

She chuckled and patted her bump.

'That's the polite way of putting it.' She grinned. 'Due next month.'

'Congratulations,' said Daniel. 'I would have thought George and the house would be enough to look after, but . . . how many is it now?'

'This will be number five,' she said.

Daniel gave an admiring shake of his head. 'You're a marvel, Effie. I don't know how you do it. Actually, I'm looking for George. Is he in?'

'Sorry, he's at the office.'

'On a Sunday?'

'You know George. He says crime never has a day off.'

'He picked that up from Fred Abberline.' Daniel grinned. 'Is the office still the same? Newgate Street?'

'That's the one. And remind him I'm expecting him home for

dinner. That's one thing about him not being on the force any more – he has more control over his hours. Less dinners ruined sitting in the oven, waiting for him to come home.'

Promising to remind George about his expected arrival for dinner, Daniel set off to Newgate Street. George had chosen a good spot for his base of operations: close to the courts, a ready walk-in for unhappy victims whose case had just failed, unfairly, in their opinion.

George's office was on the first floor over a newsagent, and he got up with a warm smile on his face and a hand outstretched in welcome as Daniel knocked and entered.

'Daniel! Long time no see!'

'I'm glad to find you in, George. Effie said you'd be here, but I wondered if you might be out on a case.'

'Treading the pavements.' He chuckled. 'I've got a couple of assistants who do the leg work for me these days. Means I can stay indoors and keep an eye on things.'

'Business must be good.'

'It is, luckily. Mostly domestic stuff. Watching husbands for suspicious wives, and wives for suspicious husbands. Investigating cases of suspected pilfering by domestic staff, or shop assistants. Nothing dramatic, but it pays the bills. Which is very necessary.' He grinned proudly. 'Especially as we've got another nipper on the way.'

'Yes, like I say, I saw Effie. This'll be the fifth, she says.'

'It is.'

'I must say, Effie looks in good health.'

'Very good. Due in a month, and still busy as ever.'

'Talking of Effie, she told me to remind you about getting home for dinner.'

Pegg nodded. 'Dutifully reminded. How about you, Daniel? Any plans for marriage and fatherhood?'

'Still on my own, George.'

'It's a lonely life.'

'It goes with the job.'

Pegg shook his head. 'The job's what you make it, Daniel. You can let it eat you up, or you can try and step back from it. Even the guv'nor got married. Twice. And there was no one more dedicated to the job than him. Except possibly you. Do you see anything of him?'

'Fred?' Daniel shook his head. 'No. But I believe he's very busy.'

'He certainly is.' He grinned. 'He's certainly moving in different circles. When I last saw him, he'd just come back from Monte Carlo.'

'What was he doing there?'

'He didn't go into details. Just that it was a job for the Pinkertons.'

'The Pinkertons!' said Daniel, impressed. 'Well, that's exalted company, and no mistake.'

'So, Daniel, I'm guessing you haven't just popped in for a social chat.'

'You know me too well, George. At the moment I'm doing some private investigation work out in Cambridge.'

Pegg chuckled. 'Not this mysterious murderous mummy!'

'You've heard about it,' said Daniel, surprised.

'It was in the London papers. Some Egyptian mummy going around strangling people.'

'I'm surprised the London papers bothered with a story like that.'

'I'm not! You know what people are like. A touch of the supernatural – they like nothing better.' He frowned. 'You're not telling me there's something to it?'

Daniel shook his head. 'No, but there's something going on.

We've had two dead bodies, and this story about the mummy is being put about to confuse the situation. At least, that's the way I see it.'

'But surely this is a local issue. Cambridge. That's a long way from London. Or is there a connection?'

'I don't know,' admitted Daniel. 'There's a man I met there, an archaeologist, who hails from London, and I'd like to find out a bit more about him.'

'Surely someone in Cambridge would be better fixed to fill you in on that.'

'No. He's been away in Egypt for a while, working on a dig. I'm not sure how much time he spends in Cambridge.'

'I don't see why you need me, Daniel. You're a better detective than I ever could be.'

'Come off it, George! If you're too busy . . .'

'Not at all,' said Pegg. 'I'm just wondering why you need someone else to nose around. You were the best at sniffing out if things were iffy.'

'Because I'm stuck in Cambridge,' said Daniel. 'And I'm not asking for any favours. This is a paying job.'

Pegg nodded. 'Very well, Daniel. I'll put my best man on it. What have you got on this bloke?'

Daniel took a sheet of paper from his pocket on which he'd written the details he'd gleaned from his interview with Sir William.

'Here you are, George. According to the Fitzwilliam, this was his last address in London, along with the names of his last two employers: one a firm of civil engineering contractors, and the Great Western Railway. He also claims to have studied at the Mannering Institute of Engineering in Greenwich.'

'Claims?' commented Pegg, amused. 'You don't believe him?'

'I'm not sure,' admitted Daniel. 'I've just got a feeling about him.'

'You want all this a bit sharpish, I suppose.'

'I'd be grateful, George.' He gave Pegg his address in Cambridge. 'Send it to me there. With your bill.'

As Daniel walked away from Newgate Street and headed back to Euston, he mulled over what George had said.

No plans for marriage and fatherhood? Pegg had asked. No plans. Wishes, possibly. But it had seemed to Daniel that it didn't fit with the job of being a detective. Out at all hours. Rarely at home. What sort of marriage was that? But it worked for others. George Pegg, for example. And the guv'nor, Abberline. As George had said, Abberline had married twice. First Martha, who'd died of TB after just two months of marriage. And then Emma, nearly twenty years ago, and still happily together. No kids, admittedly, but Abberline hadn't let marriage stop him being the best detective that Daniel had ever worked with.

No, Daniel, the problem isn't being married, the problem is you. You're afraid of being hurt.

CHAPTER FORTY-SEVEN

As Daniel came out of Cambridge Railway Station, he saw the billboard by the news-stand with the words: ANOTHER DEADLY ATTACK IN CAMBRIDGE, and underneath in smaller letters: *Fitzwilliam Killer Strikes Again?*

He took a copy and felt shock go through him as he read:

Edward Hardwicke, prominent Egyptologist and the Fitzwilliam's own star archaeologist, recently returned from Egypt, was brutally beaten on Saturday night and is currently in a coma in Addenbrooke's Hospital.

Witnesses heard shouts and sounds of the assault, and arrived in time to see the unknown attacker run off, but not before leaving Mr Hardwicke unconscious and fighting for his life on the pavement.

Only twenty-four hours before, Mr Hardwicke had been entertaining a large audience at the Fitzwilliam during a lively debate with the German Egyptian expert, Professor Waldheim. Now he lies at death's door.

Has the curse of the Fitzwilliam, which has already seen two murders recently, struck again?

So was I wrong about Hardwicke? thought Daniel as he hurried in the direction of Abigail's house. *Is he not a culprit, but a victim? If so, why?*

It was Bella who answered the door to Daniel's knock.

'Mr Wilson!' she exclaimed. Then her expression changed to one of distress. 'Have you heard the news?'

'About Mr Hardwicke? Yes. I've just returned from London and saw the newspaper when I got off the train. Is your sister in?'

'Abi's at the hospital. She went there as soon as she saw the story in the newspaper. Who would do such a terrible thing? Do you think it's the same person who killed those two men?'

'I'm not sure. I haven't had a chance to talk to the police, or anyone else. I shall go to Addenbrooke's Hospital and see what I can find.'

'Do you know where it is?'

'Trumpington Street?'

She nodded. 'Yes,' she said. Then her worried expression softened, to be replaced by a smile. 'By the way, Mr Wilson, because you left so suddenly, you won't have heard the news.'

'The news?'

'Dr Keen and I are to be married. He asked me on Friday, after the debate.'

Daniel gave her a smile. 'That is wonderful news, Miss Bella. My congratulations to you both.'

He left the house and hurried towards Addenbrooke's, taking in this latest romantic development. Dr Keen and Bella Fenton. How fast things moved in the world of romance. There had been no hint of anything between Bella and Dr Keen at the evening of the debate, no little looks or light touches of the hands. Or had there been and he just hadn't seen them? But Abigail hadn't seemed aware of any relationship between the two, or if she had she hadn't mentioned it to Daniel. In fact, her only real mention of Bella's romantic intentions had been to warn him away from her sister as 'flighty'.

He entered through the main door of Addenbrooke's and found Abigail sitting in a chair in the main reception area. She got to her feet as she saw him.

'Mr Wilson!'

'Miss Fenton. I had to go to London last night, and I've only just got back and heard the dreadful news. How is he?'

'I don't know,' said Abigail. 'I haven't been allowed to see him. It's outside visiting hours. Also, he's still unconscious, they tell me. I thought I'd wait here and see if there are any developments.'

He could see that although she was trying to present a brave front, her hands were clenched tightly together, twisting nervously, and there was a tremor in her voice. He gestured for her to sit, and she sank gratefully down onto the chair, Daniel taking a seat on the one next to her.

'Do you know what actually happened?' he asked.

She shook her head. 'Only what it says in the newspaper.'

'Perhaps Inspector Drabble will have more information,' he suggested.

'If he has, I doubt if he will pass it on to me,' she said. 'He doesn't like me and he feels I shouldn't be involved in the investigation.'

'I'm sure that's not the case,' Daniel tried to reassure her.

'Oh yes it is!' she said. 'Otherwise why would the constable he sent only ask for you?'

'For me?' asked Daniel.

'A constable arrived about an hour ago. He's one I saw with Inspector Drabble, so he knew who I was and my connection with the case. He saw me waiting and asked if I knew where you were. I told him I didn't. He said that if you arrived, Inspector Drabble wanted you to go and see him, urgently. I asked him what it was about, but he refused to tell me.' She looked at Daniel inquisitively. 'What were you doing in London?'

'Following up a line of enquiry.'

'Investigating Edward?' she demanded, her anger obvious.

'Amongst other things,' said Daniel.

'Well, I think you can safely say that he is not a suspect, not in view of what happened to him. He is another victim.'

'Not necessarily,' said Daniel. 'From the reports, it appears that this attack is different from the other two. The first, Dr Madi, was one blow to the back of the neck, possibly with an iron bar, the body then hidden. The murder of Joseph Ransome was very calculated. The chloroform, the strangulation. If the newspaper account is to be believed, this attack on Mr Hardwicke was frenzied. That suggests it was done by someone else.'

She shook her head, her expression bitter. 'I see you are fixed in your intention to find Mr Hardwicke guilty, regardless of what's happened.'

'Not at all,' said Daniel. 'At this moment I have an open mind. Perhaps Inspector Drabble will be able to furnish me with more details than the sparse few in the newspaper. Do you wish to come with me?'

She shook her head. 'I shall wait here in case there is any news on Edward.'

'Very well. Then I'll see if I can arrange for you to see him.'

She looked at him, startled and puzzled.

'How?' she demanded. 'The rules on visiting hours are very strictly observed, and rightly so. The medical staff need to be able to do their work without visitors blundering about interfering with their work.'

'I agree, but this is an exceptional case,' said Daniel.

She shook her head. 'I appreciate the gesture, Mr Wilson, but there is no reason for the hospital to make an exception in this case, and I wouldn't expect them to.'

'But you wouldn't object to my trying?'

She hesitated, and he saw her lips tremble as she said, 'No. Not at all. In fact, I would be most grateful if it could be arranged.'

CHAPTER FORTY-EIGHT

The senior nursing sister who came to meet Daniel at the main desk, following his request, was in her forties and with a no-nonsense expression on her face. Daniel sensed at once that this was a woman very used to being appealed to, cajoled, threatened and bullied as people tried to get past the outer defences of the hospital, and her firm look as she regarded Daniel showed she had no intention of allowing rules to be broken.

'Good afternoon, Sister,' he said. 'And I apologise for taking you away from your work. My name's Daniel Wilson. I've been hired by Sir William Mackenzie at the Fitzwilliam to work with Inspector Drabble and the local police to investigate the recent murders at the museum, and also this attack yesterday on Edward Hardwicke.'

'Yes, Mr Wilson. I'm aware of your position. I read about it in the newspaper.'

'How is Mr Hardwicke?' asked Daniel.

'He's still unconscious, as he's been ever since he was brought in. We suspect he may have a fracture of the skull.'

'Will he live?'

She hesitated, then said, 'I'm a nurse. The diagnosis is for the doctor to decide.'

'But a senior nurse with lots of experience,' said Daniel. His attempt at flattery was met with a look of scorn, so he changed his tone to that of formal efficiency. 'If he dies it will be another murder to investigate, which is why I'm eager to find out his prognosis.'

'At the moment he is alive and unconscious,' said the sister. 'He was very badly beaten. We shall know more as things progress.'

'Thank you,' said Daniel. 'I also need to talk to you about a Miss Abigail Fenton who's waiting in the main reception to see Mr Hardwicke.'

She nodded. 'As I explained to Miss Fenton, our visiting hours are very strict, necessary for the proper running of the hospital,' she said. 'And as she is not a relative . . .'

'She is not a relative, but she is engaged by the Fitzwilliam as my colleague in the investigation, working along with the police. I am on my way to see Inspector Drabble, but while I'm gone I need her at Mr Hardwicke's bedside in case he should wake and say anything that might help us identify his attacker, who we believe may also be the killer of the other victims.'

She frowned, uncertain.

'This is very unorthodox . . .' she began.

'Unfortunately, murder is unorthodox,' said Daniel politely. 'If you like I can get verification from Sir William. I believe the Fitzwilliam are great sponsors of this hospital. But it is vital we get any information we can, and it would be unfair to ask one of your staff to sit by his bed waiting. I do know how busy you are here.'

She hesitated, then nodded. 'Very well. I'll get one of the porters to show her to his room.'

'Thank you, Sister. We appreciate your cooperation in this matter, and if we do manage to find the culprit, I will make sure it's known that it wasn't done without your invaluable help.'

'There is no need for false flattery or meaningless silver-tongued words, Mr Wilson,' she said sharply. 'I do not respond to it, and you do yourself and me a disservice by attempting to use it. I have already agreed to your request because it is my civic duty, not to curry favour with anyone.'

Daniel gave an apologetic nod. 'You're right, and I apologise,' he said.

'Tell Miss Fenton to report to this desk and I shall see she is escorted to Mr Hardwicke's room,' said the sister.

'Which is his room?' asked Daniel. 'For when I return.'

'Room 35 on the third floor. Sir William arranged for a private room for him.'

With that, she left, leaving Daniel feeling embarrassed by her stinging rebuke. *Sometimes it works and sometimes it bounces back and kicks you*, he thought ruefully.

He returned to the main reception area where Abigail was still sitting.

'I've persuaded the sister in charge to let you stay beside Mr Hardwicke's bed. Officially, you're there in your role as my co-investigator, waiting in case he wakes and says anything.'

Abigail rose to her feet, taking his hand in hers and gripping it tightly. 'Thank you, Mr Wilson. Daniel. I don't know what to say.'

'Say nothing, but just remember to act as if you're there

officially, not as a concerned friend. Be very formal.'

She gave a wry smile. 'No fawning over him. I can assure you, Mr Wilson, that was never my attention. I do not fawn.'

But in Edward Hardwicke's case you'll make an exception if the opportunity arises, thought Daniel with a tinge of jealousy.

'I'll go and see Inspector Drabble and report back,' he said. 'I hope Mr Hardwicke recovers while you watch over him.'

Drabble was at the main reception desk at the police station when Daniel arrived.

'At last!' he said with a mixture of anger and relief. 'Where have you been?'

'I told you I was going to London,' said Daniel.

'You heard about Mr Hardwicke being badly beaten?'

'Yes. I've just come from the hospital. He seems to be in a very bad way. Touch and go, according to the doctors.'

'Yes. If he dies, we'll have another murder on our hands.' Drabble groaned. 'There's never been anything like this in Cambridge before. People are getting afraid to walk the streets!'

'You sent a constable to the hospital with a message for me to contact you urgently. Has something else happened?'

Drabble nodded uncomfortably. 'Something's come up that sounds mad. It *is* mad.'

Daniel waited, and he could tell by the unhappy expression on Drabble's face that whatever he was about to say was said with great reluctance.

'We've had two witnesses come forward who say they saw the attack on Hardwicke.'

'Why, that's excellent news! Were they able to give a description of his attacker?'

Drabble grimaced. 'That's the thing. They said they didn't see him clearly, but they could have sworn he was draped in bandages.'

Daniel stared at Drabble, stunned. 'Bandages?'

Drabble nodded, a miserable and tormented expression on his face. 'You can see where this is leading.'

'The mummy,' said Daniel. He shook his head. 'It's madness. Either they were drunk, or it's a practical joke . . .'

Drabble shook his head. 'Believe me, they didn't come in like it was a joke. They said they didn't want to come in at all because they didn't think they'd be believed and might be locked up for wasting police time.'

'Inspector, you don't really believe—' began Daniel.

'No, of course I don't!' burst out Drabble. 'But they do! Or they appear to! So what I want you to do is have a word with them. See if they're lying. Or if not, press 'em to find out what they *really* saw.'

'Why me?'

'Because they're more likely to feel intimidated by Wilson of the Yard than by me.'

'I didn't give that story to the paper,' said Daniel. 'I never described myself as Wilson of the Yard.'

'The fact is, whoever did it, it may come in useful. We don't want a panic over some raised-from-the-dead mummy roaming around murdering people. It'll lead to armed vigilantes out on the streets, and there's nothing more dangerous than armed vigilantes.'

CHAPTER FORTY-NINE

The two men were both in their twenties, both students at Trinity: Jeremiah Bingley and Erasmus Carstairs. They were sitting at a wooden table in the interview room looking very miserable and, indeed, frightened, and they leapt to their feet as Daniel entered the room with Inspector Drabble, anxiety on their faces.

'This is Inspector Wilson, formerly of Scotland Yard,' Drabble barked at them gruffly. 'Wilson of the Yard, as the newspapers call him. You won't be able to pull the wool over his eyes.' He turned to Daniel, grunted, 'They're all yours, Inspector,' then marched out.

The two students looked at Daniel, both swallowing in fear.

'We didn't have to come in!' blurted out Bingley in a burst of defiant bravado.

'No, indeed, you didn't,' said Daniel gently. 'Please sit down, gentlemen, and we'll talk.'

The two young men looked at one another in surprise, nervously wary. They'd obviously expected heavy-handed treatment from Daniel, severe bullying, and Daniel wondered what exactly Drabble had told them about this 'Wilson of the Yard'.

'I understand you saw the attack on Mr Edward Hardwicke in the town on Saturday evening.'

'Yes.' Carstairs nodded. He hesitated, then said, 'We're worried about getting into trouble. You know, for being there.'

'The college doesn't approve of us going into taverns,' added Bingley.

'Were you in a tavern?' asked Daniel.

'No!' said Carstairs. 'We were . . . outside.'

'And it was early,' added Bingley. 'Not eight o'clock.'

Immediately, Daniel realised what their fear was about. College authorities barred their students from what it called licentious activities: excessive drinking, fornication, and most things which young men came to Cambridge to seek out. *Ironic*, reflected Daniel, as Bingley and Carstairs were both at Trinity, the alma mater of Lord Byron, the most licentious of people, and Daniel was fairly sure Byron hadn't kept to a teetotal and celibate lifestyle while he was a student. He was in no doubt that the two young men in front of him had gone to that area in search of excitement and forbidden pleasure, and were fearful that if they were uncovered, their places at Cambridge would be at risk, along with extreme parental displeasure. As Bingley had said, they needn't have come to report what they saw to the police, but they had. As such, they deserved protection, but Daniel also wanted the truth of what they'd seen.

'I can promise you there'll be no risk to you from the college authorities,' Daniel assured them. 'For example, you could have been taking a shortcut on your way to a prayer meeting or any other similar activity, and I'm happy to back you up on that.'

'You would?' said Carstairs, the look of fear in his eyes being replaced by one of huge relief.

'I would.' Daniel nodded. 'If you have any problems with your college, tell them to contact me through Inspector Drabble, and I'll speak up on your behalf.' He leant forward and added intently, 'Provided you tell me the truth of what you saw.'

'We will! We have!' said Bingley.

'The figure you saw who carried out the attack. It was bandaged?'

'Around the head and arms,' replied Carstairs.

'But the rest? The clothing?'

'Rough,' said Carstairs. 'Like a workman's jacket and trousers and boots.'

'So the bandages around the head?' asked Daniel.

'Wrapped around, like when someone wraps a scarf around their face and head to keep out the cold.'

'But you felt it was a bandage, not a scarf?'

'Yes.' Bingley nodded. 'One end of it was dangling down.'

'There was a street lamp right by,' put in Carstairs. 'We could see it clearly.'

'And it was also bandaged around the arms?'

'Just the lower arms,' said Carstairs. 'From the elbows down to the wrists.'

'But his hands were bare?'

'Yes,' said Bingley. 'They were fists. Big fists.' And he shuddered at the memory.

'A big person?' asked Daniel.

'Yes,' said Bingley. 'Big and muscular. Tall. Wide shoulders.'

'And he was beating his victim when you appeared?'

'No. That came later. We were standing in the street,

looking towards the tavern, when this man came past us, all very jaunty. Swaggering.'

'Well-dressed?'

'Oh yes. He had a top hat on, very much the gentleman. He seemed to be making for the tavern, when suddenly this figure leapt out from a side alley and threw a punch at him. The man staggered back and hit a lamp post, and then this figure struck him again, even harder, and the man fell to the ground.

'Then he kicked him with those big boots,' said Bingley, shuddering again. 'I think he caught him in the head. It was awful! I'd never seen anything so . . . animal!'

'What did you do?'

'I shouted out "Stop!", and then Jeremiah here yelled out "Murder!"' said Carstairs. 'At our shout, people came tumbling out of the tavern to see what was going on. The attacker sort of hesitated, then he gave a last really nasty kick at the man on the ground and ran off.'

'I've no doubt at all that your prompt action saved the man's life,' said Daniel.

'How is he?' asked Carstairs.

'Still unconscious, I'm afraid, but alive,' said Daniel. 'Can I ask how many people you told about what you saw? Student friends of yours. It would be only natural.'

The two students looked at one another, hesitant, then Bingley said, 'We only told a few of our friends, when we got back to college. We were so shaken up by what had happened.'

'Of course.' Daniel nodded sympathetically. 'The danger is now that what you saw may be taken out of context. I'm sure you've seen in the papers the story about the murderous Egyptian mummy.'

Both men nodded.

'From what you've told me it seems fairly obvious that the attacker wrapped some sort of cloth around his head. It seems he used a length of bandage, and then did the same around his lower arms, all intended to confuse the situation. But everything else, the jacket, the trousers, the boots, the bare fists, show him to be just an ordinary man – albeit a brutal one – using them to disguise himself so he wouldn't be identified. Does that fit with what you saw?'

'Yes,' said Bingley, and Carstairs nodded in agreement

'But if someone just picks up the piece about bandages, everyone will get the wrong end of the stick, and that could place both of you in a difficult position with your college.'

Once again, the two young men looked alarmed.

'Why?' asked Carstairs. 'We've told you what we saw.'

'And very well told,' complimented Daniel. 'But if the newspaper gets word of this, they'll want to interpret it for their murderous mummy angle. And to do that they'll want your names, the reliable witnesses, and once your names appear in the paper against such a story, the college authorities won't take kindly to it. Even though I believe what you say, and will back you to the hilt with the authorities, you can imagine how the college will see it: two students in an area considered to be unsavoury, giving backing to a story about a murderous Egyptian mummy . . .'

'Never!' burst out Carstairs.

'That's why it's vitally important this story doesn't appear in the press. Or anywhere else,' stressed Daniel. 'If anyone asks you, say you just saw someone attacked, and you reported it to the police. No mention of bandages. You can say the attacker had covered his face in some sort of cloth. That's the truth, after all. But if anyone talks to you about a so-called mummy, you reject

274

the idea completely. Say you've no idea where such a ridiculous notion came from. And if any of your friends ask, tell them the same. That's vitally important if we're to protect you.' Daniel looked at them carefully as he added, 'And I don't just mean from the college authorities and your families. The last thing you want is your names getting in the paper, and the attacker finding out who you are. After all, you're the witnesses against him.'

CHAPTER FIFTY

Daniel and Drabble watched Bingley and Carstairs leave the station.

'I think you can rest assured neither of them will say anything to the press even hinting at a murderous mummy on the loose,' said Daniel.

'I'm not sure,' said Drabble doubtfully. 'You know what young men are like. They love to see their name in the paper. A bit of glory for them.'

Daniel smiled. 'I think I persuaded them it wouldn't be a good idea,' he said.

'Let's hope so,' said Drabble. 'So who did it?'

'I don't know,' admitted Daniel.

'And why attack Hardwicke? Or was it just a random attack?'

'I don't think so, not from the injuries that were inflicted on him. I haven't seen him myself, but from their eyewitness report of the attack, and what I've heard from the sister at Addenbrooke's, those sort of injuries are usually the result of deeply felt rage.'

'So it was personal?'

'That's what I feel.'

'And why use bandages to hide his identity? Why not a mask, or a scarf?'

'My guess is he was using the story in the newspaper as his cover: the reanimated mummy. If anyone saw him, that would be the story that would spread.'

Drabble nodded, then said, 'You said before that Hardwicke lied about when he came back to England, and you felt it might have an impact on the murders. D'you still think that?'

Daniel nodded. 'I do.'

'I'm guessing he's the reason you went to London, to check on him. Did you find out anything about him?'

Daniel shook his head. 'I've got a friend of mine doing some digging, but this attack on him puts things in a new light. Right now, my concern is that the attacker might try again.'

'While he's in hospital?'

'And defenceless. As I said, that attack suggests extreme rage. The sort of rage that won't be sated until Hardwicke's dead.'

'He must have done something very bad,' said Drabble.

'Yes, he must have,' agreed Daniel. 'But what that might have been, I have no idea. But if I'm right, I think there's a chance of catching the attacker. I think he'll try again, maybe tonight. I'll hide in the hospital room where Hardwicke is being treated. If I can have one of your constables to lay in wait with me, that would be excellent.'

'Why just one? Someone like this sounds like they've got the strength of an animal.'

'Because too large a police presence might scare them off.

Although it would be useful to have another couple of constables tucked away. As you say, the man who did this sounds like a real brute, so the more there are to overpower him the better. But we don't want to scare him off. Tell them to hide themselves in a sluice, or a storeroom or somewhere, out of sight, but within earshot, and only to come out if they hear a police whistle.'

'Do you have a gun?' asked Drabble.

'No,' said Daniel.

'Would you like one provided?'

'No thank you,' said Daniel. 'I've found that when firearms are involved, innocent people are just as likely to be the victims. Provided the constable you can let me have is reliable, and tough and able to handle himself, we should be alright.'

CHAPTER FIFTY-ONE

The uniformed men Drabble roped in to help Daniel consisted of a sergeant, Jed Tucker, and two burly constables, Martin and Lewis. Daniel outlined the plan of action for them.

'I'm expecting the man who attacked Hardwicke to try again while he's in the hospital,' he told them. 'My guess is he'll try and finish him off. But he'll wait until well after dark before making the attempt, when there are fewer people around, mainly just the night shift.

'Sergeant Tucker, you and I will hide ourselves in the room. Or, if that's impossible, somewhere close enough so we can observe what's going on in the room. You two constables will be out of sight, but not too far away, so you can hear a whistle if anything happens. It's most important that the attacker thinks that Hardwicke is unprotected. To that end, in case he's watching the hospital for signs of police activity, I suggest you change into your civilian clothes, and also that we go in by the rear entrance, and separately. We'll go in while it's still daylight and meet outside the room where they're keeping Hardwicke, then we can make arrangements for our positions.'

'Do we know which room he's in?' asked Tucker.

'Room 35, on the third floor,' said Daniel. 'I'll go into the hospital first, then you follow at intervals of fifteen minutes or so. If he does spot us, that should allay his fears about a police guard being on duty.'

'You've done this sort of thing before, sir?' asked Tucker.

'I was on the force for many years,' said Daniel. 'One thing I learnt is that most police work is mainly waiting. For once, at least the place we'll be waiting won't be cold or wet.'

The three uniformed men exchanged knowing grins, and Daniel realised they were as old hands at the waiting game as he was.

Preparations made, Daniel returned to the hospital and made his way to Room 35. Abigail was sitting beside the bed, her watchful eyes on the still figure lying there. Daniel came in and looked down at Hardwicke. His face was badly battered and bruised with great swathes of mottled yellow, brown and black. A thick bandage had been wrapped around his head. But he was alive; Daniel could see his chest rise and fall with his breathing.

'No sign of him waking?' he asked.

'None,' said Abigail. 'What did Inspector Drabble want?'

'He wanted me to talk to the witnesses who saw the attack. It's my opinion that Mr Hardwicke's attacker will try again, and here, while he's in the hospital.'

Abigail gave him a look of alarm. 'But he will be defenceless . . .' she said fearfully.

'Rest assured we won't let it happen,' Daniel told her. 'We're setting a trap. I and some police officers will be on guard tonight here, hidden.' He looked around the room. 'We'll find a place for ourselves. As soon as the attacker appears, we'll pounce.'

'What can I do?' asked Abigail.

'Go home,' said Daniel. 'It's important that the attacker thinks there's no one with Mr Hardwicke, that the coast is clear and he's been left alone, unguarded.'

'I'd like to stay,' she insisted.

'I know you would, but think it through. Everyone who's been attacked is associated in some way with the Fitzwilliam. That suggests the killer knows who is who. It's likely he'll know you, even by sight. If he sees you here it might alarm him and make him abandon his plan.'

She hesitated, then asked, 'You're sure he'll make his attempt tonight?'

'I think it most likely,' replied Daniel. 'He'll want to take advantage of the fact that Mr Hardwicke is either unconscious, or weak enough not to put up any resistance.'

'Very well,' she said. 'But you will let me know if anything happens?'

'I promise,' said Daniel.

CHAPTER FIFTY-TWO

The trap was set. Daniel checked the time. Half past midnight. The hospital had that early-hours-of-the-morning atmosphere: a limbo-world where daytime was replaced by the occasional clack of footsteps in empty corridors, then nothing. Now and then there was a moan, or an eruption of coughing from somewhere distant in the hospital, but in Room 35, Edward Hardwicke lay motionless.

Will he survive? wondered Daniel. Even if they caught his attacker tonight his injuries could signal the end for him. The fact that he hadn't recovered consciousness was ominous.

Daniel had decided that there was insufficient space in Hardwicke's room for him and Sergeant Tucker to hide successfully. There were screens to one side of the room, but they didn't offer the protection against being spotted that Daniel wanted. There were no cupboards in the room, and even if there had been Daniel would have been reluctant to use them as hiding place. They needed to be able to move swiftly. Plus, a closed cupboard door gave no chance for keeping observation. Instead, he and Sergeant Tucker had chosen a broom closet opposite Hardwicke's room, with a good view of the entrance to Room 35 through the door when left slightly ajar. Daniel had wedged a piece of paper under the door to prevent accidental closure. He'd done the same with the door of Room 35, putting a wodge of wet paper in the lock to prevent the door being locked from inside, just in case the mysterious attacker took that precaution.

Sergeant Tucker and Daniel took turns to sit in the one chair that afforded the clearest view of Room 35 through the crack in the broom closet door, while the other sat on a small chest of drawers. In his hand Sergeant Tucker carried his truncheon, a formidable weapon. He also had a pair of handcuffs in the pocket of his jacket. They'd been in position for nearly two hours. Constables Martin and Lewis were secreted in a sluice further down the corridor. It was now all a matter of waiting.

If he comes, Daniel thought. Say he'd been wrong. Say it hadn't been a targeted attack on Hardwicke, just a random assault. In which case, this would be a trap that wouldn't be sprung. Instead, the mystery attacker could be out on the streets of Cambridge right now, looking for another innocent victim to beat to a pulp.

No, thought Daniel, *I'm sure I'm right. Joe Ransome wasn't innocent.* And Daniel still felt there was something wrong about Hardwicke. The real unknown was Dr Ahmet Madi. Had he been innocent, or was his death retribution for something?

'This mummy business the inspector was talking about,' whispered Tucker. 'What the witnesses said they saw. And what it said in the paper. D'you think there could be anything in it?'

'No,' whispered back Daniel. 'The two witnesses saw someone

who'd wrapped a bandage round his head to hide his identity. For the rest, he was dressed normally. And mummies don't wear big boots.'

'No, I know, but . . .' The sergeant hesitated, then said, 'I was in the army before I joined the police. Out in India. You ever been to India, sir?'

'No,' said Daniel.

'We saw some strange sights out there. Things not easily explained. They got these people called fakirs. The things they can do is uncanny. I saw one being buried in a coffin and the earth was shovelled on it, and two days later they dug it up, and he was still alive. Two days! How does that work?'

'I don't know,' admitted Daniel. 'But I saw some strange things myself when we were carrying out investigations in some parts of London, particularly the areas where the Chinese and the Arabs lived. I saw a man apparently disappear into a wraith of smoke and vanish.'

'How?' asked Tucker.

Daniel shook his head. 'I don't know. A trick of some kind, but we never caught him, so we never found out. His accomplices said he was a magician.'

'Like a stage conjurer?'

'No, a *real* magician. But I knew it was a trick. The problem was, I didn't know how he did it.'

'That's what I'm saying, sir. It's like this fakir I saw in India. If he could be buried and still be alive after two days under ground in a coffin, who's to say the same ain't true of one of these old mummies from Egypt?'

'Two days is a lot different from two thousand years.'

'Yes, but it's the principle, ain't it. Who knows how long this fakir bloke would have stayed alive, buried like that. I mean, animals do it. This hibernation business. Some animals sleep

284

right the way through for six months, and if you looked at or touched them, you'd swear they were dead.'

Abruptly, Daniel held up his hand to silence the sergeant and gave his attention to the corridor outside. Footsteps were approaching, but not the overt *clack-clack* of the shoes of a nurse or a porter; instead this was slow and stealthy shuffling which moved, then stopped, before moving again, as if the person was checking rooms.

Through the crack in the door, Daniel saw a large figure appear, wearing a white hospital coat.

A porter? A doctor? Possibly, but there was something furtive about the manner of the person. As he watched, the man – because he saw that it was a man – stopped at the open door to Room 35 and peered in.

There was a flash of the white coat in the dim half-light, and then the figure disappeared into the room. It was the sight of the door being closed that brought Daniel into action.

He leapt up and hurled himself out of the broom closet and at the almost-closed door opposite. The figure in the white coat was standing over the inert form of Hardwicke, holding a pillow in both hands which he was pushing down on Hardwicke's face. Daniel grabbed the man and hauled backwards, but the man was built like a rock, his powerful muscles rooting him to the spot as he pressed down harder on the pillow.

Daniel raised a foot and slammed it hard into the back of the man's knee, and the man wobbled slightly backwards. Daniel took advantage of the man being off balance to drag him further backwards and trip him.

As the man crashed to the floor, still clutching the pillow, the shriek of Tucker's police whistle sent its deafening shrill sounding out as the sergeant smashed his truncheon down on the man, but the man rolled to one side so that the truncheon hit his shoulders instead of his head.

The man pushed himself to his feet and threw a powerful punch into Tucker's face that sent the sergeant flying across the room to crash into the wall. As Tucker slumped to the floor, Daniel scooped up his fallen truncheon, just in time as the man turned his attention to Daniel, lashing out with a punch that he only just managed to block.

The man drove an elbow in Daniel's chest, sending pain surging through him as the blow connected with his already cracked ribs. Daniel staggered back, blinded by pain, and saw the man snatch the pillow up from the floor and turn his attention back to Hardwicke, a man obsessed. Hardwicke seemed to have fallen half out of the bed, and as the man tried to haul him back onto the bed with one hand, Daniel struck him on the head as hard as he could with the truncheon. Even then the man didn't go down, and he was once again pushing the pillow down on Hardwicke's face when Martin and Lewis burst in.

'Get him off!' shouted Daniel.

Martin and Lewis rushed forward, each grabbing hold of one of the man's arms, pulling him back away from the bed. Daniel struck again, this time bringing the truncheon down hard on one of the man's shoulders and felt the bone break. This time the man screamed in pain. Although he writhed and twisted, trying to break free from the grip the two constables had on his arms, they managed to force him to the floor, face down.

'Get his hands behind his back,' ordered Daniel.

Tucker was now lurching to his feet, dazed, but he responded when Daniel held out his hand and said, 'Handcuffs!'

Daniel took the sergeant's handcuffs from him and snapped them onto the man's wrists.

By now medical staff were crowding into the room.

'Drag him out,' said Daniel, and the constables hauled the bulky body of the man out through the door and into the corridor. Daniel gestured at Hardwicke.

'Please, see if he's still alive.'

Daniel stood and watched as the medical staff gently eased Hardwicke back onto the bed and began examining him, checking his pulse and breathing. One looked at Daniel and nodded.

Daniel went outside into the corridor where the two constables were sitting on the man, while Tucker had found a length of rope in the broom closet and was tying his ankles together.

Daniel moved to the man's head and lifted it off the floor. It was someone he'd never seen before, but the man's features showed a remarkable similarity to the first man Daniel had seen on Dr Keen's table: Dr Ahmet Madi.

'Mr Kemal Madi, I presume,' he said.

CHAPTER FIFTY-THREE

They were back in the interview room at the police station, but this time Daniel and Drabble sat side by side at the table across from Kemal Madi. Two officers stood close behind Madi, ready to grab him if he started to cause trouble, but Daniel felt there was little chance of that. It wasn't just that he still had his wrists handcuffed behind him, and his legs tied to the chair he was sitting on as a further precaution, and the fact that his collar bone was broken, but all the fight seemed to have gone out of him since he'd been hauled into the police station. With his quarry, Edward Hardwicke, now out of his reach, Madi sat and looked at them, resigned to his fate.

At Daniel's request, a constable had been sent to bring Abigail in to observe the interview.

'She's part of the investigation,' Daniel had said. 'She deserves to see the closing of the case.'

The truth was that they'd caught the person who'd attacked the man Abigail obviously cared about very deeply, and she deserved to know why, and from the attacker himself, not Daniel or Drabble giving her their own second-hand version. She sat at one side of the room, away from the table, her eyes on the man tied to the chair.

'You admit that you tried to kill Edward Hardwicke?' asked Drabble.

'Yes,' said the man.

'Why?'

'Because he killed my brother.'

'Dr Ahmet Madi.'

'Yes.'

'You speak English very well,' commented Drabble.

'I also speak French,' said Madi. 'I have worked with English and French diggers for many years. It pays to speak their language.'

'What makes you so sure that Edward Hardwicke killed your brother?' asked Daniel.

'Because I was there when he did it,' said Madi.

And now the story came out, and Daniel could almost feel the relief coming from Kemal Madi as he was at last able to unburden himself of the anger he felt.

'This man Hardwicke was a crook. My brother worked with him, providing him with artefacts from digs in Egypt. I worked with my brother, doing much of the labour. My brother was always the clever one. I was better at working with my hands.

'For some time we had suspected that Hardwicke was cheating us. He told us the money came from the Fitzwilliam Museum in Cambridge and their price was very low, but we didn't believe him. Sometimes, Hardwicke didn't pay at all – he said the money hadn't arrived and we would be paid later. My brother knew the reputation of the Fitzwilliam and said they would not cheat us that way.

'And it wasn't just us. Everyone that Hardwicke dealt with suffered the same way: no money, or short-changed. Many decided not to deal with Hardwicke any more, only to work with others who were giving a fair price, but Hardwicke said if we did that he would report us to the authorities for breach of contract and we would be imprisoned.

'Ahmet was certain that Hardwicke was keeping most of the money for himself, that he was cheating both us and the Fitzwilliam. But in order to act, he needed proof.'

'Why didn't he write to the Fitzwilliam and ask them direct?' asked Daniel.

'Because he didn't know who he could trust,' said Kemal. 'Hardwicke could have people at the Fitzwilliam in his pay, and they'd report back to him about any such letters. The only answer was to come to England and find out the truth.

'Everyone who felt they were being cheated contributed to a fund to give us the money for our fare, and our keep while we were in England.'

'And you arrived at Tilbury on the Sunday?'

'Yes.'

'Did you know that Edward Hardwicke was on the same ship?'

'Yes.'

'Did he see you?'

'Yes. But we didn't speak to him, nor he to us. We were travelling in a different class to him. He travelled first class.' He scowled. 'He could afford it. He was using the money he stole from us.'

'And you travelled to Cambridge.'

'Yes.'

'And you rented a cottage.'

'Yes.'

'But the landlady thought there was only one of you staying there: your brother.'

'Ahmet thought it best if she thought that. Some people in England are suspicious of Arabs. They think we are thieves and beggars. Ahmet felt that one man – a doctor at a university – would not encounter that problem. But I stayed with him at the cottage.'

'Tell us about the Tuesday night when he died.'

'Because Ahmet didn't know who he could trust at the Fitzwilliam, he decided to go in secretly at night. His plan was to look at the account books, see how much the Fitzwilliam had paid to Hardwicke for different effects. We already knew what he had paid us for them. The difference between those prices would be the proof that Hardwicke was stealing the money.'

'How did he get in?'

Kemal smiled. 'That was left to me, to find the person who would take a bribe to let Ahmet in. There is always such a one everywhere. I visited the Fitzwilliam and talked to people, sounding them out, and found a man who would do anything for money.'

'One of the nightwatchmen?'

Kemal nodded. 'In the early hours of the Wednesday, Ahmet went to the museum and the man let him in.'

'Not you as well?'

Kemal shook his head. 'Ahmet said he did not trust this man, so he suggested I stayed outside and watched, in case it was a trick. So I took a position opposite the back door, where the man let Ahmet in.

'A short while later, another man knocked at the door, and it was opened by the nightwatchman, who let him in. By the light that came through the door I saw this other man's face. It was Edward Hardwicke.

'The door shut, and that was it. I was there for another hour, waiting and watching. At last, the door opened and Hardwicke came out, and left. I waited for Ahmet to appear, but he didn't. I waited all night, watching, until dawn came, but there was no sign of Ahmet.

'I waited until the Fitzwilliam was open to the public, then I went in, searching for Ahmet. But suddenly we were told that the museum was closed and the police had been called because a body had been discovered. I knew it had to be Ahmet.'

'Do you think Hardwicke had followed your brother to the museum?'

'He had to have. He must have been following us since we arrived at Tilbury, suspecting what we were doing.'

'Did you seek out the nightwatchman to ask him what had happened?'

'I did. He told me that Hardwicke had told him that he had private business to conduct, and that after he let him in he didn't see him again. He said the same about my brother. He said he'd let Ahmet in, then let him go about his business. He assumed he must have left of his own accord, until the next morning when Ahmet's body was discovered.

'I knew then that Hardwicke was the man who'd killed my brother. And I decided to kill him.'

'You could have told the police,' put in Drabble.

'And who would they have believed?' demanded Kemal. 'An Egyptian labourer, or an English gentleman? Hardwicke would have denied even being there. And the nightwatchman would have backed him up, for a price.'

'So what did you do?'

'The first thing I did was go to the cottage and clear out all our belongings. We didn't have many. The next thing for me was to find Hardwicke, but he'd gone, and I didn't know where. The only place I knew where I might find him again was the Fitzwilliam, so I set to work to keep watch on it. And sure enough on Thursday night he returned there.

'Once again, he knocked on the door, and the same nightwatchman let him in. He was in there for about half an hour, and then he left.

'I set off to follow him, but he knew the back ways of Cambridge better than I did, especially at night, and I lost him.

'Since then, I've been hanging around, waiting for a sight of him. I knew he would be returning when I saw the poster advertising the debate on Friday night, and I was going to get him then. But after the event he walked away with two women.' He looked at Abigail. 'One of them was this woman.

'I followed them to a house, where the women went in and then Hardwicke left. Unfortunately there were still too many people around, so I followed him as he walked, waiting for an opportunity, but the crowds were always as busy.

'Then he went into a pub. I waited outside for him to come out, but when he did, about an hour later, he had two women with him. They were drunk. They went to a house not far away, and the three of them went in.'

Daniel shot a glance at Abigail, and saw her face tighten, and knew how angry she felt – mainly at herself for having been fooled by Hardwicke.

'I waited all night for Hardwicke to come out, but he didn't,' Kemal continued. 'In the end one of the women came out of the house, and I approached her and asked her if my friend Mr

Hardwicke was still with her. She laughed and said he'd gone. He must have left by a back door, because I never saw him leave.

'I asked her if she knew where he'd gone, but she said she had no idea, but she expected him back the next night and she'd pass on any message

'Once I knew that, I knew I had him. So on Saturday night I hung around outside the same pub, and this time when I saw him approaching, I went for him. I would have finished him, too, if those people hadn't come along and raised the alarm.'

'Why the bandages when you finally attacked him?'

'Because of the story that was in the newspaper, about the mummy. I thought if I wrapped bandages around my face, even if I was seen I could get away without anyone knowing who I was. People would think it was this mummy they'd read about.' He laughed. 'Foolish, but then people can be foolish.'

'So you decided to finish the job tonight.'

Kemal nodded. 'And I would have, too, and avenged my brother, if you hadn't interfered. But I hope and pray that after all I may have succeeded. He may die tonight after what happened in that room. If there is a God, he will.'

CHAPTER FIFTY-FOUR

Daniel and Abigail were given a lift home to Abigail's by a horse-drawn police van, their arrival in the house causing a bleary-eyed Bella to appear stumbling down the stairs.

'What is going on, Abi?' she demanded. 'It's four o'clock in the morning. I heard the door close at one o'clock and I've been wondering what on earth caused you to go out at that unearthly hour.' Then she saw Daniel and said, 'Oh! Mr Wilson!'

'We caught the man who attacked Mr Hardwicke,' said Daniel.

'And discovered who carried out the murders,' added Abigail wearily.

'Who?' demanded Bella.

'Please, Bella, can we talk in the morning?' Abigail appealed. 'It is late and I need to talk to Mr Wilson.'

'No!' said Bella petulantly. 'I need to know! I won't be able to sleep not knowing!'

'The man who attacked Mr Hardwicke is called Kemal Madi,' said Daniel. 'He's the brother of the first man who was killed.'

'And the person who carried out the murders was Edward Hardwicke,' said Abigail, and Daniel saw tears spring into her eyes.

'No!' burst out Bella. 'That cannot be!'

'It is!' said Abigail. 'And now, Sister, please go to bed and we will talk more in the morning.'

There was no mistaking the firmness of Abigail's tone. Bella wavered, seemed about to protest again, then nodded to them both and went back upstairs.

Daniel followed Abigail into the parlour, where they both sank down onto chairs, Abigail burying her head in her hands and sobbing.

'I'm sorry,' said Daniel.

She looked up at him, tears streaking her face, her eyes blazing angrily.

'I am humiliated!' she said. 'I trusted him!'

'It's easily done,' he said.

'But not by you,' she said bitterly.

'I'm more experienced than you in these matters,' he told her.

'What's worse is I may have got Mr Blades killed!' she burst out, anguished. 'I told Edward that we thought Blades would reveal the identity of this expert Egyptologist he wrote about. That can only have been Edward. So Edward killed Blades to silence him, and it's my fault!'

'No,' Daniel told her firmly. 'Blades' death was nothing to do with this case. Drabble told me he was killed because he owed money to a bookie. A bookie's thug threatening him that went wrong. It was nothing to do with you.'

'But you must still despise me,' she said angrily.

'Not at all.'

'No?' she demanded. 'Why not? You should be gloating that you were right about him and I was wrong.'

'I don't gloat,' said Daniel.

'No, you don't. You are like a . . . thinking machine.'

Daniel was about to say that he was the exact opposite, especially when it came to her, but one look at the hurt and anger in her face and he decided against it. It would only lead to a massive row between them, when things would be said that couldn't be unsaid.

'You're upset,' he said. 'I'll leave you now. Tomorrow morning I'll call on Sir William at the Fitzwilliam and tell him what's happened. My advice to you is to take the day off tomorrow and catch up on the sleep you've missed tonight. I'll explain to Sir William on your behalf.'

'No!' she snapped. 'I'll join you when you make your report.'

'There's no need.'

'There's every need. I said I'd work with you, and that's what I intend to do. If you can survive without sleep, so can I. I did so on many occasions when I was at a dig in Egypt.'

Daniel nodded. 'Very well. I'll see you at the Fitzwilliam in the morning.'

After Daniel had gone, Abigail sat in the parlour and remonstrated with herself. Why did she do it? Why had she treated Daniel so badly?

Because she was angry. Angry at herself for having been taken in by Edward, in the same way she'd allowed herself to be taken in by Edgar. But both of them had been men without substance. Sham creatures, all attractive surface and show. And in Edward's case, murderous, vindictive, a user of women, a thief, a robber of honest people. But the person she'd vented her anger at had been Daniel.

Daniel, who'd been caring enough about her to persuade the hospital sister to let her sit by Edward's bed to watch over him. It had been Daniel who'd stood up for her at the debate after the verbal assault on her by Professor Waldheim. And his response had been born of indignation, spoken out loud with passion. Hardly the act of a thinking machine, as she'd called him.

I have been unfair to him. Tomorrow, I shall apologise to him and try and make things right between us, if he'll allow me to. But right now she needed to get to bed and sleep.

CHAPTER FIFTY-FIVE

There was no sign of Abigail when Daniel arrived in the Egyptian Room at the Fitzwilliam. He looked at the clock. Half past ten.

'No, sir,' he was told when he enquired about her at the front desk. 'We haven't seen Miss Fenton this morning.'

Perhaps she's decided to take my advice and have the day off to recover, thought Daniel. Sir William, however, was in, and he homed in on Daniel when he saw him at the main desk.

'Mr Wilson! I'm glad to see you! I had a note from Inspector Drabble to tell me that positive things have happened. Will you join me in my office?'

Once in Sir William's office, Daniel gave a summing-up of Kemal Madi's statement implicating Edward Hardwicke in both murders, and also in his alleged systematic cheating of the Egyptians over the relics he was sending back to the Fitzwilliam.

It was this, almost more than the murders, that troubled Sir William most.

'If this is true, it is appalling beyond words. Our reputation for honest dealing over the artefacts has been one of the reasons why we have been able to amass such a wonderful collection. Hardwicke has only been working on our behalf in Egypt for six months.'

'Long enough to arouse suspicion amongst people like Dr Madi that the right amounts weren't being paid.'

'For which he blamed the Fitzwilliam!' said Sir William, his face reddening with anger. 'I shall take action immediately. I shall send a telegram to my opposite number in Cairo telling him that I believe some of our Egyptian suppliers may have been cheated by Hardwicke. I'll choose some items and put in the telegram what Hardwicke claimed had been paid for them, and ask him to let me know what the suppliers had actually received. If there's a discrepancy, which I think there will be, then I'll instigate a financial audit of every item that Hardwicke sent to us and get Cairo to do the same at their end. If there has been any short-changing, I'll make sure it's made up.'

'You may not have much luck in getting the money back from Hardwicke,' Daniel warned. 'I get the impression he spent most of it.'

'That doesn't matter,' said Sir William. 'They will be paid what they are owed. The reputation of the Fitzwilliam is at stake.' He looked quizzically at Daniel. 'Do we know what happened to the mummy that went missing? I assume that was Hardwicke's doing. How did he get it out of the museum? And what did he do with it?'

'I'm afraid we won't know the answer to that until we get the chance to question Hardwicke. In which case, there's a possibility we may never know the answer. That final attack on him by Kemal Madi may have worsened his condition.'

'Killed him, you mean?'

'Possibly. Or caused a brain injury that may have damaged him for life.'

'It would be his just deserts,' growled Sir William. 'I am sorry to sound so harsh and unforgiving, Mr Wilson, but what this man has done has been . . .' He shook his head, unable to find words.

When Abigail woke it was like surfacing through a fog. She felt exhausted, drained from the trauma of the previous night. The revelations from Kemal Madi. The depths of depravity that Hardwicke had indulged in made her want to bathe herself to wash away any association with him. To be so gentlemanly and polite to her, so sincere, and then go off and cavort with whores in that way. Would she have been his next target for pleasure? Quite likely. And might she have given herself to him? She had to Edgar, and Edward had been far more plausible. The thought of it made her feel sick.

She pulled on her robe and made her way downstairs, surprised at the lack of noise from the kitchen. Usually Mrs Standish made a lot of clattering as she prepared breakfast, or washed up afterwards. And where was Bella? Had Bella already left for work at the library, without saying goodbye?

She entered the kitchen and stopped, stunned, as her eye fell on the clock.

Two o'clock!

She had slept right through!

She spotted a note on the kitchen table. It was from Bella.

Dear Abi. As you were in so late this morning I thought you needed to rest and recover. I told Mrs Standish to let you sleep. I shall see you, and hear all, when I return.

No! she screamed silently. *I should have been at the Fitzwilliam, reporting to Sir William with Daniel.*

CHAPTER FIFTY-SIX

Abigail hurried into the reception area of Addenbrooke's and asked to see the ward sister who'd been on duty the previous day. It was her dread that a different sister would be on duty and she'd have the laborious task of trying to explain her situation to someone new, and come up against a wall of resistance as she had done before. She was relieved to see that it was the same ward sister.

'Miss Fenton,' the sister greeted her.

'Sister.' Abigail nodded. 'I apologise for taking you away from your duties, but I'm here to check on Mr Hardwicke's condition.'

The truth was, she was here to try and catch up with Daniel. She'd gone first to the Fitzwilliam to see if he was still there, and had been told by Sir William that he'd left, his next point of call being the hospital.

'Mr Hardwicke recovered consciousness this morning. He is still in a weak state, but the doctors hope he will make a full recovery.' She hesitated, then her expression grew grim as she added, 'A police constable has been placed on duty outside his room, in view of the fact that he has been charged with serious offences. I believe they include murder.'

'Yes, they do,' said Abigail. 'Has Mr Wilson been here today?'

'He called earlier and spoke to the constable,' replied the sister.

'Did he give any indication of where he was going to next?'

The sister shook her head and said, 'I must return to my duties now, Miss Fenton.'

'Of course,' said Abigail. 'Would it be possible for me to talk to the police constable?'

The sister hesitated again, but then nodded. 'As you are part of the investigating team, I don't see why not. Mr Hardwicke is still in Room 35.'

Abigail made her way up to the third floor. A police constable was sitting on a chair outside Room 35, reading a newspaper, and to her relief she recognised him as one of those who'd been in the interview room when Daniel and Drabble had questioned Edward in the early hours. It saved her having to make lengthy explanations as to who she was and why she was there.

'Good afternoon,' she said.

'Good afternoon, Miss Fenton,' said the constable, getting to his feet.

'Abigail! Is that you?'

The sound of Edward's plaintive call from inside the room filled her with rage and the desire to go in and attack him, but she swallowed, bringing her anger under control.

'May I see him?' she asked the constable.

'I've been told no one's allowed in except the medical staff, but seeing as it's you, miss, go ahead.'

'Thank you,' said Abigail.

She entered the room. Hardwicke lay in the bed, propped up on pillows, his head still heavily bandaged, his face badly bruised.

'There's been some terrible mistake!' he appealed to her. 'Abigail, you have to make them end this nightmare!'

Abigail fixed him with a steely stare. 'The nightmare is of your own making, Mr Hardwicke,' she said. 'The mistake you made was in thinking you could get away with cheating the Egyptians out of their money, and then killing those two men.'

'They're lying!' said Hardwicke imploringly. 'It's a conspiracy against me!'

'If that's so, I'm sure a judge and jury will be able to determine the truth,' said Abigail.

She turned on her heel and left the room, ignoring Hardwicke's plaintive cry of 'Abigail! You have to help me!'

'I understand Mr Wilson was here,' she said to the constable. 'Did he say where he was going to next?'

'No, miss,' said the constable. 'But my guess would be to see Inspector Drabble to wrap things up. With the murderer caught, I'm guessing he'll be off back to London.'

Yes, I suppose he will, thought Abigail.

She thanked the constable and walked back down the stairs, her mind and heart a mixture of confused emotions. Seeing Edward in the bed, listening to his desperate appeals to her, she felt only disdain. He was a pitiful creature, a liar to the end.

She wondered what to do. Should she go to see if Daniel was still with Inspector Drabble? But to what purpose? She felt as if she was trailing uselessly around Cambridge after him, and constantly missing him. And what would she say if she saw him? She felt the urge to apologise. No, more than that, she wanted to tell him how she felt about him. Something she'd been denying to herself. She'd allowed herself to be diverted by the showiness of Edward, but much of that had been because she felt that Daniel didn't see her in any other way than as a colleague. If anything, Bella had had more chance of capturing his heart, until Dr Keen stepped forward with his offer of matrimony.

No, she thought. *I've just been exposed as making a fool of myself over one man in front of Daniel; what would be his opinion of me if I started blurting out that I had feelings for him? He would despise me as shallow, flitting from one man to another, the same as I accused Bella of doing.*

Now the case is over, he will leave. And he'll leave thinking badly of me.

And I deserve it.

CHAPTER FIFTY-SEVEN

Daniel picked listlessly at his breakfast. He'd told Mrs Loxley that this would be his last day staying with her, that now the case was over there was no further need for him to stay in Cambridge, so he would be leaving that morning.

He was disappointed that he hadn't seen Abigail. He wondered why she hadn't turned up at the Fitzwilliam yesterday morning, as she'd promised she would. He could only guess the humiliation she felt over Hardwicke was too much for her to deal with at this moment. And she hadn't made any attempt to get in touch with him yesterday; he'd checked with Mrs Loxley to see if she'd called while he was out at the hospital and seeing Inspector Drabble, and been told she hadn't. Which meant she was avoiding him. And if that was the case, Daniel felt that if he were to go in search of her to say goodbye he would not be received welcomingly.

Sadly, whatever he felt for her, it was not to be.

He was interrupted in his thoughts by Mrs Loxley appearing with an envelope.

'This has just arrived for you, Mr Wilson,' she announced. 'Special delivery.'

It was a report from George Pegg. A note attached said:

Dear Daniel. I told my man it was urgent so he got this done at speed, which is why it's brief. Hope it's what you want.

Bill enclosed, as agreed.

Yours sincerely,

George

It was indeed brief, just a few lines on a piece of paper, but it gave Daniel the background he wanted on Hardwicke which showed he'd lied about almost everything. He read:

Hardwicke enrolled at the Mannering Institute, but left after just one month there. There's nothing in writing, but my man gained the impression that he was asked to leave after certain things went missing. There was no prosecution because the Institute didn't want the bad publicity that would have happened as a result.

He did work for Great Western Railway, but in a ticket office, not involved in anything like digging up remains. He was also just a clerk at the firm of civil engineers.

My man's checking the address he gave in London and will let you know more as he finds it.

Daniel made a mental note to send a reply to George thanking him for the swift work, at the same time letting him know that

Hardwicke had been arrested, so there was no need for any further digging into his background.

One thing was positive: the report from George gave Daniel an excuse for returning to the Fitzwilliam to deliver it, and George's bill, to Sir William. And perhaps he'd see Abigail there.

As Daniel walked up the steps of the Fitzwilliam, he considered showing George's report to Abigail, but decided against it. She'd suffered enough; this report detailing his lies would only make her feel worse about herself. Instead, he went straight up to Sir William's office.

Sir William was studying a telegram as Daniel entered his office, and he offered it to Daniel.

'From Cairo,' he said grimly. 'It backs up what Kemal Madi said. Hardwicke was cheating both the Fitzwilliam and the Egyptians.' He shook his head. 'How could I let myself be taken in by that creature?'

'You weren't the only one, Sir William,' said Daniel. 'This morning I received this report on Hardwicke from my man in London.'

He passed the piece of paper to Sir William, who read it, and then dropped it on his desk with an expression of disgust.

'The man seems to have made a profession of chicanery and fooling people!' He sighed. 'A pity, because he did send us some wonderful artefacts from Egypt. If only he'd stuck to the one thing he was good at.'

'Based on this, Sir William, I wonder how much of the work he did in Egypt was his own, and that he didn't steal from others,' said Daniel thoughtfully. 'He's certainly capable of it.'

'Yes, true,' said Sir William. He tapped the piece of paper and muttered, 'I wonder what's the best thing to do with this?'

'My advice would be to keep this confidential,' said Daniel. 'It shows that Hardwicke lied about his qualifications and work experience, but it won't be needed to prove that he murdered Dr Madi and Joseph Ransome; we have the evidence from Kemal Madi, which will be enough to convict him. But I don't believe it would be good for the reputation of the Fitzwilliam if this report leaked out.'

'You're right.' Sir William nodded. 'I shall keep it under lock and key.' He picked up George Pegg's bill and added, 'Leave this with me and I'll send Mr Pegg a cheque for his work.' He looked at Daniel. 'Has Miss Fenton seen the report?'

'No,' said Daniel. 'I got the impression that she was particularly trusting of Hardwicke because of the vast amount of antiquities he was sending back for her to catalogue. Anyone would have been impressed by that. I didn't want her to feel any more disappointed in him than she already is.'

Sir William nodded thoughtfully. 'Yes, that will have been hard for her. I'll take your advice and keep the contents of this report to myself. But thank you for your work, Mr Wilson. You not only solved the murders, but with your discretion, you've kept the reputation of the Fitzwilliam intact. I assume your work here is now over?'

'It is,' said Daniel. 'I shall be catching the next train to London.'

With that he shook hands with Sir William, said goodbye to Miss Sattery, then went down the stairs to the Egyptian Room to say farewell to Abigail.

She wasn't there, and the steward he spoke to said he'd seen her briefly that morning, but then she'd gone out.

'Did she say where she was going?' he asked.

'Sorry, sir. She just put on her coat and went.'

Daniel thanked the man, picked up his overnight bag, and left.

Goodbye, Fitzwilliam Museum, he thought as he walked down the steps. *Goodbye, Cambridge. Goodbye, Abigail Fenton.*

CHAPTER FIFTY-EIGHT

Daniel arrived at Cambridge Railway Station to find a notice saying: 'Trains to London delayed due to cows on line.'

He found a porter to get more clarification and was told, 'A herd of cows wandered onto the line just as the train from London was coming round the bend. Luckily, the train wasn't derailed, but a load of the cows were killed. We've got a couple of men working with the farmer to round up the others and get the dead cows off the line. It's going to take a couple of hours.'

A couple of hours, thought Daniel. Whether to return to the centre of Cambridge to spend some time there, or wait here. Aware that there was always the possibility of the cows getting cleared from the line earlier than expected, Daniel elected to stay. Most of the benches on the station seemed to be full of people also waiting for the next train for London to depart, so Daniel settled himself down on a wooden crate that was waiting to be put into the goods van.

He'd been sitting there for an hour when he spotted Abigail pushing her way through the throng towards him. He stood up and nodded.

'Miss Fenton.'

'You decided to leave without saying goodbye?' she demanded.

'I looked for you, but you weren't to be found,' said Daniel.

'I would have thought a well-known and experienced detective like yourself would have been able to track down someone like me with comparative ease,' she said curtly. 'I assume you did not look very hard.'

Daniel was about to snap a retort asking how much she wanted to be found by him, but decided against it. Instead, he said blandly, 'But we meet now.'

'Yes.' She looked coldly at him as she demanded, 'Why did you not show me the report on Edward Hardwicke from your friend Mr Pegg?'

'You've seen it?'

She nodded. 'Everything he said was a tissue of lies. His qualifications. His experience.'

'Yes, it was. But he was very plausible.'

'To me, not to you.'

He almost said: *But I wasn't emotionally tangled up with him.* Instead, he said, 'Call it a copper's intuition.' Cautiously, he added, 'I'm surprised Sir William showed it to you. I got the impression he was going to keep its contents for his eyes only.'

She hesitated, then admitted, 'He didn't show it to me. I was waiting for him in his office and I saw something with your name attached on his desk. I was curious and looked, and found the report under some other papers. When I saw the title "Mr Edward Hardwicke", I looked at it. Fortunately, it was short so it didn't take me long to read. I'd replaced it by the time Sir William entered the room.' Angrily, she burst out, 'You should have showed it to me! You showed it to Sir William!'

'Sir William had paid for that report. It was his.'

'But we were partners in this investigation! That's what you said!'

'Indeed, we were. But I felt if you were to read it, you would be hurt. You were already hurt enough when you discovered he was the killer, and he'd wormed his way into your friendship. I felt revealing all this to you would have been . . . even worse for you.'

'That was for me to decide!' raged Abigail.

'No, it wasn't,' said Daniel. 'I was aware that you harboured feelings for him—'

'How dare you!' snapped Abigail. 'I did not!'

'Yes, you did,' said Daniel doggedly. 'You may deny it now, but you did. And I could not see you hurt any more than you already have been.'

'Why not?' Abigail challenged him. 'You were right and I was wrong about him! I stand by what I said before: you have the right to gloat.'

'And as I said to you then, if you think I am the kind of man who does that then you have misjudged me, and you don't really know me at all,' said Daniel. 'In which case, maybe it's better that we part on these terms. You angry and misjudging me. Me, hurt in my own way, and obviously misjudging you.' He looked at her politely but coldly. 'It has been a pleasure to work with you and know you, Miss Fenton . . .'

314

'For God's sake, don't be such a sanctimonious prig!' she shouted at him, and then she sank down onto the crate, dropped her head into her hands and burst into tears.

Immediately, Daniel sat down beside her, anxiety on his face.

'Oh God,' she moaned. 'Tears! There goes the last vestige of my dignity!'

'Miss Fenton . . .' began Daniel awkwardly.

'Abigail! My name is Abigail!' she shouted, wiping her eyes with a handkerchief. 'And I don't want you to go! And not just on these terms! I want you to stay!'

Daniel stared at her, stunned. 'But . . . but . . .' he stammered.

'You may be a bloody good detective, Mr Wilson, but when it comes to recognising a woman's true feelings you are useless!'

'You want me to stay?'

'Yes! Alright, not for ever. I know you have work which will take you to many different places, but for the moment I want you to stay. With me. I think you are the best man I have ever met, and right now I want you to hold me and kiss me and tell me you care for me . . .'

'I do care for you!' said Daniel earnestly. 'If only you knew how much! From the first moment I saw you.'

'Then why didn't you say so?' burst out Abigail.

'Because . . . because we're from two different worlds. Because you are smart, intelligent . . .'

'For God's sake, talk to me later. Right now, if you feel it, hold me and kiss me.'

And he did.

As he enveloped her in his arms and kissed her passionately, feeling her kissing him back, he heard a woman's voice say in disapproval, 'Well, Maude, will you look at that! You'd think respectable-looking people like that would be able to control themselves in public.'

As their footsteps moved off, he thought, *I don't care. I have met the woman I want to be with.*

JIM ELDRIDGE was born in central London towards the end of World War II, and was blown up (but survived) during attacks by V2 rockets on the Euston/Kings Cross area of London where he lived. He left school at sixteen and did a variety of jobs, before training as a teacher. In 1971 he sold his first sitcom (starring Arthur Lowe) to the BBC and had his first book commissioned. Since then he has had over 100 books published, with sales of over three million copies. He lives in Kent with his wife.

jimeldridge.com

To discover more great books and to
place an order visit our website at
allisonandbusby.com

Don't forget to sign up to our free newsletter at
allisonandbusby.com/newsletter
for latest releases, events and exclusive offers

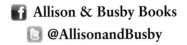 **Allison & Busby Books**
@AllisonandBusby

You can also call us on
020 7580 1080
for orders, queries
and reading recommendations